CROWN TOURNEY

Ten tales of deadly damsels, cursed castles and edged weapons

TANSY RAYNER ROBERTS

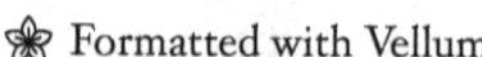 Formatted with Vellum

Contents

On fairy tales (and tansy)

I've always stolen from fairy tales. Not exclusively fairy tales — Greek myths and Roman history have contributed plenty of grist to my mill, and I'd be here all day if I had to list all my literary influences.

But writing fantasy, especially fantasy with humour, means that fairy tale tropes are always within reach. Grab a handful, twist and toss it into the stew.

(Stone stew, obviously.)

The heroine of my first published novels, Kassa Daggersharp, was entirely a creature of fairy tale — not specific stories, but the witches she was descended from were clearly the storybook variety, with a few twists here and there. In *Liquid Gold* (1999), she encounters a most distressing gingerbread house which is damp, saggy and rotting and yet somehow still has a witch living in it.

Another character from my Mocklore series, Bounty Fenetre, is entirely constructed from fairy tale narrative: in "Hobgoblin Boots," (2004) she plays Puss in Boots to her childhood friend's Marquis De Carabas, which comes a bit of a shock to him. He thought she was his romantic lead; she had firmly put herself in the "helper" zone. A sequel Bounty story, "Queen of Courtesans," (2016) is shaped around one of my all-time favourite fairy tales, The Twelve Dancing Princesses.

Some of my first published short stories include "Cendrillon and the Chromium Prince" (Machinations 2002) and "Fairy Godmother Express," (ASIM 2002) the latter being based around a mail order training program for Fairy Godmothers.

Undermining favourite old stories, treating them with sarcasm and twistiness while mining them for parts, is one of my favourite writing techniques. I've done it with classics like *The Three Musketeers** and *Pride and Prejudice*,† I've done it with Shakespeare‡ and oh, have I done it with Greek myth.§

But there's something about fairy tales.

More than any other kind of story, it was fairy tales that taught me about adaptations — about retellings and different versions. I've always been fascinated by how stories change when they get retold in different formats. I don't have many specific book memories of fairy tales from my childhood, possibly because I was reading novels so young that I barely recall any picture books. I have an ancient vintage paperback of Perrault, but I couldn't tell you if I acquired it when I was 6 or 16.

The fairy tales I remember absorbing as a child were from other places — not Disney, really, my childhood

---

* *Musketeer Space* (2016) by Tansy Rayner Roberts
† *The Season of Dragons* (2024) by Tansy Rayner Roberts
‡ most recently, *This Enchanted Island* (2024) by Tansy Rayner Roberts
§ *Gorgons Deserve Nice Things* (2023) by Tansy Rayner Roberts

Disney content was pretty much *Mary Poppins* over and over with a side helping of *Bedknobs and Broomsticks*. Despite my heavy reliance on VHS rentals, I was never especially interested in that version of Snow White or Cinderella or Sleeping Beauty — but I have powerful memories of a vinyl record of a Hansel and Gretel opera which burnt that story into my head. There were plays a plenty — my acting debut was as the cow in Jack and the Beanstalk — and *Faerie Tale Theatre* caught me at a very impressionable age. I remember several of those productions, though the only one I owned on VHS was *The Twelve Dancing Princesses*. I watched it over and over, until it was basically imprinted on my ribs.

(It's likely that I read Roald Dahl's *Revolting Rhymes* ahead of some of the stories he parodied; certainly, I knew about the darker side of the stories from early on. I always knew that the grandmother really got eaten and that the stepsisters cut off their feet — I'm not 100% sure that Dahl was the one who told me this. My mother is a likely culprit.)

On my first visit to London at 10 years old I discovered the history of Pollock's Toy paper theatres, another mild obsession that has ticked away inside me ever since. Their version of Cinderella (*Cendrillon*) was far more interesting to me than picture books.

Was that the beginning of my obsession with fairy tale frocks? Hard to say. But I do love a magical fashion parade.

Jim Henson's *The Storyteller* and Rik Mayall's *Grim Tales* cemented fairy tales for me as a visual medium — perhaps people with stronger memories of the picture books they read had that association all along. The images have stayed with me even more strongly than the stories.

I tell a lie. I do remember a picture book, of sorts. At some point I acquired an Arthur Rackham colouring book which included actual fairy tales retold, along with his classic illustrations — I read and held and loved this book, barely even attempting to colour the pages. That wasn't the point of it. The drawings excited and delighted me.

Years later I realised that what I had internalised as Rackham's clear, beautiful black and white line art style had been simplified for colouring pages, not the actual artwork. By then the damage was done — his real art, which I do love, often feels a bit cluttered and over-drawn to me. I'm uncomfortable with him in full colour, happier in black and white and silhouettes.

(Silhouettes never let you down. Any wonder that I keep chasing Kathleen Jennings, asking her to take on just one more art commission?)

Rackham's versions of all the fairy tale characters are printed on another of my ribs.

By the time *Beauty and the Beast* hit cinemas, I was a teenager, and a lot more interested in fairy tales than I had ever been as a child. I discovered Robin McKinley and Terry Pratchett, and learned that there were authors who could take a bare bones tale, add real characterisation, and worldbuild it into a novel. This process captured my attention deeply.

(I recall McKinley's *Beauty* being a soothing balm for those of us who were outraged when the lovely beast got transformed into a stupid prince at the end of the Disney movie — my friends and I, a cluster of 13 year old girls, literally cried out in protest.)

By the time I finished university, I was reading Marina Warner and Jack Zipes for fun. Analysing fairy tales, and learning about their history, expanded whole new worlds for me.

A trip to Rome in 2002 gave me two important milestones in my love for fairy tales: on the plane over, I read *Rose Daughter*, in which Robin McKinley took the fairy tale had provided with revolutionary treatment when she wrote *Beauty*, and did it AGAIN. This time, drawing on two more decades of experience being a person, and a new perspective from learning about gardening in the intervening years.

This blew my mind: that an author would have the sheer confidence and creative majesty to write two separate novels in response to the same fairy tale felt like magic. One was published in the year I was born, the other in my early adulthood.

(Robin McKinley is magic, never forget: she led the way.)

The more I learned, the more I loved. The first 15 years or so of the 21st century for me is wrapped up in the growing Australian SFF scene. At its peak of local publishing, there were some extraordinary books published, all by Australian women, with their own takes on particular fairy tales.

Margo Lanagan's *Tender Morsels* (2008) added claws and teeth to Snow White & Rose Red, a similar treatment to what Robin McKinley had done with Donkeyskin in her heart-breaking *Deerskin* novel.

Kate Forsyth has devoted a whole era of her career to big literary novels balancing dark eras of our history with classic fairy tales: the first of these and still my favourite was *Bitter Greens* (2012) which explores historical witchcraft in Italy alongside writer's salons in France alongside the fairy tale of Rapunzel.

Then there's Juliet Marillier, who was writing fairy tales all along, from the exceptional *Daughter of the Forest* (1998) based on The Six Swans to *Wildwood Dancing* (2006) based on those Twelve Dancing Princesses (always my favourites).

Fairy tales often make me angry. I want more justice than the stories themselves allow for — versions which point out the cruelty of the men or the viciousness of the villains often make me happy. It's extraordinary really that I didn't see *Into the Woods* until quite recently, because I would have adored its narrative choices so much in my teens.

Fairy tales make more sense to me when they are under interrogation. When I had kids, I found that I wasn't able to read fairy tales to them without my own commentary. The picture book of Snow White which my son had as a child was a version without the non-consensual kiss, but was weirdly *worse* — the dwarves gave Snow in her glass coffin to a random prince passing by just because he asked to take her! They all then dropped her coffin, dislodging the apple. My kid got a short lecture (every time) on why it was inappropriate for Snow's friends to be so cavalier with their friend's "dead" body.

Our version of Red Riding Hood was even better — because the grandmother of the story was replaced by Glammer, my kids' own grandmother who *as we know* has strong muscles, chops her own damned wood, and isn't going to be anyone's victim.

(My mum is 82, and still chops her own wood.)

I love a shared world fantasy, when it comes to fairy tales — *Shrek* was probably more enjoyable to me because I hadn't seen *Into the Woods* yet, but it works on many levels. I also really enjoyed the worldbuilding and character work of *Once Upon a Time*, which is full of terrible people making terrible choices but also weirdly great. Our family didn't make it all the way through the show the first time around, but we recently revisited it with youngest (now 15). At its worst, it is schlocky melodrama but at its best it's such an epic, ambitious show that gives no fucks about any preconceptions you might have about its characters. The redemption/unredemption arcs get exhausting with the villains (who are all the best characters) but it's such sheer fun to see the characters played with so shamelessly, especially because they are clearly the Disney versions and we're used to the idea that Disney is all about shiny IP control, not wild soapy experimenting.

In true Robin McKinley style, *Once Upon A Time* is unafraid to retell a fairy tale more than once when a new idea comes along.

For a while there, my *Castle Charming* series sucked up a lot of my creative feelings about fairy tales — this was a series of novellas that became a fix-up novel and it remains one of the most sympathetic portrayal of fairy tale princes I've ever written. I wanted to write something that felt Young Adult and fun but also addressed the fact that... being in royal families screws people up in the real world, so would that do in a fairy tale world?

I love a bit of modern Ruritanian romance, or trashy palace dramah like *The Royals* or *The Princess Diaries*. My broken messy princes in *Castle Charming* are just sad little rich boys, but I fell in love with them as I always do when I write about damaged fictional men.

I wanted *Castle Charming* to feel modern — with its tabloid newspapers and casually queer young adults and so on — but still be set in a magical kingdom. I pulled in all my favourite iconic fairy tale tropes — Cinderella and her glass slipper, Sleeping Beauty and her spindle, the beanstalk, the pumpkin coaches...

And the Twelve Dancing Princesses again, only this time it's *one* prince, and he ends up in a skeevy fairy nightclub, not a fancy underwater promenade with gold and silver fruits hanging from the trees...

When I wrote *Castle Ever After*, an epilogue to farewell my beloved *Castle Charming* reprobates, I chose the Snow Queen and added some Nutcracker for good measure — sure, *Frozen* reinvented that story for a new generation, but that didn't mean I couldn't take a stab at it. Especially as I'd stolen Kai's name from that story in the first place...

In assembling the stories for this collection, I noticed there was a huge gap between older fairy tale stories I wrote early in my career, and a new wave of available reprints from the last five years. There are many reasons for this — for a while there I was heavily into writing stories inspired by other sources. But a big part of that "gap" is because all my fairy tale ideas and impulses flooded directly into *Castle Charming*, a five year project which concluded in 2020 with *Castle Ever After* and a Kickstarter including commissioned artwork and special hardback editions.

Kai will always be my Sleeping Beauty, and Dennis will always be his prince. (Reciprocated pining!) Ziyi will always be my angry Cinderella, and Camilla my even angrier Rapunzel. Chase and Cyrus will always be my favourite damsels. The King and Queen of Castle Charming represent all my feelings about how fairy tales never allow parents to be good at the job.

I love them so.

Still, it's nice to know that I have new feelings and thoughts about fairy tales to keep churning into story meat. Most of this book is made up of stories from the last five years, as my post-Castle Charming fairy tale feels crept up on me all over again.

I included some of my older pieces "from the vault" to remind myself that fairy tales have always been woven into my fabric.

I'm sure there are more Cinderellas and Prince Charmings and wolves and witches and fairy godmothers in my story futures, too. You wait all your life for an enchanted castle to come along, and three arrive all at once!

TANSY RAYNER ROBERTS, 2025

TOWERED

Day 1

I think I'll grow my hair.

Day 2

Should my hair be growing this fast? I wish I had someone to ask. Yesterday, it was above my shoulders, and today... well, today, it's brushing the small of my back.

How does hair even work, anyway?

Day 3

I've got really good at braiding.

Day 4

I'm baking bread. We're all baking bread. I live at the top of a tower block of apartments, twenty floors high. The scent of fresh-baked bread comes in through the vents, through the barely cracked windows, through the floorboards.

I eat bread, and braid my hair, and watch the tiny people out of my window.

This is my life now.

Day 5

They used to explain why, with every lockdown, every enforced isolation period. There used to be charts and maps and lists. TV—remember TV?—was a non-stop broadcast of why, and when, and what to do next. Who was essential enough to leave their homes. Who must stay put, until told otherwise.

This time, there wasn't much at all. A leaflet under the door. A siren in the air.

I think perhaps they don't want to explain because then they'd have to admit what is happening. It's not a virus this time. It's something else, something no one wants to say out loud.

I can't say for sure. But last time I looked out the window, watching the tiny people below, the small handful of emergency personnel (uniformed, masked, geo-tagged) or licensed delivery people allowed to walk across bridges, cross each other's paths, exist in the real world... I'm certain I saw one of them transform into a bear.

A while later, another grew large, too large, teetering on giant feet.

One security guard outside our own building grew so small I could no longer see them at all. Shrunk to the size of a mouse? Or actually transformed into a mouse?

I'm so high up. I can't be sure.

And yet.

I *know*.

Day 6

It's possible I've been reading too many fairy tales.

Day 7

Can anyone ever really read too many fairy tales?

Day 8

I do not consider myself a collector, and yet I have so many books, in every room. Fairy tales, all of them: classic collections, picture books, vintage tomes, modern retellings.

If I'm a collector, does that mean I'm not an obsessive?

All I have to read is here. Which is fine, because this is all I have ever read, for as long as I can remember. Fairy tales on fairy tales on fairy tales.

But now we can't go out, now the broadcasts have turned into static and the internet has given up the ghost...

(How many bars do you have? My devices flatlined on Day 1.)

Now we live in a new world order where ordinary citizens can't leave our apartment towers, and those essential workers still allowed outside keep transforming into things that aren't people...

There's no way to get new books.

So, this is it. All the books I'm ever going to read, here against my walls in shelves and stacks. This is the final collection.

And I wonder: if all I have to read is fairy tales for the rest of my life, then either that's a terrible coincidence, or somehow I knew the future was going to look like this.

Day 9

It's possible I am in fact a collector of books about fairy tales. What other explanation is there?

Day 10

I saw a person today. He flew past my window, tiny as a bird with buzzing wings. His face was quite clearly the same as the last delivery person who brought me noodles from the local place.

(The local place no longer answers my calls. I still have a landline, but no one's ever on the other end. It rings and rings.)

Perhaps if I make friends with the tiny flying people, they'll bring me acorns and sugar water and keep me alive.

Day 11

My grocery order, made by phone eight days ago, finally arrived. I did not see who delivered the bags to my door, but I heard hoof beats and what sounded like a horse's neigh just around the corner, heading for the lift.

I have to think it was a magical horse. I don't think anyone's ever convinced a non-magical horse to use a lift in a tower block.

At least I have ramen, and apples, and eggs. Life could be worse.

Day 12

Today it rained rose petals, from 11am until 4 in the afternoon.

I have questions.

Day 13

Today I turned a teacup into a frog.

I turned an egg into a tiny baby dragon who hid from me behind the spoons.

I turned a handful of my own hair into a plate of short-breads that I couldn't quite bring myself to eat.

Apparently, I am a witch now.

That feels like progress.

Day 14

My hair is now so long that it doesn't always follow me from room to room. It swirls around the lamp and the chair, stays put while I walk from the bathroom to the fridge and the bookshelves and back again.

At bedtime I have to walk backwards, retracing my steps, to unravel myself from the furniture. It's time to cut my hair.

Day 15

Cutting my hair was a mistake.

Day 16

Yes, yes, every time I cut it, it grows faster, I get it now. I've read that story.

Thanks very bloody much, E. Nesbit.

Day 17

Today I pushed my hair out of the window. It billowed and fell in tumbling, golden waves. Some of it braided. Some of it tangled. Some of it threaded through sleeves of garments and indoor plants and sewing projects I'll never see again.

My hair fell and it kept falling, over the edge to the street below.

I'm not getting out of this tower any other way. I know that now.

Day 18

Last time I walked as far as the lift, the buttons failed to respond. There used to be a set of emergency stairs, but the door has disappeared.

That was days ago, before I gave up on escape. When I thought perhaps my final hope was pushing my hair out the window.

Maybe someone would climb it. Maybe someone would solve my problem for me. Maybe someone would pull me to my death.

Fairy tales are all about innovation and hope. Aren't they? Sometimes they're about kindness.

I've read so many fairy tales, it's possible that I failed to take the most important message of all away from them.

Stories are not real life.

No one's coming to save me.

Day 19

Today, I climbed out of the window.

I wound my hair around and around the curtain hooks to hold it fast, then I hung from it, so I could cut myself off my hair and not the other way around.

Then I climbed out, clinging to the window ledge, as my body began to grow instead of the hair. Faster and faster. I grew heavy, leaden. My limbs extended. My weight made the building creak.

Finally, large enough, I stepped down into the street.
Safe. Free.

Now I am a giant woman, standing astride the city, still growing.

I saved myself, but who will save the city from me?

Are you wondering how I knew I could make myself grow? The answer is simple: I read it in a book.

Day ???

Here we are again.

What did you miss?

I grew so large that the city broke beneath my weight, so large that air went thin and breathing became impossible. When I fell, I became a force of nature. Destruction. Damage. Earthquake. Cavernous ravine.

I fell, and the continent screamed beneath me.

Act of—well, no. Not god. Fairy tale, perhaps.

Act of fairy tale.

Do I regret it?

Ask me again in the future.

After I fell, I slept. And when I awoke—now, whatever day this is—I found that someone, some brave and hardy soul, had cut my hair in my sleep. Don't ask me what they used. Helicopters? War planes. A single axe, over and over, cutting through a single hair like it was an ageless redwood. Something clever like that.

Now my hair is growing again, and I have returned to standard human height. Here I sit. Weighing next to nothing, comparatively speaking. Trapped in another tower.

This one is not an apartment block.

Someone built this tower out of the remains of a city that fell to the fairy tale plague. It's made from spindles and gold balls and thorns and dead wolves. It's made from straw and sticks and bricks.

My hair whorls out beyond the walls and windows, ever-growing, an ocean of myself, pushing outwards. The world will drown in my hair, eventually.

Here I remain, trapped inside, with nothing to read.

Day 31

They sent a prince to solve the problem that is me with mathematics and measuring. Apparently, he read the solution in a book. A good sign all around: people still read fairy tales.

I probably shouldn't have turned him into a frog, but I was having a bad day.

Day 47

Today, no one came to save me or to kill me, which makes a change from recent events.

It's time to save myself. Again.

If that means saving the world from me at the same time, well. Things can be two things at the same time.

They have left me nothing—no food, no water. Nothing I could possibly work magic upon. Nothing I could transform. Except the tower for itself, the hair on my head, the skin on my bones.

I bit a piece of fingernail from my hair, and transformed it into a gleaming, shining sword.

And then...well.

You know what I did next.

You probably read it in a book.

I cut my hair from my head, and my head from my hair, at the same time. The sword swished. The blade cut.

And after that...

I was unstoppable.

Author's Note: Rapunzel, Melisande, Towers

I like Disney's *Tangled* movie just fine, though I spent a lot more time with the *Tangled* Playstation game which digs deep into the aesthetics of the film, especially Rapunzel's flowers, her artistic flair, and her use of hair as a weapon, all of which is pretty great.[*]

When it comes to Rapunzel iconography, I've always been more enamoured of the Tower than the Hair. (Let's not even talk about the prince, usually so dull, the smartest thing Disney did with that film was to replace him with a rogue.)

There's something chilling and cozy in equal measure about Rapunzel's imprisonment. Sure, she can't leave, *but*... (I love a tower in a story almost as much as I love a ball-room or a library or a library the size of a ballroom).

I went through a phase where my chosen writing

---

[*] I love a computer game that lets you play in a magical world and collect shiny things, I don't understand why there aren't more of these. The Hercules Playstation game was EXCELLENT.

mentors (via blog posts and podcasts) were Lani Diane Rich and Jennifer Crusie. I went from knowing almost nothing about romance in stories to understanding the structure and purpose of romance: why it works and especially why it doesn't. (I don't know if their podcast analysing romantic comedy films is still available but I ate it up with a *spoon*.)

One gem of writing insight I took from them — I think it was Lani who said it first, though it could as easily have been Jenny — was about the Tower. Specifically the Tower in tarot card readings, and how it means destruction and crisis, but also liberation and renewal.

Lani talked about how the key she had found to writing satisfying women's fiction was to 'tower' her heroine up front. Wreck her old life in chapter 1, then write a story that shows her strength in recovery.

I've kept this with me for years (maybe decades?) — especially the concept of 'tower' as a verb.

To tower your heroine/to destroy her life so she can be remade.

(It's not just women's fiction, obviously, it's a solid structure often used for heroes in action movies. And *Batman*.)

"Towered" was published in 2022, so it's a Covid story. It feels like everything written from 2020 onwards was either a Covid story, a Covid response story, or a Covid denial story. Do we put it in our stories at all? Do we carry on writing a world where it never happened?

Five years on from the beginning of Covid it feels like we have a clearer idea now on how to write about it. Like other life-changing historical tragedies — whether it's 9/11, or the Port Arthur Massacre — it takes time to understand what has changed forever and what is basically the same a few years later. (Not to mention the disconnect where some people behave as if nothing changed and others can't un-see the changes.)

There's a language to shared past experience, and a huge event like Covid leaves patterns we can recognise. In the most recent Doctor Who Christmas Special, Nicola Coughlan's character unloads about the trauma of knowing her mother died alone in hospital, getting angry all over again about how many other people casually broke 'the rules' for selfish reasons. She doesn't specifically mention that this was during Covid lockdowns — she doesn't have to. The language is there.[*]

I've always liked writing stories that are time-stamped — containing little details about life that you might have otherwise forgotten ten years later.[†] Whether you experienced lockdowns vicariously, or long-term, or only had to deal with them for a few months because your entire state was locked down for nearly a year (hello, fellow Tasmanians!) there are little details that bring back that time. Sourdough starters pinned to lampposts. Soft toys left in windows to make private walks feel more friendly. Memories, buried in fiction.

---

[*] Forty years from now, it's likely that podcasters (or whatever we have instead of podcasters, I guess just injectable fannish wisdom) will have to explain diligently about the relevance of Covid in the 2020s, just as Doctor Who fans now earnestly explain the relevant of 1970s era strike action to the Peladon stories.

[†] I diligently wrote a short story about motherhood in the year each of my children was born, conscious that I would forget most of what I felt back then… and I was right. But I still have the stories.

Towered is not a Rapunzel retelling, all towers aside. It's a Melisande retelling.

For many years, I remembered Melisande as one of the fairy tales written by Oscar Wilde. I owned it as a tiny illustrated book and I was so sure he was the author whenever I recalled it.

But no, it was Nesbit all along. Thank goodness I wrote a story to remind myself of this important fact.

"Melisande: or short and long division"* is often cited as a fairy tale parody, but I don't think that's quite true. It's a fairy tale that uses tropes from other fairy tales, but that's true of literally all fairy tales — they're constantly eating each other.

Reading it, the story feels just as true and funny and strange as any other. It is a fairy tale in which the characters know they are in a fairy tale, and can reference other fairy tales, and think this means they are smart enough to get away with it.

The plot, in short:

The baby princess is cursed to be bald at her christening, and is allowed to cash in her father's spare wish at the age of 5. She asks for golden hair that will grow twice as fast when it is cut, which leads to a whole bunch of problems through her adolescence, both physical and mathematical... and it gets worse once a prince tries to solve the problem by cutting the princess off her hair, because *she* starts growing.

---

* found in *Nine Unlikely Tales* (1901) by E. Nesbit but, perhaps most importantly, available on Project Gutenberg.

The solution involves timing, a sword and a very large set of weighing scales, but as with all fairy tales the end is never the interesting part. The body horror concept of hair growing so fast you can never be rid of it is almost as grim as a trapped princess using her hair as a ladder for other people, and a prince being pushed off a tower into thorns...

I kind of love this story. As with all Nesbit's writing, it's funny and sharp as a knife. But I still remember the shock and surprise of realising that fairy tales could be written by real people — not only real people hundreds of years ago. Twenty-four years of Edith Nesbit's lifespan overlapped with that of my grandfather. She was a modern writer!

If she could do it, why not me?

The Princess went on growing. By dinner-time she was so large that she had to have her dinner brought out into the garden because she was too large to get indoors. But she was too unhappy to be able to eat anything. And she cried so much that there was quite a pool in the garden, and several pages were nearly drowned. So she remembered her "Alice in Wonderland," and stopped crying at once. But she did not stop growing.

— "MELISANDE: OR LONG AND SHORT DIVISION," E. NESBIT.

DEATH OF SNOW

Cinders

This week, our hotel smells of apples. Every dish that comes out of our restaurant kitchen includes the same ingredient: sliced, diced, roasted, stuffed. Didn't think it was possible to turn apples into soups, omelettes, kebabs, a nine course degustation for one?

Our chef will show you otherwise.

You don't even have to read the menu, just grab a copy and inhale the scent.

That's what comes from hiring witches, I suppose. They're crafty, but single-minded. Our last chef was all about the pumpkins for breakfast, lunch and tea. Fritters and casseroles, pies and curries.

Before that, we had months with a chef who only worked with the same leafy green: I never did figure out if it was a herb or a lettuce, but by the end of it all I was sick of the taste of rapunzel.

I suppose apples aren't so bad. We get more walk-in guests these days, drawn in by the heavy aroma of fruit and spices.

"Do you have any rooms free? What *is* that delicious smell?"

I'm at Reception, checking in a nice middle-aged couple to the Coral Room. Halfway through the tidal warnings I am obliged to provide for the underwater bathroom, my sister Silla breezes past. "Don't forget it's your turn to clean the Snow Suite!"

Bite me.

I turn up my smile brighter to Mrs and Mrs Johanssen. "Can I just check your swimming certification before I give you the keys?"

We have four suites in the hotel: Snow and Glass and Godmother and Queen. No one likes cleaning the Snow Suite. It's hard to manage hospital corners on the sheets when your teeth are chattering from cold.

No other suite requires a shovel and a pickaxe to complete routine housekeeping.

When I'm done with that, my other jobs for the morning include picking arrows out of the walls of the Forest Room, thinning the bulrushes in the Frog Room, and loading up the washing machines in the cellar with towels and sheets.

After all that, I deserve a cheeseburger, but my lunch

options are apple pancakes or Waldorf salad. I take the pancakes.

Back to Reception after that, smiling and nodding. There are worse jobs in the world. Jobs that don't provide pancakes. If I didn't have to share an attic with the three people in the world who hate me most, I'd consider myself happy.

In the middle of the afternoon, Ms White arrives with her cherry red suitcase, and my smile becomes a lot more natural. She's my favourite regular, and I don't care who knows it.

Ms White looks around my age, though I catch a hint from time to time that she might be older. Her hair is black and shining, her skin glows like she's living in a moisturiser commercial, and her eyes are both knowing and mysterious.

"How long is your stay?" I ask, for purely professional reasons.

"Oh, a few weeks. Longer if you'll have me. I booked a suite?"

Sometimes Ms White prefers one of our smaller rooms, and she always prefers a new experience over the familiar.

"We have the Snow Suite ready," I say without having to check the computer. She's never stayed in that one before.

Ms White winces, then tries to cover it with a dazzling smile. "Not that one. Is anything else available?"

"The Glass Suite is free. Or the Forest Room is available for a longer stay, if you'd prefer?"

"Glass," she says, turning her smile up from dazzling to incandescent. "I like the sound of that."

"Will you be dining with us this evening?"

She sniffs the air. Her perfect mouth forms something I have never seen before upon her face: a frown of disapproval. "Apples?"

"Our new chef."

The smile comes faster than the frown, whisks it away as if I never saw it. "I love the taste of apples."

Inspector Wolf

I was called to attend a suspicious death at 2:45am in the morning, at the Stepmother Hotel on Slipper Street. The hotel owner was not in attendance.

The hotel receptionist, Miss Cinders, escorted me to the landing on the second floor. She was visibly distressed, with tear-stained face and hands that trembled. She spoke too quickly, all at once, as if she was nervous in the presence of the police.

"I don't know what happened," she said, over and over. "I can't think how, or who — she was so *beautiful*."

Miss Cinders is not ruled out as a suspect.

The victim is 5 foot 6 inches tall, with curling black hair. She was discovered lying on the staircase, wearing a red dressing gown over a French silk negligee. Her feet were bare. In one hand, she held an apple (red) with a single bite taken out of it. I have requested our forensic team investigate whether the bite matches the victim's teeth, but they have not yet got back to me with an answer.

According the hotel register, the victim's name was Ms

Snow White of no fixed abode. She is a regular customer of this hotel, and on this occasion was staying in the Glass Suite.

While awaiting the representative from the coroner's office, I investigated the suite in questions, and discovered that Ms White's suitcase was empty. She arrived at the Stepmother Hotel with no spare clothes, or even a toothbrush.

Miss Cinders insisted that Ms White was wearing a coat and other clothes when she arrived, which suggests the dressing gown and negligee were in the suitcase originally. There was no explanation for Ms White's missing clothes, or lack of personal items/toiletries beyond those supplied by the hotel.

The apple was originally provided from room service on request of Ms White.

Other staff on duty that night included Miss Silla and Miss Milla, daughters of the (absent) hotel owner. Both claimed to be asleep during the room service call. Miss Cinders received the call, collected the apple from the kitchen at 12:08, and delivered it personally to the Glass Suite.

The hotel chef had left the hotel at 10:45 the previous evening, and cannot be contacted for interview at this time.

My investigation continues.

Witch

I imagined a dozen ways to end her life. I stole her breath with tightened stays, I cut her heart out with a knife, I poisoned apples by the bushel.

Every time I baked a pie I thought: this one could be my murder weapon.

I dreamed her death so many times. I always woke with a smile upon my lips.

I took this job to be near her. Every apple peel was intended to wrap around her white and fragile throat. Every loaf of bread or slice of cake was baked for her to choke upon.

Snow White, my nemesis.

Beautiful daughter, dead.

I only exist to end her life.

And yet.

This time. It wasn't me.

Snow

I only haunt the best hotels. If you're going to die, do it in style: high thread count and after hours room service.

I've never died at the Stepmother Hotel before. Which is odd, when you think about it. I try to spread myself around, but there's no denying this place is one of my favourites. The odds were in favour of it happening here, sooner or later.

Since I first escaped the witch, the castle, my old life in another world, I've died thirty-seven times. Usually in the luxurious surroundings of a glamorous hotel suite, restaurant or bar. Sometimes a museum, if it comes upon me during the day. Once, on the runway at Fashion Week. Once, in the back of a taxi cab.

I move from city to city, country to country. Back and forth. Glamour, always. I try my best to avoid all sites of past deaths. Nothing worse than trying to check into a hotel only to terrify the staff because they remember cleaning your blood off the bathroom floor.

It is what it is. It's a long time since I've been angry

about it, or even sad. Tonight, I'm both. Because I'm dead on the staircase of the Stepmother Hotel, one bite from a perfect apple lodged in my throat, and that means I can't come back here, ever again.

I'll never get to flirt with Cinders at the front desk. Never ride up in the Art Deco elevator. Never get up the nerve to try the Snow Suite after all. (How bad could it be?)

I'm done here.

Nothing to do but wait.

Twelve hours after my most recent death, I awake on a bright green mountainside, gasping for air. At least, it looks like a mountainside. Sometimes it's a riverbank, or a desert. Sometimes a long, grey beach. Sometimes a forest so deep you can barely see out of it.

Never snow. I have a memory of snow (and ravens, black wings flapping), but it doesn't belong to this world, or the one where I have died so many times. When I remember snow and ravens, it's as if I am a child trying to hold on to a place that no longer exists. I'm not ready to accept the memories that would flood back if I saw snow again.

And so, the mountains are green, even at the top-most peaks. There are no ravens here.

I'm breathing, at least. My throat is clear of the fragment of apple that cut off my air. Still, I'm not out of the woods.

I call this the other place, the in between. I usually have to wait here until my earthly body is disposed of. Burial, cremation, whatever it takes. It might be days or even weeks, especially if the police take an interest. They can keep you longer than you'd imagine, in a morgue.

When I return it's instant, a snap of the fingers and I'm back on a train or the back of a taxi with my cherry red suitcase, heading for the next glamorous location. I don't question these things, not any more. I don't know why I am the way that I am.

I don't know who murders me, every time.

I do know that this mountain is getting chilly, and there's no way off but through.

I also know that I'm the only person who does this. The only person like me in the world. Constantly ricocheting between life and death, with barely enough time in between to freshen my lipstick.

So, why am I not alone this time?

She walks up the mountain towards me, her sneakered feet crushing the soft green grass and wildflowers. She looks calmer than in real life, her pretty face framed by bright golden hair. Usually she is rushed off her feet, dragged in three places at once, but then she'll sees me and smile. It's like I've given her a glass of iced tea on a hot day, and I'm the only one who can offer her a moment of respite.

Not today. Today, she looks wall to wall calm, like being here is the best thing that's ever happened to her.

"Ms White," she says. "*There* you are."

"Cinders," I say. I want to rage at her, to surround her with questions: *what, who, where?* How can she be here? Is she dead too? Instead, I say: "You can call me Snow."

And then I'm awake.

No, that's not the word I meant to use. Not merely awake. I'm *alive*.

My throat is sore, like I've been fighting to breathe. I'm sprawled awkwardly on a staircase, the edges digging into my neck and back and half a hip. I roll, push myself into a seated position. My head swims for a moment of dizziness, and I spit that damned knot of apple into my hand.

"What did you do?" I ask through a burning, swollen, angry throat.

Cinders, crouched a little way from me, looks horrified. "I kissed you," she whispers. "Oh my god, what a creepy thing to do, I know that. You were dead. For hours. How could I..."

"You kissed me."

Stunned, she nods.

"You saved me."

"I don't see how," Cinders bursts out. "How could that possibly have worked?"

"I don't know." I stretch my neck, let it crick once. "But it's different this time. I wonder why."

Inspector Wolf

The suspect, referred to at her place of work as 'the chef' or 'the witch,' resides in a small bedsit flat at 175 Redgrave Street, on the nineteenth floor. As I entered the suspect's flat with her permission, I observed a strong smell of apples and cabbage.

The suspect, approx. 4 foot eleven inches, with long straggly grey hair, was visibly distressed and unable to sit still during the questioning.

I observed a bulletin board on the far wall of her studio, covered with various photographs of the victim, Ms White, and several newspaper articles depicting a series of unfortunate and mysterious deaths of a woman meeting Ms White's description.

A serial killer, then. Seeking out and murdering women of a particular physical type.

"Did you kill these women?" I asked.

"All of them," confessed the suspect without hesitation. I've killed her thirty-six times. But this time..." She turned and stared at me with an expression I can only describe as *desperate*. "I poisoned every other apple. Not this one."

This seemed an appropriate juncture to arrest the suspect, and bring her into official police custody for further questioning.

Cinders

I've never raised anyone from the dead before. Not with a kiss. I'm not even that good at kissing, I've only ever practiced with Robbie Buttons behind the bike sheds and sometimes on my own hand when I was thinking about movie stars.

Ms White... *Snow, she said I could call her Snow*... looks none the worse for her adventures. Her eyes are bright as ever, her skin as pale and glowing, her lips so dark red...

Well, I'd better stop thinking about lips for now. Don't want to get distracted.

She's distracted enough for the both of us, marching up and down the staircase landing, her dressing gown gaping open just enough to show off all the pretty silk and curves beneath. "An accident," she mutters. "Could it really be an accident? After all this time? It's usually murder."

"That's what the Inspector reckoned," I chime in. "Inspector Wolf. He's gone to interview the chef, what with the apple and all."

"Chef. Apples." Snow spins around, her eyes fierce. "She's not a witch, is she, your chef?"

"I assumed so. I know it's rude to judge, but she looks like... Well, you know. Crone aesthetic, and all that."

"Crone," Snow murmurs. "Can it really be her, after all this time? Was it always her?"

She makes a flit for the door. "Time to talk to this inspector of yours."

"Dressed like that?" I yelp.

"Oh, yes." She glances down, shrugs, and suddenly she's wearing her trim red jacket again, over a suit and fresh nylons. Her shoes are the colour of toffee apples. "Is the police station near here? Let's go!"

Inspector Wolf

That's a turn up for the books and no mistake.

Our murder victim, Ms Snow White, arrived at the station at 7:15am, demanding to speak to the person in charge of the investigation: myself. She was accompanied by Miss Cinders, the former suspect who had discovered Ms White's body.

After I had ascertained that Ms White was indeed alive and no longer classified as a murder victim, I attempted to question her about the previous night's movements. She refused to co-operate with the authorities until she had the opportunity to interview the suspect known as 'the witch,' who was at that time in police custody.

In the name of keeping the peace, and in full acknowledgement that this was an exceedingly unusual situation, I allowed Ms White and Miss Cinders to enter the interview room with the witch. I accept full responsibility for this decision.

"It's you," said the murder victim, Ms White. "You're the one who killed me. Thirty six times!"

The witch appeared to confirm this statement with her silence, and a small nod of her head. "Would you like to hear a story?" she asked.

Witch

Once upon a time, in another world, I was a Queen. Oh, yes, you wouldn't think it to look at me now. I was young and beautiful and vain. I had magic, too, enough magic to fill a palace and a country with prosperity and happiness.

Instead, I used the magic to keep my skin fair, my wardrobe fine, my figure trim. And with the rest of it, well. Every lady needs a friend. Mine was my mirror.

One day the mirror said to me, "The child is growing up. Soon she will be prettier than you."

I could not have that. Could not see beyond my own face. The mirror said: "Cut out her heart and eat it." And I tried, oh, I tried.

Our world, the world we come from, it bleeds curses. If you use magic for selfish means, that magic bites you back. I knew that once, but I had forgotten, or I thought myself too powerful to be concerned.

The moment I drove that knife into her heart, I was cursed, along with my magic. I woke up here, in this world of loud automobiles and call waiting and microwaves. I knew in my heart a single mission: to kill Snow White. And so I did. I was good at it.

I had enough practice, after all.

I baked the pies, I pulled the stays, I choked you, beat you, shot you through the heart. It was a good day's work, over and over. Thirty-six times. I grew uglier with each of your deaths. Older. Crumbling to dust.

As it turns out, I don't mind. Murder is far more satis-fying than beauty ever was. Your blood tastes sweet, every time I let it fall.

I have no regrets.

Snow

There is silence, after the witch stops speaking. Cinders looks like she is about to be sick. Inspector Wolf stops writing his notes and stares at the ceiling.

I look my murderer in the eye. "You know what? I think it was an accident this time."

"Impossible," croaks the witch. "Someone stole your death from me…"

"Cinders gave me the apple. And I was distracted. Thinking about her pretty eyes. I took too big a bite, and it caught in my throat. I stopped breathing. You had nothing to do with it." I stand up, raising myself to my full height and grace. "I don't think I need you any more. I'll be more careful. *I'll see you coming if you try.*"

The witch — my mother once, and my queen, though I had forgotten both these facts until now — unfurls her shrunken body. "You never see me coming. Your deaths are everything to me."

"Not any more. I'm not yours to kill."

She's desperate, clawing at the table like she wishes it was my throat. "I am nothing without killing you."

"Then be nothing," I tell her.

It's enough. She falls apart, like a cloud of ashes on the air, and crumbles away until there is nothing left of her but curls of apple peel, scattered on the floor of the police interview room.

"Retirement," mutters Inspector Wolf between his teeth. "Or a holiday at least. Somewhere warm."

"You're free," says Cinders, sounding dazed. "Free of her. Free to live whatever life you choose."

"I am," I agree. "I need a holiday. Not warm, I think." I smile at Cinders. "Your Snow Suite... it actually has snow, I think?"

She swallows a laugh. "So much snow! People are usually surprised..."

"No more surprises for me. But I think I'm ready." I reach out carefully, and take her hand. "Show me your Snow Suite. And we'll go on from there."

I can already taste the crisp, familiar scent of a frozen winter, and hear the beating of raven wings upon the air. *Home*. It won't be home. But it might taste a little like it, for a while.

Tomorrow, I'm going to have to learn to live in this world.

Author's Note: on Snow White, Cinderella, Wolves and Witches

I love a fairy tale mash-up. Who doesn't? From *Shrek* to *Once Upon a Time* and all the way back to *Into the Woods* (this is the actual order in which I consumed these productions).

I always loathed *Fables* (first published in 2002) — far too grimdark & misogynist for my tastes, and the thing that drove me up the wall was how the creator was lauded as some kind of genius creative force for his terribly original idea when putting all the fairy tales into a shared universe AU is like the most *obvious* thing to do with them.

Each Peach Pear Plum, anyone? *Witches Abroad? Castle Waiting?*

Anyway, I love a shared universe. The MCU might have given us all ice cream headaches from too much of a good thing, but the idea of characters I know all crossing into the same fictional world has always excited me.

This story is my take on the 'fairy tales meet crime fiction tropes' subgenre that is hugely popular in children's fiction — including the Sesame Street sketches where Kermit the Frog interviews fairy tale characters as a news reporter, trying to get to the truth of their dramatic life events.

For the record: my favourite version of Snow White was *The Charmings*,[*] a 1980's family sitcom that I came across when living in England and still can't believe actually existed.[†]

My favourite version of Cinderella is a cross between *Ash* by Malinda Lo, *Ella Enchanted* by Gail Carson Levine (I remain embarrassed how far I got through the book before I realised it was Cinderella) and Season 7 of *Once Upon a Time*.[‡]

My favourite version of Red Riding Hood is every Teen Wolf fanfic where someone draws attention to Stiles canonically wearing a red hoodie.

My favourite fairy tale witch is always Granny Weatherwax, except when it's Nanny Ogg.[§]

Diana Wynne Jones did it better than anyone (she always does) in *Howl's Moving Castle*, creating a world where fairy tales are accepted history, and guidelines for the future:

> *In the land of Ingary, where such things as seven-league boots and cloaks of invisibility really exist, it is quite a misfortune to be born*

---

[*] I am well aware that its status as my favourite relies heavily on me never watching it again in the 21st century, despite the existence of YouTube.

[†] Sister Monica Joan/Judy Parfitt from *Call the Midwife* plays the wicked queen!

[‡] I still think it's bizarre that the Bridgerton novel *An Offer from a Gentleman* is based on Cinderella when none of the other books are fairy tale retellings, doesn't everyone else get thrown out by that???

[§] Though if we're going to be 100% honest here, my favourite fairy tale witch is my mother.

the eldest of three. Everyone knows you are the one who will fail first, and worst, if the three of you set out to seek your fortunes.

Sophie Hatter was the eldest of three sisters. She was not even the child of a poor woodcutter, which might have given her some chance of success...

"It's not fair!" Lettie would shout. "Why should Martha have the best of it just because she was born the youngest? I shall marry a prince, so there!"

— *HOWL'S MOVING CASTLE* (1986), DIANA WYNNE JONES

WAKING FLORA
A JONTY AND ROLAND ADVENTURE

a tale of towers, too many castles,
and the best of all possible squires

I never expected inheriting a castle to cause such a fuss!

One does have to be alert to the possibility of peril and what-not when it comes to castle-acquisition in this day and age. I've heard some stories, I can tell you. Dragons and ghouls and poisonous cabbages... my cousin Whippy, you know, Sir Wythbutnot, he had a whole business to sort out with evil stepmothers and a blighted apple orchard when he came into his castle.

Still, one can't turn it down. It's an honour and a duty, our family likes to say, as if this is a tradition that's been passed down for generations, and not simply a deuced nuisance that came about after the enchanted kingdoms fell under the rule of a megalomaniacal tyrant. Or, as I call him, Uncle George.

Uncle George always had a bee in his bonnet about chivalric duty. I suppose one isn't born a tyrant. It sneaked up on him after a handful of decades muttering about inheritance laws and Eldest Sons Letting The Side Down, and

the Good Old Days when knights were green, and royals
were all trying to kill each other with daggers.

No one can say the signs were not there. My childhood
and that of my cousins involved rather too many forced
drills when Uncle George was around, not to mention all
those meaningful looks over bed-time stories whenever a
noble knight came up against a wicked giant, or a prince got
a chance to tell everyone how much charm he had to offer.

My cousin Daffy wasn't the least surprised when Uncle
George/her Pa went full overlord about a decade ago,
beheading our little kingdom's perfectly harmless king and
taking the reins. Not that Daff got much of a chance to say:
"I told you so." Once the dust settled, all of us younger
family members were princes and princesses, whether we
liked it or not. Every single one of my unmarried female
cousins was shut up in her own tower until rescued by a
suitable suitor.

(Took the almighty negotiating powers of several aunts
to calm things down after that, I can tell you, and I wouldn't
say 'calm' was the end result. We still can't all eat a civilised
lunch together without someone losing their temper.)

I think some of Daffy's sisters are still in towers, actually. Someone should look into that. Daffy herself stationed
a well-bribed maid with a golden wig at her window, and
ankled off to the nearest Bluestocking College. Last I heard,
she was on track for a doctorate.

Where was I?

Castles!

Not content with being a small-scale tyrannical despot
who chops off heads and locks up daughters, Uncle George
set off on a mighty crusade to bring every enchanted
kingdom under his thumb. He won a goblin army in a late

night card game with one of his less respectable friends in the warlord business, and that only encouraged him. Bang, snap, swish, before you knew it, our little kingdom had swallowed up twenty or so neighbouring principalities, including an aggressively long list of bespelled castles, cursed palaces, haunted manors and similar examples of feisty architecture.

(Leaving magical surprises behind in the brickwork has become a favourite pastime for recently-conquered king-doms. I can see why. It makes for an effective spot of passive aggressive vengeance.)

Next came the paperwork. So much paperwork! No one ever warns a would-be-tyrant how much bureaucracy is required to hang on to all the jolly old conquests once they've been conqed. I suppose no one's pay grade is high enough to break that sort of news to a known head-chopper.

Uncle George sweated bricks over how to fund the payroll for his Grand High Wizard Secretariat, when the bills for his various invasions started rolling in — even despots have to lump out the gold purses for the johnnies who do the real work behind the scenes. Wizards who know the difference between a binding contract and a budgetary spreadsheet are well aware of their own value, and not the least bit intimidated by the Dread Threat to Behead.

What with all the magic-users making bank in the Grand High Wizard Secretariat and planning the next wave of conquests, that left no one to sprint around tidying up the hex-happy castles dotted around the recently conquered countries.

Someone had to do the bally job.

And that was when good old Uncle George remembered

how many newly-crowned princes he had lolling about the place.

One of the joys of hanging from a branch (however low-hanging) of the Family Nouveau Royal, is an inheritance clause that kicks in once a chap turns twenty-one. So far, eleven of my older cousins have "come in to their castle." The chaps, that is. As established earlier in my tale, all the princesses of the realm get is towers and/or marriage contracts. Bit of a rummy deal, one might suggest, though considering how many princes have been maimed by their castle in recent years, the girls might be getting off lightly.

Conrad's castle was dragon-infested. If he hadn't quickly married a witch with a talent for reptile-repellence, it might have been curtains for good old Conrad, though he lost two fingers before the banns were read.

Beety scored a moat full of eels and three haunted cellars. He lost a leg and two squires in the first week, poor fellow!

Whippy of the aforementioned evil stepmother + blighted apple orchard shenanigans — astonishingly — still has all his limbs and has turned the whole business into a thriving cider industry. He's our success story. Best not ask about the emotional scars and night terrors.

Torquil got bats in the belfry — quite literally, not a metaphor, though I don't mind telling you, we were all placing some heavy misinterpretations on his letters for a while there. He only ever wears turtle-neck jumpers these days.

In short, I was prepared for tribulation when I came into my castle. But I was confident I could handle it. After all, I had a clear advantage over my cousins, when it came to the good old Prep For Trib.

I had my squire, Roland.

Ah, says you, but what good is a mere squire in the face of dragons and ghouls and all the other enchanted disasters that might be awaiting you in your recently-inherited castle, young Jonty?

To which I reply: clearly, you have not met Roland.

It's a joy to watch my squire work. Put him to serving up goblets of mead or greeting guests at the feast, and he's an artist, exactly the correct amount of smooth and smarm. Mention that the castle's a bit chilly these days and point him at the woodshed, he'll chop you a year's worth of fuel in an afternoon. Give him a prince with nothing to wear to the latest royal wedding, and he'll produce an acceptable doublet and hose out of thin air.

Put him in the way of a castle surrounded by impossibly thick, wildly tangled, definitely cursed thorn hedges, armed with nothing but a short-sword, and oh...

Watch Roland *slice*.

I know my place when there's hero-ing to be done — never mind the royalty, you'll find Sir Jonagold (Jonty to my chums — it should properly be Prince Jonty, but everyone's spent the last decade forgetting I'm a prince, why stop now?) bringing up the rear, carrying a hamper and on occasion, toting my squire's cloak.

Roland takes on so many duties that should be mine, strictly speaking, if I didn't have the knightly talent of a smaller-than-average pudding bowl. It's the least I can do, to carry the bags. He doesn't approve of me performing menial tasks, but what can he do about it when his hands are full of sword?

If my uncle hadn't conquered two dozen enchanted kingdoms and made himself Supreme Overking, my fate would have been extremely modest. Based on my actual skills, I'd have ended up a minor bard at best. Perhaps a tailor, or a landscape painter. No one would ever have looked at my fresh little face and declared 'let's put this one in armour!'

But the expectations of princes are rather high around here. Luckily, I have Roland to make up all my shortfalls.

That's us caught up! On with the tale.

Imagine the scene: the turrets of an enchanted castle peeping out over the top of high, cursed thorny hedges. A sunny day. Roses in bloom. A landscape painter might call the whole thing *picturesque*, if not for Roland and his sword, hacking his way through the shrubbery.

(I myself would suggest that Roland's sword-wielding competence and general muscular silhouette rarely makes a scene *less* picturesque, but let's keep personal confessions to a minimum for now.)

Rose petals billowed in the air above him, great clouds of floral confetti heralding my squire's general prowess with a blade. Muscles flexed beneath rolled-up sleeves.

If I was a bard, I'd write him a ballad.

"You have noticed, squire, that the thorns are closing in behind us?" I called out to this paragon of chivalry. It was for this reason that I was standing rather closer to his shapely behind than I usually dared.

I have always had a more nervous disposition than my squire, but even Roland showed a touch of concern as he wiped sweat from his heroic brow. He sent a hard stare at the hacked-up thorn hedges, even now reassembling themselves in our wake.

"Better not stop for a noonday repast, Sir Jonagold," he noted in the calmest of tones. "We wouldn't want to get entangled in the defensive spells."

"Jolly good," I agreed. "I'll pass you a chicken leg to gnaw on as we go, shall I?"

"I think that would be most efficient, Sir Jonagold, if it's not too much trouble."

And on he chopped.

It took around six hours to finally break through to the castle — and my, she was a beauty! All of those bedtime stories had set my expectations high, but no one could deny my dainty castle was a corker. Twisty towers, spiralling stairwells, and those little pointy roof bits, all in pale lilac brick and cerise tile right out of the illustrated pages. The sunlight had dimmed into the late afternoon, but that did not detract from the beauty of the castle, nor that of my strapping young squire.

"I say!" said I.

Roland, not looking even slightly tired, retrieved his cloak. No squire would dream of entering a castle under-dressed. "Time to survey your inheritance, sir?"

"Yes, indeed," I agreed. No time to bask Roland's mighty works now, though I would certainly encourage some appropriate basking at a later date.

"Shall I go ahead of you to check for traps, sir?"

"Indeed, yes, *yes*," for Sir Jonty is no fool.

Roland led the way, in that inimitable way he has, somehow restraining his bold heroic nature so that it would be apparent to any onlooker that he was the servant and I the master. I don't know how he does it, considering his shoulders are so much broader than mine.

"All clear, sir," he said finally, in a most reassuring voice, having defeated three traps of the 'snapping metal teeth' variety merely by being clever with a stick. What a man.

"Righty-ho," I replied, following my squire's shoulders into an ornate central courtyard.

A courtyard full of corpses.

"Oh," said I, stricken at the sight. Men, women, chil-dren, dogs. Laying about on the cobbles as if a mighty storm had struck them all in a single blow. "Oh," I breathed again, staggering back a little. "*What has that monster done?*"

When one's uncle becomes a fearsome despot, rampaging across the land and crushing the peasantry beneath his boots, well. The only way you stay sane under such circumstances is to tell yourself stories.

Stories like: *of course, they all fled before he took yet another kingdom for his own. They'll be huddled in cottages of distant rela-tions, safe and well.*

These folk had not fled. They hadn't even had the chance to be afraid. They were strewn about like dolls, as if they had fallen suddenly asleep in the middle of their daily work...

"Sir Jonagold..."

And here was I, the worst of fools, carrying on like all this was a mere inconvenience, something to be wry and long-suffering about, not a soul-crushing blight that Uncle George had brought upon our lands. Brought upon his own family. Making us complicit in his wretched, wretched crimes...

"*Jonty*."

I blinked. "Roland?"

"I think they're alive," said my squire, leaning over a grey-cheeked cook whose apron was covered in cobwebs.

in which Flora is awoken by a
squire and his charming prince

⁂

As it turned out, the reason that the castle folk looked
asleep was that they were, in fact, asleep. My doughty squire
and I were unable to wake them from that slumber.

This was almost worse, I thought as I patted the arm of
the sleeping cook, half-hoping she would spring alert and
tweak me for my impertinence. They might not be dead,
but there was still some sinister spell holding them all in
this state.

"Your uncle didn't do this to them," Roland said,
attempting to reassure me. "I think they did it to themselves. A form of protection..."

"And who," I raised my voice in anger. "*From whom*
would they need to protect themselves?"

It was rare for Roland to allow himself anything like the
look of pure frustration I saw in that moment. He was
usually the calm one, the soothing presence. He devoted so
many hours to telling me how I should be politic, stay calm,
appear as harmless as possible...

Nephews of the tyrant who go about muttering "It isn't

right" or "Someone should do something" tend to come to a sticky end, and I mean that literally.

It happened to my little cousin Feggles (Sir Fenwyck of Gaunt), before he was even old enough to come into his castle. He snapped something sarcastic to Uncle George over supper about daughters and nieces and towers and how certain tyrants should buck up their ideas. None of us ever heard from poor old Feggles again.

No one expected me make trouble, not when every rebellious streak I'd ever entertained was thoroughly muffled by my smooth-talking, fire-extinguishing squire.

There were times I almost resented Roland for being so dashed good at keeping me safe.

In this moment, looking around the courtyard full of sleeping souls, I felt a rising outrage that even my paragon of diplomacy would not be able to extinguish.

And, for once, the look on Roland's face suggested he would not even try.

"Let's break the spell," said I.

In the tallest tower, we found flowers. Flowers on every step of the curving stair, as fresh as the day they'd been picked, scattered like a carpet.

At the very top, well...

You know what we found.

You've read this story.

Her name was Princess Flora. You couldn't miss it. Someone had made a banner that hung from the ceiling above us. The tower room was lined with tapestries, devoted to this fair damsel's mighty deeds.

It was as if her people had thought none of them would be left alive to tell the world who this princess had been, and they jolly well wanted to be sure that future generations got the gist. Perhaps she might awaken in a century or two, all alone.

Uncle George's tyrannical rule began elevenish years ago, and his goblin army had swept across the wider lands ever since. At most, this castle had been under this spell for a decade.

I might have worked that out even if I didn't recognise the young lady.

My cousin Sassy was at school with a Flora. Robust girl, good at sports. Handy with a sword. She'd visited one summer hols, the year Sassy did the debutante thing (two years before Uncle George became a tyrant, turned our lives upside down and stuck poor old Sassy in a tower). I'd no idea Flora was a princess from some other kingdom, but back then I wouldn't have cared a lick.

If Flora was the same age as Sassy, she'd have been ten years older than me that summer — tiny Jonty, a mere shrimp of nine-and-a-half, who thought nothing of girls unless they were sneaking off on fishing trips without including him.

We'd be about the same age now, if Flora had spent a decade in this bower, protected from the world outside by magical roses and thorns and sleeping charms.

It looked like the same girl. She had a familiar solidity to her, like if she socked you in the arm, it would hurt for at least half an hour afterwards.

I remembered those rosebud lips, curved around words like 'push off, small fry, we're going fishing without you!' (It was almost certainly Sassy who said that to me, but a wounding remark is a wounding remark, when you're nine-and-a-half. At the very least, Flora was an accessory to the crime.)

According to the tapestries — and what sort of chump would take the time to embroider fibs — Flora was a mighty warrior, a noble ruler of her people, and an excellent fast-bowler at cricket. She took on thirteen fairy gifts at birth, and let me tell you: fairies provide more useful gifts than silver rattles and rag dolls, when they think there's a destiny on the horizon. They'd front-loaded this one with some serious fire power.

Princess Flora lay in her bower, hair spread wide over silken pillows, heart-shaped mouth pursed in anticipation of a kiss. Even asleep, she was brimming with magic. She lay beneath a quilt strewn with cut flowers that, like the blooms on the stairs, were not only still alive after a decade, but glowed with fairy dust.

Under Flora's name was a smaller banner, clearly stitched in a hurry. *Her righteous fury will save the world*, it proclaimed.

"Jolly good," said I. "Righteous fury is exactly what we need. Better wake her up."

I looked in expectation at my squire.

"You realise," said Roland, in that world-weary-yet-effortlessly-polite way he had about him, even after six hours of swording thorns. "*You* have to kiss her."

Honestly, dear reader. It hadn't occurred to me for a *moment*.

My squire and I rarely argue about anything more serious than whether the new tabard design is appropriate for a prince to wear in public, or whether I honestly have to purchase flowers for Aunt Hildebrand's favourite saint *again*.

I usually give in, after a bit of bargy for the sake of it, because it does not pay to disagree with one's squire. They always know best. Mine is endowed with an enormous brain and a sensitive heart, which is a jolly good combination when sensible choices are to be made.

However, in the matter of kissing young ladies to break spells, it turns out that my squire is a colossal fat-head.

We argued about it for about twenty minutes, doubling our previous record for disagreeable banter ('twas the matter of the long tippet sleeves, and I regret how easily I gave in).

My erudite and faultless argument was this: Roland had put in all of the knightly puff by getting us through the thorned hedge, and stepping in front of steel traps, not to mention all the other heroic things he did on a daily basis to cover up for my inadequacies. If someone was going to kiss a princess awake and take part in her fairy tale ending, it was not going to be I.

(It would break my heart, of course, to see him swallowed up into Princess Flora's story of destiny and vengeance, but that only made my heart harden to the inevitable sacrifice. I'd always known I would lose him to a worthier love than mine sooner or later, and this sturdy princess was both epic and deserving, if her tapestries were to be believed.)

Roland's argument, mundane and disappointingly bourgeois, (as if I hadn't caught him reading tracts of revolutionary poetry on his days off, who was he trying to kid?) was that as the legitimate heir of princely blood who had inherited this dashed castle, I should be imposing my willowy frame upon this blameless and unconscious young lady in order to fulfil the destiny *he* had always believed I would somehow blargle blargle, chivalric potential, I don't know, I tuned out after I realised he was speaking nonsense for the first time in his life.

It had to happen eventually. The poor sap was due to snap.

And snap he did.

I was getting up a good head of steam about how "a title isn't worth a pot of beans when you're handed it by an uncle tossing them around like popcorn, and if so-called royal blood is what counts, why don't I call in Aunt Hildebrand to do the smooching…" when Roland finally — for the first time in five years of loyal service — gave into frustration and flung his shapely torso in my general direction.

Which is to say, smooching occurred of the fiery, passionate and entirely requited variety, and while it was happening, my squire and I forgot there was a princess to be rescued at all.

It was magic.

But also:

Oh, dear. It was magic.

You wouldn't think there was a great deal of wiggle room in the fairy tale tradition of "awoken by a kiss" but there you are. There we were.

There she was.

Awake.

I've always admired a certain sort of girl. You know the sort — or perhaps you don't. Dashing damsels, I call them. With a heavier weight on the *dashing* component, as the *damsel* is mostly ironic.

Dashing damsels are sporty and loud, with far more confidence than yours truly. They wear what they want, they eat what they want, they laugh with great cheer at the feasting table, and if anyone's pulling together a friendly game of Pillage-the-Fields (that sport with the ball and the stick and the other stick and all the bellowing) then she's the lass you want on your team.

I have quite a few girl chums along these lines — which is perfectly jolly, as long as aunts don't get the wrong idea and start humming matrimonial songs, grasping completely the wrong end of the stick.

(You might have surmised as much re. above: passionately requited embrace with one's squire.)

The best fun about having strong-minded girl chums is the part when a fellow can sit back and watch forthright young ladies plough through crowds to get exactly what she wants, whether it's a particular horse, a particular bridegroom, a prize ribbon at the arm-wrestling festival, or the last mug of cider before the barrel is tapped.

The trick to staying chums with such dashing damsels as these is to keep to the edges of the room so as not to be ploughed over, shout 'huzzah' when a 'huzzah' is called for, and make it *very* clear that Sir Jonty is not on the marriage market (he will, however, be an utter sport when it comes to introducing her to any eligible chaps she fancies, as and when required).

All of which is to say, when Princess Flora rose from her bower, all glowing righteous fury and lacy nightgown and eyes burning with rose-coloured flame, the first thing she said was:

"TAKE ME TO THE TYRANT KING AND LET ME BE HIS DOWNFALL."

In that moment, with the tower shaking to its foundations, the tang of fierce magic in the air, and the encouraging taste of my squire still lingering on my lips, I knew exactly what my role was in the final act of this melodrama.

It was to hold Flora's cloak, and shout 'huzzah.'

Flora cleans house, Roland makes
good choices, and Sir Jonty is
merely pleased to be included

If you live within coo-ee of the enchanted kingdoms, you know what happened next. At last count there are twenty-five ballads and I'm sure the number will rise by the end of the month. Roland features in about half of them, which *he* thinks is none too shabby considering he's not of noble birth.

Pox to the nobility, says I in return, smothering him with kisses. And pox to all beastly bards who think that putting my beloved in their song might put them in for a chance with him. He's taken!

In case you're not up to date on the ballads, I can summarise events thusly: Flora cleaned house. She and her blazing pink eyes, her flaming swords (literally every sword in the vicinity bursts into flame when she strides past, which is rather thrilling the first dozen times, and something of a tiresome safety hazard after that), her singing flowers (all flowers burst into song when she strides past, a fun party trick which also serves as an early warning system) and her epic, epic destiny.

That's Chosen Ones for you.

By the time we made it back to King George's court, at the heart of the enchanted kingdoms, Flora had an army behind her. Not an especially rugged or professional army — ordinary people on the march, don't you know, inspired by the princess with the flaming eyes who had come to save us all from...

Well. Uncle George.

The goblin army did their best to stop her, but Flora blasted them with fairy dust and rosebuds until their nerve broke and they scarpered for the hills.

The towers went next: some were already empty, thanks to socially-approved knights rescuing a handful of my cousins with courtly marriage proposals; others were still being used as princess jails.

Flora brought every tower down into heaps of glittering rubble. Once released, my cousins Sassy, Squiffy, Whinny and Olivia came marching alongside Flora and her army of righteous fury.

(By now, Roland and I had slipped towards the back of the march, not wanting to call attention to ourselves, but still available for the occasional well-placed Huzzah! We also took responsibility for water and sandwiches to be supplied every time we stopped for a spot of tower-destruction, because someone has to pay attention to these matters and Flora already had Being an Avatar of Justice on her plate.)

Uncle George met Flora in the courtyard of his own castle, surrounded by guards, face twisted into a cruel smile.

"I see you've turned my family against me," he said. "Which of my useless sons and nephews is your champion?"

"I don't need a champion," said Flora Awoken. "I'm right here."

(Quietly, back in the ranks, Roland squeezed my hand. We had agreed that neither of us would press the other to be even slightly heroic, no matter the provocation. This was not our story.)

Every single person standing witness to that moment believed that Flora would cut off Uncle George's head. That was what he'd done to his predecessor, after all.

According to the local bookie, a goodly portion of the audience were open to a more whimsical resolution — quite a few locals had bet on Flora transforming him into a geranium.

But violent justice, oh yes. What else was a mob for if not that?

Flora surprised us all when she laid down her flaming sword, and put Uncle George on trial. Within three weeks, her court found him guilty of tyranny and egregious land theft, after consulting and cross-referencing the real estate laws of every kingdom he had ever conquered.

Next, Flora split the enchanted kingdoms back into their original property division, returning every square of turf back to the people, *not* the former royal families.

Finally, for good measure, Princess Flora outlawed

royalty. The Grand High Wizard Secretariat, recognising a lifetime's source of paid administrative duties when they saw one, flocked to Flora's side, quills and ink at the ready. With their help, she dotted every I and crossed every T.

It was terribly legal, officiously official, and perfectly dull as downfalls of tyranny go.

Still, the ballads keep coming. Humans always get the stories they want, even if they have to wait for the bards to come up with versions that scan better than real life.

It's been a year now, since Uncle George was toppled, and my prince card was formally revoked by the most impressive damsel to ever damn her way across the enchanted kingdoms.

I'll admit, I floundered a little in the aftermath, wondering what use a chap like me could possibly be in this brave new world, without a princely title and a rich uncle. Once you've seen a girl like Flora Awoken achieve her destiny, it's easy to view oneself as A Tad Insignificant.

Luckily for me, I still had a squire. Roland's never short of ideas.

We considered the whole knight errant business, biffing around with quests and whatnot. Bit awkward, though, that only one of our duo was qualified to perform heroic quests, and the other one was me.

We did our duty for a bit in the mean time, volunteering for the Enchanted Kingdom's first presidential campaign (obviously Flora was a shoo-in candidate, but she did insist we do the whole thing by the book though no one wanted to run against her — my cousin Daffy finally threw her own hat in the ring for a lark. I've never seen anyone so relieved as Daffy was to lose that election!).

Roland and I considered running a tavern, starting a newspaper, and adopting a dog.

President Flora offered us both positions in her ministerial cabinet, but we put her off by laughing maniacally at the very idea until she left us alone.

Only last night, Roland made a new suggestion. "They're starting the tourney circuit again," he said softly, trailing fingers across the back of my neck. "New rules, for the new era — you don't have to be of noble blood to compete."

The thought of it perked me up. I've never lost my taste for pageantry. I might even be brave enough to pull out the old vermillion tabard with the bells I'd been hiding in the cedar chest beneath my collection of printed ballads featuring my beloved. "So, you'd ride around from place to place, jousting and such and showing everyone how brilliant you are?"

"I wasn't sure you'd like the idea?"

"It sounds marvellous."

"There might not be much for you to do, Jonty," Roland warned. "Won't you be bored?"

"Nonsense, darling," I said, and pressed my lips to his heroic brow. "I'll be terribly busy, don't you know, holding your cloak, and shouting huzzah."

Author's Note: on Wodehouse, girls in towers and a century of cryosleep

Is Tansy over her Wodehouse obsession yet? Possibly not.

This was a fun experiment with voice, and I do love a story where the source material and the tones are radically at odds with each other.

Then again, what was Wodehouse writing when he created his eternally cheerful 1920s, untouched by the trauma of World War I, if not fairy tales?

I am starting to find more of my favourite fairy tale tropes as I comb through these stories! Towers, yes! Enchanted thorns, always. Capable princesses, certainly. Princes not to be taken seriously, essential.

A lesson I learned from reading Robin McKinley over and over in my teens is that, to turn fairy tales into fiction that feels real, you need to look at the spaces between the story.

It requires clever worldbuilding to take a story beat like an enchanted spindle or a princess locked in a tower and create a world where that story beat *makes sense.*

Or you can just make fun of it, which is just as good.

The part of the Sleeping Beauty story that always gets me — the part, I think, that makes it stand out from other fairy tales — is the discovery of the sleeping castle folk. *Everyone* falls asleep, not just the cursed princess. It gives me the shivers.

I've retold parts of Sleeping Beauty before — so many iconic moments, how can you not — notably in *Castle Charming*, where I found the nerve to do it twice.

My Queen Ella is a tragic figure: having secured a royal marriage Cinderella-style, then losing of one of her babies in a kidnapping plot, she is lost in an enchanted sleep for nearly twenty years while the lives of the castle move on without her...

Spindles are an actively malign object in this world, with a taste for royal blood. When one roams loose in Castle Charming, the royals know to protect themselves... but a young newspaper reporter named Kai who does not know he is their lost prince gets stabbed by the same spindle that cursed his mother...

And of course, the sleep that they fall into is *not what it seems.*

Returning from an enchanted sleep to a world forever changed is a fascinating idea, and it's something I often return to. It's quite a science fictional idea, explored in various SFF properties over the decades — from *Doctor Who*, *Blake's 7* and *Star Trek* to *Red Dwarf*, *Futurama* and *Captain America*.

Mary Shelley did it in a story called "Roger Dodsworth: The Reanimated Englishman" which was published in 1863, 12 years after her death.

One of my favourite examples of this trope is the YA novel *When We Wake* (2014) by Karen Healey. A teenager in 2027 is accidentally killed at a protest rally in 2027 and awakens 100 years later, as part of an experiment in cryogenesis.

The book explores one of the most essential and fascinating story questions at the heart of the Sleeping Beauty fairy tale: how much can the world change in one hundred years, and what would it do to a person who finds themself stranded in their own future?

A DAREDEVIL DUCHESS'S GUIDE TO CASTLE HAUNTINGS

Hire The Best

❧

"Here we go," said Perroquet as we drove my bright green Grenouille roadster down the tree-lined road leading into the village. "Pitchforks at dawn."

My polka-dot headscarf came loose again, and I had to snatch it from the air before losing it under the wheels. "Don't be silly. The villages don't whip out the pitchforks until the middle of the night. Otherwise they wouldn't need the flaming torches."

Tartouf, who was driving, snorted at us both. "You're both snobs. You've forgotten how to connect to ordinary people."

"I think referring to anyone who isn't us as 'ordinary people' makes you the snob," I remarked.

We were certainly turning heads. The locals of the village favoured drab clothes and muted colours, and they stared as we drove past. Perhaps it wasn't the car. Perhaps it was Perro's red leather coat, or my bobbed strawberry blonde hair that caught their attention. Perhaps it was simply that that we were newcomers, or foreigners, or because there wasn't much to stare at in a village like this.

Nothing but the haunted castle, which was what had brought us here.

Perhaps that was it. The locals were burning the image of us into their memories so as to properly tell the tale of our demise later on, after their local ghost had their way with us.

My name is Charity Hathaway Du Motte, also known as the Daredevil Duchess. Ghosts have to get up pretty early in the morning to get the better of me.

Our first stop was the inn at the far end of the village, the last building before the winding road that led up to the castle. The castle's jagged towers were barely visible thanks to the thick trees and the fading sky, but there would be plenty of time for that.

We're great at castles, me and my team. Castles and ghosts go together like grilled kippers and buttered toast.

Our landlady greeted us with a wary warmth, doing her best not to look as if she was mentally noting our relative heights and widths on behalf of the local undertaker. She showed us to our rooms — a cozy twin for Perro and Tartouf which she probably would not have offered if she knew they would push the beds together as soon as she left, and her best room for me, because that's the sort of privilege reserved for ladies with posh Artemisian accents and useless titles.

There were handmade quilts on the bed, framed embroideries on the wall. No obvious draughts from the window, or mouse-holes in the wainscoting. All terribly cozy. I can slum it if I have to, but I have no objection to comfort.

"Will his Grace be joining us?" the landlady asked with a flutter.

"His Grace is somewhere over the Tethysian Ocean in a hot air balloon full of reporters and politicians," I assured her, with a smile to soften the sharpness. "I wouldn't hold your breath."

Don't Let Your Past Hold You Back

I knew I was marrying an adventurer. I went into it with my eyes wide open. You don't marry a man who creates newspaper headlines like Death Defying Duke without expecting challenge, adventure and the need for a sturdy pair of walking boots.

Lytton had other ideas. During our courting days, I believed his sweet talk about wanting a partner in crime, a sturdy adventuress to stand at his side... but as it turned out, what he wanted was to keep his derring-do in a separate sphere to his respectable wife.

Respectable *Artemisian* wife, I realised too late. That was what he wanted from me. A foothold in my country after being exiled from his own; an exiled Balvorian duke would never be entirely accepted in the republic of Artemisia, a country that tossed all aristocratic titles out the window about fifty years ago. Lytton needed a local wife to justify buying up Artemisian property (a country estate, several town houses), making friends with important Artemisian gentlemen, and setting up accounts and loans with Artemisian banks to finance the next expedition, and the next, and the next.

He expected his duchess to hold down the fort while he dashed around the world doing whatever he wanted. Every time I suggested Lytton invite me along on his dramatic voyages (about which you can read in any popular newspaper) he would kiss my cheek and buy me another house, or a lap dog, or an opera box.

I got the message, eventually. It was one of the greater embarrassments of my life, but we mustn't dwell on such things. I moved on. In my family, curse-breaking and archaeological digs and deep research were par for the course... and while I've never been a great reader, I've always been excellent at putting theory into practice. Why not launch my own career of daring escapades?

Some might argue I went too far, what with the parachuting out of biplanes and the cliff-climbing championship and that time I swam across the Phretien River with a dying vampire strapped to my back, but what is the point of a life half-lived?

These days, my newspaper headlines war with those of my husband. Once a year or so, our paths cross in a new foreign country and we play the doting couple. In front of the reporters and the cameras, he does so love to tell the world how much he admires his Daredevil Duchess.

I pretend I'm not hoping that he chokes on my fame and success.

You're Only As Good As Your Team

I did not intent to become an expert in hunting the supernatural, but once you stumble a haunted castle or twelve and live to tell the tale, expertise builds up. Opportunities come knocking.

Such as the offer I received last year from Sanguine & Dance Publishing Ltd. to write a book about the monsters of Mulgrave, one of my favourite sinister continents. What's a duchess to do, turn an offer like that down?

(My husband, I mention for no particular reason, has never written a book.)

I keep my team lean, and loyal.

Perroquet, with the rosy cheeks and flyaway dark curls, has been my assistant and safety officer for six years now — he's the one who ties the ropes, assesses risk, checks for traps and occasionally stabs zombies in the neck when my back is turned. A literal lifesaver.

Tartouf, our newest addition, is my official photographer. He's lean and tall, with red hair and a flat expression more suited to a disgruntled bodyguard than an artist; it took Perro about a week to lure him into bed. (Honestly, that was six days longer than I expected.)

My secretary Gloria, lifesaver and guardian angel, essential cog in the wheel of our team, had not joined us on this particular outing. She was currently waiting for us in a five-star hotel on the coast of Chauritz on the grounds that she could manage my correspondence more easily from there, and she suspected the Byreft hospitality wouldn't be up to her usual standards. Gloria likes her champagne chilled and her breakfasts continental.

Our current job was to investigate Castle Blanchette, a haunted edifice overlooking a tiny village in Byreft, the country between Ichandry and Chauritz. Byreft often gets left off the map because it's barely worth colouring in such a slender dash-and-dot.

I get a great many letters begging for my help these days. Since the book deal, it's hard to decide which jobs are worth taking. There was something about this one that caught my eye. A tragic history, a royal connection, some extraordinary visuals... and if we were very lucky, an undead cat.

Readers love cats.

At First, Approach By Daylight

It was a strangely sunny morning — the most sunshine I'd seen since we crossed the border. Considering that Byreft is largely made from trees and shadows, I hadn't expected anything so cheerful.

The castle knew how to do its job of looking spooky and sinister. It loomed up out of the hillside like it had been built by a team of cultists serving an ancient spider-god.

Everything about the castle was pointy: the towers, the turrets, the thin, angled windows. The preferred aesthetic of the original architect seemed to be: "I know spikes are fashionable right now, but let's take it way too far."

Tartouf was snapping pictures before Perro parked the roadster; the walk from the village wouldn't have killed us, but we like to have our gear close when we're dealing with creatures from beyond the grave. "This is no good," Tartouf complained. "Looks like the castle's about to host a teddy bear's picnic. We'll have to come back at dusk when the light is lower."

It's rare for a photographer to complain that the light is

too good, but Tartouf earns his living by making creepy castles look downright diabolical; sunshine is not his colour.

"We may as well have a look around while we're here," I said, a little sarcastic. "If it's not too inconvenient?"

You always approach a potentially haunted site by daylight the first time around. That way, when things go terribly wrong at midnight, at least you know where all the walls are supposed to be.

We surveyed the outside with due diligence, and finally approached the large oak front door with an iron key that the mayor of the village had left for us with our new landlady. It was a gnarled and twisted thing which turned too easily in the lock; ghost or no ghost, this suggested regular visitors to the castle.

Luckily there had been at least basic security; often the locals assume their superstitions are enough to keep everyone out, and the interiors turn out to be not so much haunted as wrecked by the travelling homeless, or drunken local youngsters.

Inside, the narrow windows meant that even the blinding sunshine couldn't prevent a general air of gloom; Tartouf made a few excitable noises and started snapping images of the shadows looming across the hallway.

So far, the interior featured your standard haunted castle props: empty suits of armour pinned to the walls, dusty portraits of grim relatives, a wide break-neck staircase designed for dramatic reveals and occasional homicide...

A white cat, perching on the landing and staring directly at me like she wanted to set me on fire with her eyes.

"See something interesting?" Perro asked me warily.

I nodded upwards. "Exchanging pleasantries with the mistress of the house."

Tartouf lowered his camera. "Duch, what exactly are you looking at?"

"Oh," I said, realising with an uneasy shudder. "So, neither of you see the cat?"

The white cat yawned and plotted my death.

Fairy Tales Are Rarely Helpful

There are many tales told about Castle Blanchette; I'd done my due diligence in several Chauritz libraries, or rather I'd read the notes provided to me by Gloria, who was far better than I at sifting through troves of leather-bound books for the juicy details.

The most popular version was this: the king of Byreft had three sons and sent them on foolish quests to test whether any of them were worthy to rule. The first challenge was to find the tiniest, most adorable dog in the land — which is a pretty good one, I'll admit. Never mind magic harps and buckets of gold, a king who sends his sons on a year-long quest to find a cute dog has to have something going for him.

The youngest son got lost, because youngest sons in these sorts of stories tend to be equal parts stupid and lucky. He found himself here, a tiny village in the middle of nowhere, and called on the castle... where he met a magical cat who welcomed him (possibly) or kidnapped him (almost certainly), and maybe even seduced him (best not to think about it too hard).

As Gloria noted in her perfect purple handwriting, it probably wasn't this castle. If this story is real (which it isn't), then *this* castle is in the wrong place to belong to that story, and it's not old enough — the castle is two centuries old, the fairy tale was popularised a century before it was built, and if the fairy tale was based on real people, then Byreft hasn't had a royal family for five hundred years.

Somewhere along the way, some smartarse villagers decided to name their local fortress "Castle Blanchette" after the fairy tale, in the hopes of luring in cat-loving tourists or some such nonsense.

The one thing we were certain of, heading into this situation, was that there would be no enchanted cat waiting for us.*

"Ghost cat," muttered Tartouf, taking pictures of the landing which appeared to him completely empty. "Best kind."

"You can't see it at all?" Sometimes he can see the supernatural through the camera lens if not with his bare eye, but it wasn't a given. I was more concerned that Perro could not see the cat. He's the most magically sensitive of the three of us.

Me, I jump out of biplanes and stumble into haunted corridors while the other two howl at me to stand still and

---

* None of these facts would prevent us from including the fairy tale in the book. It's a great story. It goes on forever, there are three separate quests, and several romances. The white cat lets the younger son hang out in her castle and provides him with all the magically special items he needs, and then tells her elaborate backstory and the whole thing keeps going and going and... it could fill a chapter or two, is what I'm saying

stay safe. I'm not used to being the one who sees more than everyone else.

The cat blinked at me.

I blinked at the cat.

"Do you think ghost cats like sardines?" I wondered.

"Bold of you to assume this town can scrounge up a tin of sardines," said Tartouf. "We're a long way from the ocean."

Gloria was probably eating sardines right now, pan-fried with salsa verde along with a glass of the local sparkling white (or, it still being morning, a tall glass of freshly squeezed juice). Why couldn't haunted castles be located in the middle of cities with excellent restaurants?

"We should check the upper floors while it's still light," I said, my gaze fixed on the cat, who sniffed at me and licked its paws. If it wasn't for Tartouf and Perro swearing blind they couldn't see it, I would never have imagined the cat was a ghost.

"How big is this cat?" asked Perro. "Do you think it could push you down the staircase?"

The white cat sneezed at me and looked superior.

I hummed between my breath. "I feel that it wants to."

We took the back stairs.

The trouble with fairy tales is, they're rarely helpful. They rely on rules that do not apply to real life: choose kindness and you are rewarded, fulfil three quests and your heart's desire is guaranteed, talking animals always have something important to say.

With my family history, I know better than to expect a happy ending no matter how many quests I fulfil, or undead mysteries I solve.

The Castle Blanchette fairy tale would have you believe that the white cat not only provided the prince with a handsome dog small enough to leap through a wedding ring, but also a walnut that when cracked gave forth a silk tunic fine enough to thread through the eye of a needle.

It would have you believe that on the third year when the prince returned to report that his father would have him bring back a beautiful maiden as his bride, the white cat revealed herself to be a cursed queen who already loved him because the prince looked exactly like her own long-lost love.

It would have you believe that the prince and the transformed cat found their happy ending together.

Fairy tales are tidy like that.

But if this particular fairy tale had any basis in truth, why would a white cat still be haunting these halls?

Ghosts are symptoms of trauma, of unresolved pain, of chaos and unfinished business. Ghosts are messy, and they make their own rules.

That's what I love best about them.

Use Your Senses

There are many signs that a home is haunted: unexplained sounds and smells or patches of unrelenting cold. Witness reports often mention whispering voices, shadowy reflections, eerie music, or objects that move without explanation from room to room.

All of these signs are commonly known; enough that they are often used by locals trying to authenticate a false haunting. We've come across plenty of pretenders in our line of work; nothing like a hint of spookiness to lure in the tourists or cover up a mundane crime.

"How many deaths connected to the castle?" I asked as we made our way through chilly room after chilly room on the upper floors.

"One or two every few decades," said Perro. "Six in the last three years." Tartouf's hand tightened on the strap of his camera. "That seems like a lot of bodies," he said, alarmed. "Is that a lot? I think that's a lot."

Perro and I, hardened veterans of the ghost-hunting business, glanced at each other and shrugged. We forget sometimes, because Tartouf looks tougher than both of us put together, that he hasn't been here for most of our scrapes; Perro still looks sweet and innocent, like the shorter version of a prince from an illustrated fairy tale (he has freckles on his nose!) but he once cut my arm free of the jaws of a werewolf who had literally bit more than he could chew.

"It's not excessive," I said, remembering the skeletons we once found in the cellar of the Balvorian embassy.

"How is that —"

"It depends, love," Perro said in a gentle voice, patting his sweetheart's arm. "Often the ghosts are *because* of the bodies..."

"That's the best-case scenario," I added.

"Well, obviously."

"The best case — oh," said Tartouf, swallowing. "Because if death leads to the creation of ghosts, that's better than when the ghosts are the ones who..."

"Ghosts can't kill," I said shortly. "Not without human assistance."

"That's not as reassuring as you might think!"

I hadn't been trying to sound reassuring, merely accurate. Death by ghost came in many forms: hypothermia, being driven from heights, literally being scared to death. These were usually accidental side effects of haunting, unless possession came into it.

Possession was always a deliberate act.

"They're skilled at creating accidents," Perro muttered. "Did I mention that all six of the recent deaths are young men between the age of twenty and twenty-five, all dark haired, all pretty?"

There was an awkward pause between us.

"Thank goodness I'm ginger," said Tartouf after a moment, with a hollow laugh. "And you, darling —" Dark haired, pretty, it wasn't *not* a description of Perro. "Thank goodness five-and-twenty is a distant memory for you."

"Get stuffed," Perro said, but he was laughing too. He'd been worrying over the crow's feet he spotted in the mirror a month ago; hopefully this would help him appreciate them a little more.

I stopped in the middle of the room; this had been the royal chamber once, though there was now nothing remaining but a bed frame with all the gilding worn away, and a mirror someone had covered with a cobwebbed cloth. The chandelier featured many tiny crowns; astounding no one had stolen it, though it would be tricky to smuggle a chandelier that size past all the noses of the villagers.

It was cold here, directly under the chandelier. Cold like ice. I saw the white cat sunning herself on the window ledge. "What are you trying to tell me?" I asked her.

She farted genteelly; the scent wafted across the room and I saw both Perro and Tartouf react as it smacked them both directly in the nostrils.

"Oh, good," I said. "I'm not hallucinating."

Or, at least, if I was hallucinating, I wasn't the only one.

Do Your Homework

We returned to the patchwork inn in time for tea and the sort of hearty spread one is only ever offered in the country: bright orange-yolked eggs, buttered bread and fruit preserves either made by your hostess or traded from her neighbour with bountiful plum trees.

Tartouf dedicated his evening to charming our landlady into letting him use one of her out-buildings to set up a temporary darkroom. Perro carted in boxloads of our (that is to say, Gloria's) research notes to review.

I found myself writing my own notes over hers, green ink adorning her signature purple handwriting.

Most of my notes were questions.

> *Legends of a white cat: ghostly animals are almost always white*
>
> *(Is this because no one can easily see the darker ones at night?)*
>
> *Is white a creepier colour than tabby or grey?*

(All cats are grey in the dark)

Why did the king ask the prince for a tiny dog anyway?

If the prince wasn't a prince, who was he?

If the prince wasn't a prince, why were there three of them?

Ask about the cloth that was fine enough to go through the eye of a needle.

(Clearly a metaphor)

If this isn't the real Castle Blanchette, does the real castle from the story have a different ghost?

"This seems useful," said Perro, waving a notebook. "Reported sightings of ghosts at the castle."

"How does that tie in with the recent deaths?"

"That's a different notebook." He seized that with his other hand, which required him to put down the bowl of walnuts on which he had been snacking; our landlady was of the opinion that all men required constant provisions of food in order to keep up their strength.

"I'm starting to explain why Gloria demands such a high stationery budget."

"She's worth every penny." He tossed me the deaths notebook, keeping the ghost notebook for himself. "The ghost isn't always a cat."

That was almost interesting. "Is it sometimes a beautiful princess?"

"Opinions are divided. There were a few claims of a white lady, a few more of an eerie voice without any visuals... one of three handsome naked men, but that was put down to Mrs Baggle from the village drinking too much plum wine and misinterpreting her interaction with a cartful of travelling peddlers."

"Sounds like quite a night."

"Oh," he said in a different voice.

I glanced up from the list of the dead (Kristoff Landerson (seventeen years old) was the most recent; a local miller's son who was found at the foot of one of those spiky towers with his neck broken). "What is it?"

Perro winced. "No group approaching the castle has ever reported more than one of their party seeing a white cat. And the person who does see it..."

No, that wasn't my spine shivering at all. Must have been a draught from the window. "Let me guess. They're the ones who end up dead?"

"Nine times out ten," admitted Perro, looking at me with wide eyes.

I've faced worse odds.

Castles Are Spookiest After Midnight

Perro and I once surveyed a castle that was daisies all the way down. The stone was butter-yellow, and the turreted tops of the towers had been filled in with earth, so flowers could grow there. The flowers poked out of window sills and the cracks between flagstones, and the whole thing looked like something out of an illustrated edition for good little children.

At three minutes after midnight, a headless woman screamed her way out of the top window, fell four storeys and enacted the most grotesque scenes of her own five-hundred-year old murder until Perro threw up in a flowerpot.

(It was probably for the best that we didn't have a photographer with us at the time; no one needs to see that.)

There's something about midnight that brings out the ghouls and the poltergeists. It's symbolic, and spooks love symbolic. Superstition is literally their life blood.

Perhaps if humans believed that breakfast time was

more monstrous than the middle of the night, we might have wraiths interrupting our morning coffee.

In any case, my team returned to Castle Blanchette at a quarter to midnight. Perro was armed with the usual business: ropes, a rifle full of rock salt, and all manner of protective amulets. Tartouf carried three cameras and a portable lighting rig; his priority was getting good pictures, not saving our lives.

I wore comfortable clothing — a pair of day pyjamas in black silk, and a dark beret to match, with low-heeled boots — but otherwise my equipment consisted mostly of an electric torch, and my spirit of adventure.*

The cat was nowhere on the lower floor. I posed for a few 'Daredevil Duchess investigates' shots with all of the long shadows and sinister shapes that Tartouf had been hoping for.

We made for the stairs — with no white cat anywhere in sight.

"What's the betting that a clock chimes loudly at midnight?" whispered Perro behind me.

"Did you see a clock anywhere in the castle when we searched the place?" Tartouf whispered back.

"Not during the day, obviously." Perro is particularly invested in the 'castles are at their most haunted after midnight' theory.

We made our way up the main staircase, sweeping floor after floor with torchlight to see no sign of a cat, white or otherwise. Tartouf grumbled about us not lingering on

---

* I had a few silver curse-breaking daggers spirited about my person, but doesn't everybody?

some of the more interesting floors, but I was all about the Royal Chamber.

As we pushed open the heavy door to that enormous, dusty room, the sound of a clock chime reverberated through the floorboards.

"See?" said Perro.

"Maybe they kept it in the larder," mumbled Tartouf.

The cold spot under the chandelier was still several degrees chillier than the rest of the room. I proceeded to the covered mirror.

"Wait!" begged Tartouf, setting up his tripod in the corner. "Just a minute to get the lenses ready…"

"Still no cat?" asked Perro, peering under the skeletal bed frame.

"Still no cat," I confirmed.

"Turn back to me for a sec," said Tartouf. His camera clicked over and over as he took photographs of me standing in front of the mirror, about to pull the cobwebbed cloth away.

Finally, I turned back and tugged on the cloth. It slithered away, revealing clear reflective glass.

Mirrors are Inherently Sinister

There's a reason that so many fairy tales and supernatural stories involve mirrors. It's not that they are naturally magical objects, exactly. But humans believe that they are, and that's enough to give fate an encouraging kick in the pants.

If you don't know anything about anything, then mirrors feel like a magic trick. Why else would you see your own face staring back at you, but not quite your own face, not exactly as other people see it. Everything reversed; turned out wrong.

It's that wrongness that makes mirrors inherently sinister. Nothing looks exactly right in the polished silver.

Sometimes you see things in the mirror that can't be seen with the naked eye. The room behind me was filled with smoke — thick, twisting plumes of white.

My feet felt frozen to the floor; I didn't dare turn my head to see if my vision was true. But in the mirror's reflection, those white coils of smoke gathered around the figures of Perro and Tartouf, taking on rather peculiar shapes:

Perroquet looked like a parrot with wide-sweeping wings and a pointed beak; Tartouf, hunched over his camera, looked rather like a dog with long ears.

I wrenched my attention back to my own image in the mirror. That was wrong, too; my strawberry blonde hair in its tidy bob (so fashionable, so practical) had become long, spiralling tresses. No beret in sight. My eyes shone green instead of blue. Wrong, all wrong.

I opened my mouth and a voice not my own came spilling out:

"Don't think for a moment, my prince, that I have always been a cat. Let me tell you now how I came to haunt this castle. My father was a king, so long ago that I can barely remember him, and he lost me to the fairies when I was but a baby..."

Sometimes, You Are the Ghost

Just like that, I was inside the mirror. Or perhaps, inside the ghost.

This was not my first metaphysical transportation; not even my tenth. Somehow, whenever ghosts get the urge to seize a human and spill their secrets in vivid technicolour, I'm the one who gets picked.

(Perro says I ask for trouble; Gloria calls me catnip for spooks.)

I drifted along a corridor of a castle; not this castle. That would be far too easy. No, it was another castle, another time. The ghost's voice unravelled as I floated past golden tapestries and silken rugs that looked impossibly new despite their antique style.

The voice of the ghost echoed in my ears (perhaps not my ears any longer), telling the story of her origin.

My mother, driven wild by her cravings, was desperate to taste the fruit...

The fairies cursed them both unless they paid for their greed...

And so I became a slave before I was even born...

Trapped in an enchanted palace for eternity, my only companions a hound and a parrot...

Rescued by another king, a beautiful young man with dark hair and eyes...

My love, he looked just like you.

I blinked, realising that the ghost of the lost queen was no longer speaking. I was back in Castle Blanchette, standing on the turrets of the highest, spikiest tower, my waist-length hair and long white dress fluttering in the night breezes.

The youths came, laughing and dancing. One of them played a guitar; another carried bottles of wine. There were four of them, all young, all beautiful, and one near enough in appearance to my long-lost love that I crept forward, longing to hear his voice...

Not *my* love. My husband was off risking his neck in some warmer climate, with newspaper reporters awaiting breathlessly to hear of his latest exploits. (Lytton had blond hair, a reddish beard when he was careless about shaving, and flinty eyes.)

This boy, though, the boy with the guitar. He looked like *her* love. The ghost liked him. She recognised something in him. When he swayed drunkenly close to the edge of the parapet... the ghost pushed herself inside the skin of the pretty girl nearest to him. She leaned forward in this borrowed body, wanting to touch him, wanting to push...

I pulled back from the ghost, desperate to return to my own body, but the thoughts of husbands and personal

history were so fresh in the front of my mind that even as
the scene from the turrets faded around me, I found myself
standing before a very different mirror, staring at a different
face.

I saw my husband. Lytton stood in a small wash house,
halfway through shaving his traveller's beard into something
more debonair and appropriate for a duke who wishes to be
invited to a better class of party. His head was half-turned,
chatting to another man in the doorway, who wore a style of
jacket I recognised as Ichandrian. He had not seen me at all.

Goodness. Was Lytton in Ichandry? I had thought him
busy on his quest to travel around the Tooth Cape in a hot
air balloon. Could he really be only one border away
from me?[*]

Turning back from his conversation to pay attention to
his razor, Lytton stared directly into the mirror, pale as if...
oh, as if he had seen a ghost.[†]

I lifted a hand in greeting, in case he could see me — in
case it was me he was staring at in such horror, and not a
white cat perched directly behind my head.[‡]

The world blurred around me. When it stilled, there

---

[*] Not that it mattered. We might as well be continents apart, the way our
marriage was going.
[†] Someday, perhaps we would laugh about this. Probably not at the same
time.
[‡] My hand was transparent. I could see my husband's face through it.
Funny, the things you notice at times such as these.

was no mirror. Or at least, there were so many mirrors that one did not signify.

I stood in a different castle. Hovered, that is; I was still the ghost, and she was flesh and blood.

A queenly lady with long white hair lounged among cushions and coverlets, reaching her arms out to a pretty young man with dark hair falling in his eyes.

"Now you know my story," said the lady in white, her fingers toying with his hair. "My king and husband is gone, but you, my love, look so like him. It is almost the same."

Sick with love, he gazed back at her. "Will you leave your castle and come with me, to meet my father?"

The white cat — the white-haired woman — the lost queen — the stolen princess — smiled at him with all her teeth.

"I would follow you to the ends of the earth. But to win your father's throne? Oh, yes."

All Backstories Are A Little Tragic

♥

"It's a beautiful story," I remarked to the white cat. "A little messy in places, and I'm not sure where the parrot fits in. But three centuries ago, that sort of fairy tale was terribly fashionable."

The white cat licked a paw and gave me her death stare; back to normal, then.[*]

"A shame it's not true," I went on.

The white cat hissed.

"Oh, come on. Kings and tiny dogs and forbidden magical plants and way too many castles for a country this size? I don't believe a word of it. Ghosts may be real, but fairy tales? Never."

The cat blinked at me in what could only be described as a threatening manner.

"Fairy tales," I said slowly. "Don't leave footprints on the

---

[*] I could not feel my fingers, did not know if it was warm or chill, I was a little concerned that this ghostly state might be everlasting. Best not think about that now. I was getting better at ignoring it altogether.

ground. They don't traumatise people so badly that they end up haunting the living. The story of the white cat is fine for a storybook, but it's not real. It's not your story. So, why don't we start again? Tell me why you're here."

The cat became a beautiful silver-haired queen.

"No."

The cat became a beautiful silver-haired child, with a bright parrot on one shoulder and an adorable moppet of a dog in her arms.

"No."

The cat became a handsome, dark-haired prince.

"Closer, but no."

The cat became an elderly woman in wide, stiff skirts, settled in an ornate chair. The gown was white (or had been white before it aged into a sullen grey) punctuated with pearl cabochons and ivory ribbons. A silvered wig covered her hair. The hem of her skirt was heavy with dust and cobwebs, as if she had been walking up and down a thousand attics for a thousand years. Her fingertips were stained with ink.

She looked human, at least, and not something out of a storybook.

I narrowed my eyes. "That dress dates you. Did you live three hundred years ago?"

"That sounds about right," said the ghost in a heavy, awkward accent.

"Still too old for this castle."

The crone gave me a flinty look. "They built it over my grave."

"Oh." I considered. "That would do it."

"So glad you approve."

I found a chair — perhaps the ghost of a chair — and sat

opposite her. My limbs were not tired, and my head did not ache (there were benefits, it seemed, to living among the ghosts) but it is difficult to have a conversation when one sits and the other stands. "Tell me about the white cat," I entreated.

"It's only a story. I wrote it to amuse the duke."

I cast my thoughts back to Gloria's copious research. Byreft, unlike my own country, did not remove all aristocratic titles when they rid themselves of their monarchy. They only had a few aristocratic families, but they clung to them until the lines died out. "The Duke of Taulion?"

His castle was to the north of here; in far greater disrepair than this one, practically fallen to ruins, and not a single ghost to be heard of.

She nodded gravely. "My husband was a lesser baron of his court."

"You're the Comtesse des Fées." Inventor of the fairy tale format — or at least, the lady who popularised it across the Mulgravian courts. Stories of fairies and lost queens and magical gowns and talking animals. .

"They called me that," she admitted. "Among other things."

"How is it that your grave was left unmarked?"

She gave me a tired smile. "Would you say it is unmarked? They dropped a castle on me."

And filled it with fairy tales. Perhaps it had been intended as a tribute, when first built. But two hundred years passed, and the town — the whole *country* had forgotten why they did it.

"You've been murdering young men," I noted.

"I don't mean to hurt anyone," she sighed. "My life feels

such a terribly long time ago. But I do remember a young man."

Pretty, dark hair. "Not your husband, I presume?" Marital fidelity was not in vogue in the time of Taulion's court.

Her expression softened a little. "From before my marriage. I carried the memory of him into my stories. He was every prince, every king, every lover."

Tall, dark and handsome. No fairy tale heroine ever seems to appreciate a fair-haired gentleman, or one of medium height.

"Visitors come to *this* Castle Blanchette so rarely," breathed the lady in white. "Sometimes I see one who reminds me of my lost love. I do not mean to hurt them... but if I could only touch him one more time..."

Six in the last three years was not what I would call rare. Her body count was escalating, and she did not seem aware of it. Once ghosts are more than a century old, it's hard to make them change their ways by appeal to their better nature; this one had little restraint left if she could kill so many merely by snuggling closer.

"Why this story in particular?" I asked. Castle Blanchette wasn't the Comtesse des Fées' most popular story. Not even in her top ten. And yet, clearly it was on her mind for her to take cat form here in the castle — according to witnesses, she had been doing so on and off for as long as the castle stood.

The lady in white smiled at me. Somewhere from within her enormous court dress, she produced a shrug. "Readers love cats," she said simply. "When you tell my story, keep that in mind."

So, there was some deliberation in her actions. Not quite a confession, but not far off.

"Is that why I'm here? To tell your story?"

"No," said the lady in white. "That's why you're going back."

Readers Love Cats

I burst back into the land of the living, my lungs aching from lack of use; my eyeballs dry as a bone. I coughed and could barely stop coughing. There was so much dust.

A strong pair of arms held me up. A familiar figure in a lilac suit darted before me, her dark hair piled into a tidy bun. She thrust a thermos flask of lukewarm tea at me with her usual air of extreme competence. I sipped and then gulped, until my eyes started watering. "Gloria, what are you doing here?"

The strong hands released me. "Charity, what happened?" growled a male voice, utterly familiar and yet impossible.

"Lytton?" I could barely wrap my head around Gloria having left her four-star comfort in Chauritz to bring me a flask of tea, but my husband? "What are *you* doing here? How did you find me so quickly?"

Even if he had been in Ichandry when we saw each other in the mirror, it would have taken him hours to cross the border, far more than that to locate where I might be...

I did not exactly keep him up to date with my travel plans. His best course would have been to find Gloria first and demand she tell him where to find me...

"Quickly?" snarled Lytton Du Motte, Duke of D'Aulnoy. Frustration creased his craggy face. "Charity, you've been lost in this damned castle for *three months*."

There was a sound on the stairs and my Perroquet scrambled into sight, his lovely face butchered by the most distressing beard of sadness. Perro let out a low cry and flung himself at me, nestling into my bosom like a squirrel seeking comfort. "Duch," he moaned. "We lost you."

"Nonsense, I was right here." I patted him on the head.

Tartouf emerged at a stately pace, lifting his camera. "Of course, I missed the reunion," he complained. "I don't suppose you can do it again, for the pictures?"

"I think not," rumbled Lytton. "Let's get out of this mausoleum."

My first step was shaky, and my husband — having apparently lost all decorum in my absence — scooped me into his arms and carried me down every flight of stairs in the castle.

We burst out into the sunshine — oh, spring sunshine, time had passed indeed — and my husband did not let me go even after he had tucked me into the back seat of a sleek black car that was certainly not my bright green Grenouille roadster.

"I'm fine," I muttered.

"You were lost," he snapped in return.

"I have work to do, Lytton, you had better not get in the way of it..."

He stared at me, and then sighed. "What do you need?"

"An appointment with the mayor, probably some sort of

town meeting, a bath with very hot water, and a slice of that pie that the landlady makes, the one with layers of onion and potato and home-cured bacon."

Lytton's mouth twitched; it was the first time I had seen him look anything other than impatient or fake-for-the-cameras in years. "Is that all?"

"And a notebook. And Gloria. And Perro. And Tartouf."

Lytton raised his reddish-gold eyebrows a little; I rather thought his crow's feet had deepened a little, since we last saw each other. They were a great deal more noticeable than Perro's. But terribly distinguished. "And?"

"I suppose you can stay," I murmured. "If you really wish to be useful."

We left Byreft a week later: the Daredevil Duchess, the Death Defying Duke, Gloria and Perro and Tartouf. The mayor and the town had been advised to follow the following recommendations, to soothe their resident ghost and keep her from killing further young men:

1. Castle Blanchette was to become a museum dedicated to the works and history of Madame Marie-Britt De Blanchet, also known as the Comtesse des Fées, author of such popular tales as *Queen Hippolyte's Salon, Cunning Cinders, Le Chevalier Belle-Belle* and, of course, *Castle Blanchette (or: The White Cat)*.

2. Young men of a certain profile (age range, hair colour) were to be barred from the doors of the

museum and, if they insisted upon entry, must wear a cap to hide their hair and a sturdy knitted vest to protect them against the first flush of ghost chill. Ugly beards, such as that modelled by a certain Monsieur Perroquet, were encouraged.

3. No one under the age of thirty was to walk on the parapets.

4. Sardines were to be left on the window ledges twice a week, to appease the cat and/or the ghost; flowers were likewise to be left in the cellars near the spot believed to be Madame De Blanchet's resting place, though recent experimentation had proven that she liked sardines better.

5. When my book was published, it was to be made available for purchase at the village shop for those interested in learning more about the castle's history and that of its infamous host.

6. As long as Madame De Blanchet and her history (not to mention the site of her grave) were treated with respect and culturally-appropriate memorial traditions, the ghost was unlikely to cause further turmoil, but if she did...

7. They were to write at once to Lady Charity Hathaway Du Motte (the Daredevil Duchess), and I would return.

My husband, you may not be surprised to learn, was unimpressed by this last clause, but I insisted upon it. My insistence upon anything I wanted came up against very little protest from him these days. I was not sure how long his attentiveness would last, but I intended to make the most of it.

(Does it count as romance if one's husband only realises he cannot live without you after believing you eaten by ghosts? Ask me again on my next anniversary.)

If in turn I was cajoled to spend a few months on our home estate to recover my health before returning to the field of supernatural investigation, well... I have always had a healthy respect for the art of negotiation.

Besides. I had a book to write.

The Haunting of Castle Blanchette (and other ghostly adventures of the Daredevil Duchess) * was a best-seller upon release, a year to the day after I escaped the castle's ghost.

One of Tartouf's clever photographs, capturing a cat-shaped shadow in the deepest halls of the castle, was displayed upon the cover of the paperback edition. Readers lapped it up. Cats+ghosts=the hottest read of the year.

During that twelve months, my husband did not leave my side. Indeed, he proved most useful during the writing process, taking so many day trips to various libraries on my behalf that I wondered for a time if he planned to write a competing manuscript, detailing his own adventures...

Gloria assured me he was merely assisting with our research, every time I wondered aloud about my husband's intentions. Eventually, I stopped asking.

If Lytton's dedication encouraged me to spend more

---

* Available by request at your local bookshop

lazy mornings in our shared bed, well, that is a matter best left to the imagination.

We first launched the book in Artemisia, alongside family and friends. While the reporters did all but invite Lytton to take credit for my work, he only reiterated how proud he was of my achievements.

"You do not have to give up your adventures, you know," I remarked in bed one morning, as we plotted out the coming tour: my book was already selling off the shelves in multiple continents. We had so many invitations to visit as guest speakers; the trick was to decide which to accept. "I will not disappear the second you step into a hot air balloon."

"Won't you, though?" he murmured, kissing my shoulder.

"I won't stay at home," I laughed lightly. "But that doesn't mean anything bad would happen."

"You will continue to hunt ghosts, unlock supernatural secrets, and generally hurl yourself into deadly danger, once the lure of public discourse about Castle Blanchette has waned?"

To tell the truth, I was already exhausted at the thought of travelling the world to talk about ghosts I had already dealt with. I would far prefer to get my hands on a *fresh*, juicy haunting. Gloria had been saving the most interesting letters for when I had a little free time...

"I will," I said firmly. Our marriage vows included a promise of honesty, after all.

"It seems to me, my duchess, that the easiest possible way to find adventures would be to stick with you for a while," said Lytton, his large hand covering my own. "What do you think?"

I thought about Madame De Blanchet and her lost love; the endless parade of similar young men in her stories; the bodies found dead at the castle. Sometimes, it is best to let go of the hurts of the past and move forward.

"Husband," I said in my most seductive tone of voice. "Have you ever met a banshee?"

Lytton's eyes lit up as they always did when a new adventure began. I had seen that light many times before, on his way to leaving me behind. It was the first time he had directed this particular light in my direction. "I have not."

"Well, then," I said, scattering maps as I leaped out of bed. "Let me tell you now: you're in for a treat!"

DON'T MISS TOMORROW'S EDITION:
DAREDEVIL DUCHESS & DEATH-DEFYING DUKE
BATTLE BANSHEES IN BALVORIA.
EXCLUSIVE INTERVIEWS AND PHOTOGRAPHS!
YOU WON'T BELIEVE YOUR EYES!

Author's Note: The White Cat

Here's a life lesson for you: if you volunteer to retell a specific fairy tale for a project, *read the story before you are committed*. Vaguely remembering a past version doesn't count. Read the words.

As part of an experiment in self publishing, I joined a collaborative author anthology which became the blink-or-you'll-miss-it volume *Castle of Secrets* (2024). The theme was dark fairy tale retellings. Two years before delivery, we were asked to nominate our chosen fairy tale.

The trouble was a) most of the good ones had already been taken and b) I had already written my own versions of most of the Big Name fairy tales. I did a quick search, and decided after some research to choose one of the stories written by Madame D'Aulnoy. Thanks to Marina Warner and Kate Forsyth, I have a long fascination with the women of the fairy tale salons of Paris who wrote and popularised so many of the 'court' fairy tales, i.e. the ones about frocks and crowns rather than the ones about hiking through forests.

I'll always choose a castle over a forest.

I selected "The White Cat" which I vaguely recalled being an interesting story, and decided to myself that I'd do some kind of heist story with it. I wanted to add to the lore and world of my Lyceum/Artemisia curse-breaker stories[*] so I decided this would be my Daredevil Duchess story. I ordered a pretty illustrated edition of Madame D'Aulnoy's stories (*The Island of Happiness*, translated by Jack Zipes) and then *I did not think about it for two years*.

Please do not copy my creative process. I wouldn't wish it on anyone.

When it came time to write my White Cat retelling, I discovered that the original fairy tale is a) insane and b) not at all what I remembered. It is a complex, tangled Scheherazade of a story concoction, with far more talking animals than I personally enjoy.[†]

I feel like my version captures the essence of the original tale as coherently as possible, though I cut out many layers and strange sequences. Yes, there are multiple princes, quests, dogs and timelines. Also, there are fairies. The occasional snippet floats by that feels like a familiar story (oh, the pregnant queen needed to eat from that

---

[*] In "Curse of Bronze" (2020) Bella Hathaway inherits the family curse-breaking business and solves her aunt's murder in a tale that owes a lot to Beauty and the Beast, talking furniture and all. She has two older sisters, who in true Robin McKinley style, are also named after virtues: Faith the war reporter and Charity the daredevil duchess. Faith's story is told in "A Taste for Skulls" in which she returns from war with some damage and steps into the role of Jeanne Watson, assistant to a female Sherlock Holmes (2024).

[†] My preferred number of talking animals is zero. I felt like such a fraud when I wrote a talking cat story one time and rather enjoyed it. But I can stop any time I like.

fairy's personal garden, did she?) only for the carpet to be tugged from under you.

The surreal, vivid illustrations of Natalie Frank in this particular edition only added to the sense that The White Cat is a fever dream, not a fairy tale.

(There is a dog called Toutou and a parrot named Perroquet.)

They transformed all the lords and ladies of the kingdom into cats, left only the hands visible of the rest of his court, and reduced me to the deplorable condition in which you found me. Finally, they informed me about my birth and the death of my father and mother, and told me, "You will be released from your cat-like form only by a prince who exactly resembles the husband we have just eliminated."

"It is you, my lord, who bear that resemblance," she concluded. "You have the same features, the same air, the same voice. I was struck by it the moment I saw you."

— "THE WHITE CAT," BY MADAME D'AULNOY, TRANSLATED BY JACK ZIPES

In reading The White Cat with all its questy goodness, I was most reminded of one of my all time favourite Enid Blyton novels: *Tuppeny, Feefo & Jinks.* *

It's not one of the famous ones, not part of a series, and not reprinted at the same rate at *The Wishing Chair, The*

---

* (1951) previously published as *The Green Goblin Book* in 1935

Faraway Tree, or all those crime-fighting children. I had an op shop copy as a kid which I lost track of during the garage sale years. For a long time, this one book was emblematic of my adult quest to replace beloved books that I regretted letting go of.

I have a lovely vintage edition now!*

The plot of *TFJ* is rather similar to that of *The Goodies*. Three young goblins find each other and set up a dear little shop, promising to sell unusual items — which leads them on the kind of adventures you might have if you were offering a service to do Anything, Anytime, Anywhere.

They befriend a fairy, get into a scrape with a rubbish portal bucket (solved with an Aladdin style 'new lamps for old' heist), chase down a magical Bluebird in Dreamland, climb a sugar mountain on a camel to face down a giant on behalf of a dwarf, and eventually fall in love with fairy princesses (one each) to accomplish their happy ever after. So many fairy tale tropes in one book!

The story in the book that most reminds me of The White Cat is the Adventure of the Surprising Blue Table-cloth. Our goblins meet Fairy Tiptoe's Uncle Hoppety who challenges them to find the Wonderful Tablecloth owned by

---

*   Literally while writing this note, my thoughts went to the One That Got Away, another childhood book that I sold and was never able to find again, largely because it has a title shared with many more recent and popular books, and I couldn't remember the author. I thought I'd give it one more go, spent some time hunting via Google (no dice) then through GoodReads and finally FINALLY several pages into the search found The Blue Umbrella (1968) by Carol Beach York. This book has lived rent-free in my head for at least 40 years and I'm so excited that I now have a copy winging its way to me. Ironically, it's about a child who runs a bunch of side hustles to save up for a beloved object, and I'm pretty sure she holds at least one garage sale.

Nobbly the Gnome. This cloth will, when commanded, cover itself with a marvellous spread of food and then clear away the dishes, only to replenish itself over and over.

The deal is done easily (the goblins by now have a palace to trade for the magical item), but they are conned by local innkeepers who steal the magic tablecloth and replace it with a similar one.

Upset that the magic no longer works, the goblins return to Nobbly who offers them another of his magical treasures — a black cat who purrs pearls and then, once the innkeepers pull the same trick, a red whip that whips your enemies.

This third time, the innkeepers are thoroughly rewarded for their wicked work, thanks to that red whip, and the goblins end up with all three treasures since Nobbly the Gnome is so happy with his palace!

I don't know why this story in particular has stuck in my head for so many years, but there's something about the lyrical fairy tale quality of the items themselves — and the rule of three, of course. The pearls are reminiscent of the good sister in Diamonds and Toads, who does a good deed and is rewarded by jewels falling from her mouth. The magic tablecloth is a reminder of the magic porridge pot without the 'cautionary tale' aspect of the story.[*] And of course, the red whip is a more violent version of the harp

---

[*] One of the most glorious examples of a fairy tale being told as performance is Rik Mayall's Grim Tale of "Sweet Porridge" (1989). If you've never seen it before, go look it up on YouTube right now. I'll wait.

(waits)

I KNOW, RIGHT?

which, when stolen by Jack, calls out to warn its owner that it is being stolen.[*]

Part of the genius of Enid Blyton's stories[†] is how she takes familiar elements and tropes and reassembles them into stories that feel as if they have existed forever.

While I'm ruminating on classics from childhood, I want you to know that Charity drives a roadster because of Nancy Drew, and her hair is strawberry blonde because of Trixie Belden.

---

[*]   Anyone else suddenly hear a cry of "I belong to Chrestomanci Castle" in their head or is it just me?

[†]   I know she was a horrible person, but there's no scraping her off my ribs now, I read way too many of her books when young to avoid being affected by her fictional choices for the rest of my life.

CRIMSON AS A RUBY
(WAS THE HEART)

Ruby

Dear Crimson

I never thought the colour red would betray us. Isn't that stupid? It was our colour. We were the best friends named after the same colour.

It was ours.

Whenever I imagined the Day of Sorting, I never thought we'd be separated. Not for an instant. I know you worried about it, but I never did. I was so sure — white or red or yellow or blue. Whatever rose stem my hand closed around, yours would be the same.

I pricked my finger on the stem, did you know that? I was so busy looking at that drop of blood, I didn't even think about the colour of my rose, and then I saw it was red. And I was so relieved, because nothing had to change. We didn't have to give up our little two bed apartment, we didn't have to go somewhere new and scary.

Then I saw your face.

I saw your rose.

Maybe it's white that betrayed us, by picking you. Red is

fine. Red is solid. Red is right here, on the ground, waiting for you.

What's flying like? Are you making friends?

I miss you.

Ruby

Crimson

Dear Ruby

I'm sorry it's been so long. We don't have a lot of time to ourselves Up Here. I've been working hard, training. Flying is not as easy as it looks. Humans don't have the right muscles to operate full wings, not at first.

It's good, though. I'm making progress. I'm not unhappy. You should see my shoulders now, they're so strong!

We all live in these long dorm rooms, with weirdly large beds. You need that space, for the wings. It's so uncomfortable at night: they ache when they stay in the same place for too long, but turning over in bed is such a performance. It's like sharing a room with a bunch of grumpy owls, everyone fluttering and groaning and swishing whenever they shift around in bed.

The food is good — lots of it, basic stuff. Not as bad as the stories say.

(I miss your cinnamon cakes, and breakfast cereal. Everything here is health health health, veggies and protein and supergrains, properly blended for maximum efficiency and power.)

I'm honoured to be here, making a difference. Doing my duty. But I miss your face.

Hugs,

Crimson

Ruby

Dear Crimson

I saw two angels today. A local gang tried to roll over the stallholders at the market, and one of them pulled a knife. Within seconds, the angels were there, catching up the gang-members and wrapping their wrists in glowing gold thread. I ran up to them, thinking maybe — *maybe* one of them was you.

They wore feathered cowls, and the same bright white uniform. One was female-shaped — she could have been you. But when I came closer, I realised: not your chin, not your shoulder.

It only made me miss you more.

Of course, they wouldn't let you down here on duty so soon, I know that. But part of me couldn't help hoping.

Your

Ruby

Crimson

Dear Ruby

I killed my first demon today. I didn't even mean to. I don't have my certificate yet.

We're fresh meat so we get to tag along on patrols some-times, nothing lower than Level 90. Light duties, no crime expected. They call it the Cake Walk. No one pulls knives or silver bullets on Level 90 or higher, because they're all so fancy and refined. (And the 24 hour constant camera feed in all public areas doesn't hurt). The only crime that happens up here in the clouds is the kind that happens behind closed doors; the kind we're not allowed anywhere near.

I was paired with an archangel called Sabbath. A tough customer; forty-eight demon notches on her belt from a twelve year career. She goes Down Below every other week. She's harder than I could ever be.

She didn't see them coming.

The demon got the drop on her from above, literally: releasing a crate of ration batteries that slammed her to the ground. She shook it off, swinging her wings as she took off after the creature (they never get demon infestations that high in the clouds, no one knows where he came from).

I realised three blows in that she wasn't going to win the fight. She was sluggish, bleeding from one eye. (Concussion, they said later, and three broken ribs from where the crate landed on her, it's amazing she got back on her feet at all)

I saw the demon's blade slide into her stomach, soft as honey. And everything went... I don't know. Red. Hazy. I don't know what I did.

When it was over, the demon was dead, Sabbath was alive, and there was blood everywhere. I had it in my hair, in my wings. The paramedics said I'm the reason Sabbath made it to surgery in time for them to save her.

I'm writing you this because I need to tell someone how much it hurt. It felt awful. I could barely breathe for days afterwards, like the world was made of darkness and fire. I kept flashing back to that moment, those actions. I kept seeing what I did to that demon all over again, like it was something worth remembering.

But now...

They give me pills, little blue ones, and somehow it doesn't hurt any more. I still remember what I did first thing in the morning, and last thing at night, but the rest of the time? It's become a funny story, something I tell to make the other fresh meat jealous that I saw action before they did.

I'm pretty sure, in another week or so, I won't remember the bad parts at all. It's something about this place. I suppose it makes sense. We couldn't keep the peace if we were always falling over ourselves in grief and guilt about the nasty shit we have to do.

But I wanted someone out there to know that the first time I killed a demon, I felt really bad about it.

I don't know when I'll see you again. Maybe I'll have killed another dozen by then. Maybe it won't even matter.

I miss you. I miss who I used to be.

Sorry to be such a downer. I promise, next time, I'll write about something happy.

Love,

Crimson

Ruby

Dear Crimson

I've been training. Running every day. Lifting weights. I didn't know, before. I didn't want to go anywhere, so I didn't even try to better myself. No wonder you were chosen, and I wasn't.

I get another chance. One more chance, on my nineteenth birthday. To be re-Sorted. To trade my red rose for some other future.

Three months to go.

Maybe I'll see you soon.

Your

Ruby

Crimson

Dear Ruby

Don't come here. Please. I want to be with you more than I can say, but I don't want you *here*. I don't want you to wear the wings. It's not the magical dream we thought it was, Up Here.

Maybe I'm selfish, but it helps me get through the day to know exactly where you are, that you are living our old life. That you're the same. I wish I was there with you.

Please don't give up your peace and safety for a chance to join me. They wouldn't let us stay together anyway, and... I'm not the person who left.

You'd be disappointed, I think, in who I have become.

Crimson

Ruby

Dear Crimson

The rose was red again. So, I suppose I'm not good enough anyway.

(And it doesn't matter, because you don't want me there in your fancy world of angel wings and demon wars.)

I wish I'd got my chance to prove you wrong.

Your

Ruby

Crimson

Dear Ruby
I miss you more today.

Crimson

Dear Ruby
You haven't written back. Don't think I haven't noticed. We always said we wouldn't drift. We said nothing could separate us, not even space and time. You promised.

Crimson

Dear Ruby

Are you alive?

Crimson

Dear Ruby

I know you're trying to make me hate you. I see you. I refuse to believe you just forgot, or have been putting it off, or that you hardly even think of me any more. I know you're doing this deliberately. I know you.

Your

Crimson

Always

Ruby

❧✿☙

Dear Crimson

I know it's been a while. I wasn't...

I didn't stop writing to hurt you (of course I did)

I stopped because I didn't know who you were any more.

I stopped because you didn't want me to change.

I can't be your perfect photograph of another time, before you went away. I get to change too. I get to grow up. Maybe I'm not killing demons, but that doesn't mean I'm exactly the same person I was I was two years ago, when your rose turned out to be white and not red.

I'm pregnant. How's that for change?

Ruby

Crimson

Dear Ruby

I'm so happy for you! That's amazing.

When are you due? I might be able to apply for a visit home in a few months but I can put it off longer if it means I get to meet your baby.

I've missed a lot, it seems. So many questions!!

Are you happy?

Crimson

Ruby

Dear Crimson

It's not a happy story, at least it didn't start out that way.

Everything's fine now. And the baby is — well. There's going to be a baby. I'd rather you came home to visit *me*.

I don't know where to start talking about all the things you've missed. I know that's my fault mostly, because I stopped writing. But I wanted to figure out who I was, beyond the person whose best friend flew away to become an angel.

And this is it.

The baby's due in two months. Come when you like. Or don't.

Ruby

Crimson

❧

APPLICATION FOR PERSONAL VISITATION BELOW CLOUD LEVEL: Approved

Dear Ruby

Thank you so much for letting me visit with you and your daughter. She's beautiful. I'm sorry it took so long for me to organise the paperwork. Wish I'd come sooner.

(I'm sorry there were so many awkward silences.)

It's so strange, isn't it, seeing each other after all this time? Of course we've both changed. I'm sorry I ever made you feel like... I was leaving you on a shelf, expecting to return to exactly the same person, the same moment in time.

Your edges are sharper in some places, softer in others. I suppose mine are too.

And now, I miss you all over again.

Crimson

Ruby

APPLICATION FOR PERSONAL VISITATION
BELOW CLOUD LEVEL: Approved

Dear Crimson

Two visits in the same year, you must be doing well at work for them to let you go so readily.

This one was better, I think? We're getting better at filling the silences.

I think you made more of an impression on Feebe this time around. Her eyes brighten when I talk about you, or point at your picture. You're Aunt Crimson now, by the way, sorry not sorry.

I hope you can come again. I never quite manage to find time these days to sit down and write like I used to (yes, I know, it's been weeks already since you left, my thank you note is so late you'll probably visit again before you receive it).

I liked the look on your face when you sat in my little kitchen, like you had found a safe place to land. Like you belonged there. But it made me worry about where you are the rest of the time, what you're doing Up There. It's a long time since I even let myself think about that.

I don't want you to hide that world for me, or pretend it has nothing to do with you and me, with Feebe, in a kitchen.

So, killed any demons lately?

Ruby

Crimson

Dear Ruby

After a while, the blood and death and fear all blurs together. Many of our days are boring. Law enforcement, flying, paperwork.

But the bad days are really bad, and you're right: I don't want it to touch you and Feebe. Not at all.

I carry on, knowing my work is important, knowing I'm trained to do a good job. Knowing that everything I do might be the difference in keeping you and your little family safe.

Keeping other people's families safe.

I've been here nearly four years. Retirement for anything other than near-death wounding in the field kicks in at twenty years. There's a long haul yet. I can't think about it too much, can't wish away all the moments between here and there.

I love flying. But now I know what I'm missing out on. I want to come home.

I'll visit more often. There's a promotion looming, and that comes with perks. I'll be there when I can.
Love,

Crimson

Ruby

Dear Crimson

White. The rose was white. I knew I shouldn't have let her do it so young, applied for the extension for study plans, or family special circumstance, though both of those would be a lie. There's no extension option for 'mother isn't ready to let go.'

She's sixteen, and she wanted this. Wanted an adventure. Wanted — though she never admitted it to be until she had the rose in her hand — to fly Up There with you.

I don't blame you. I don't. I can't, or my heart will break and letting that happen twice in one day would be excessive.

My daughter is going to be an angel.

She's packing her bags.

I wish I hadn't coaxed all those terrible stories out of you for all these years. I wish I didn't know the dark side of what she will face up there. I wish I didn't know how heavy her wings will be on her back.

I wish.
You'll see her soon, before I see you next.
All my love,

Ruby

Crimson

Dear Ruby

I applied for retirement. That is, I filled out the forms. I have so many kills on my belt, so many years of excellent service, my choices are really only two: promotion to the executive, or retirement in good standing.

I'm so ready for this.

Two months. If they approve my application, I could be home in two months.

But.

But Feebe is coming Up Here, and that changes everything. I know it matters to you that I'm here too. I know it would make it easier for you, knowing I can guide her through those hard early months, the first year. Good mentorship made all the difference to me when it came to surviving this job, and thriving.

Good mentorship made me the angel I am, and I didn't get it until later than I should have done.

I can be here for Feebe. I want to offer you that.

But I'm selfish, too. Turning my back on the retirement

option now might mean years before I get the chance to step away again... so I need to you to ask me to do this.

I need to know this is what you want. For all three of us.

You know what I want.

Love always,

Crimson

Ruby

Dear Crimson
   (I'm sorry.)
   (I hate to ask you.)
   (I hate that you made me say this.)
   Please stay, for her sake. Just a little longer. Be there for her. I'd do it if I could.
   (I'd have done it for you, if it was possible.)
   Your

Ruby

Feebe

Dear Mother

I killed my first demon today. I was partnered with Aunt Crimson, which I know is not a coincidence, but I can't complain about it because every recruit in the Fresh Meat intake is wildly jealous of me. She's such a badass.

It was supposed to be a Milk Run (that's what they actually call it), but a gang of demons was waiting for us. They'd been tipped off, I think? Internal investigations are underway.

There were five of them, and two of us. I'm not even certified to kill demons yet.

I didn't kill all of them, obviously. That was Crimson. She's beautiful in the field, hard as nails but light, too. Like a paper dart on the air. As soon as she knew we were in trouble she pushed me behind her, took them all on.

One leaped over her head. I stabbed wildly as he came down. We struggled, but I got my blade into his throat. When it was over, and I shoved his body off me, I saw Crimson in the thick of it, spinning in blood, her blade bared. Red flecked over her wings and cowl. She didn't even look angry about it all, just empty. Like she has been doing this so long, she can't even feel it any more.

I can't wait to be as good as her.

But I think...

I don't know what you said to her, to make her postpone her retirement. But she never talks any more about going home. Even said I could have her scheduled leave next month, to get home and see you.

(I'm not sure this is healthy.)

I love her. I love you both. But I think it might be time for her to stop, before she can't.

And she won't do it, unless you ask. She's always listened to you. Everyone up here is all serious business. I don't think the angels are really friends with each other.

She needs a friend, Mum. We're her family, right?

Anyway, she'll be in hospital for a few weeks. One of them slashed a tendon in her leg, and it's taking ages to drain the curse magic out of the wound to the point they can do proper surgery. I have a visitor's pass, but I asked and I can sign it over to any other family member. If you want... if you were willing to come Up Here, maybe you could come visit her?

I think she'd like that.

Thanks for the socks and the chocolate.

Love,

Feebe

Crimson

❧❀☙

APPLICATION FOR CIVILIAN VISITATION ABOVE CLOUD LEVEL, SPECIAL CIRCUM-STANCES: Approved

Dear Ruby

You shouldn't have come.

Crimson

Ruby

Dear Crimson

You've done enough for Feebe. You can come home now. Please. I want you to come home.

Love,

Ruby

Crimson

Dear Ruby

Let me tell you what happens when an angel retires.

It takes four sets of surgery to remove our wings. They do it under local anaesthetic because they need the patient's feedback throughout the process, to ensure they are not taking too many nerve endings during the removal. Muscular damage is common.

We have ten mandated, company-authorised sessions of physical therapy scheduled in as a default, to help us learn to move and function without the heavy weight of the wings. Fourteen mandated psychotherapy sessions to process the emotional loss of flight, of duty and purpose, of going through process that everyone refers to as, not retirement, but The Fall.

An angel does not lay down her blade and trot off home to grow roses around her cottage door. An angel Falls, and it is spoken of with a haunting sense of accusation and regret.

It is, I have been told, like having your sense of self-worth torn from you, feather by feather.

I should never have put it on you, made you feel guilty that I stayed here for Feebe. The truth is, I could have come up with another excuse. I came up with a dozen before I even filled in the forms, the first time around.

I'm not ready to let it go.

I'm not ready to Fall.

I'm not sure I ever will be.

Love,

Crimson

Ruby

Dear Crimson

You are stronger than you think you are. The kettle's hot. *Come home*.

If you really must think of it as a Fall, then make the leap and I will catch you.

Trust in our future.

I want you here with me.

Always,

Ruby

The Angel Executive

ANGEL AGENT CRIMSON
    RECOMMENDATION FOR PROMOTION
TO THE EXECUTIVE:
    Approved

ANGEL AGENT CRIMSON:
    RECOMMENDATION FOR RETIREMENT
IN GOOD STANDING:
    Approved

Dear Agent Crimson

It is rare for one of our angels to be approved for promotion and retirement simultaneously, but you have always been exceptional. Given your service history, the Executive have agreed to a further ten days for you to make your decision.

We hope you appreciate this opportunity to choose your own future, and we trust that you will make the right decision.

Honourable regards,

THE ANGEL EXECUTIVE

Feebe

Dear Mother and Aunt Crimson

Today was a good day. Three lives saved, two arrests. No one died.

I love you both, and I'll see you when my leave is approved.

I'm so glad I have you both to come home to. I hope you're taking good care of each other.

Your

Feebe

Author's Note: On Oscar Wilde and Nightingales and Crimson and Ruby

The title of this story is a quote from an Oscar Wilde fairy tale, "The Nightingale and the Rose" which is, you should not be shocked to hear, heartbreaking.

(Definitely not for children or bedtime, Oscar!) *

It's the tale of a nightingale who overhears a lover's lament and goes above and beyond to help make a romantic wish come true… but mostly it's about how young people in love say stupid things and you probably shouldn't listen to them.

You know the phrase 'don't set yourself on fire to make someone else warm?' This nightingale kills itself to turn a rose red so that a random student can use it to claim a dance from the girl he loves… but the girl turns out to be ungracious (wanting jewels instead) and the student abandons love as quickly as he acquired it.

------

* I was rather charmed to learn that Wilde published a second collection of fairy tales, A House of Pomegranates, three years later, which he said was "intended neither for the British child nor the British public."

Meanwhile, the nightingale is dead, having imagined its sacrifice would be worthwhile.

Oh, Oscar.

So the Nightingale pressed closer against the thorn, and the thorn touched her heart, and a fierce pang of pain shot through her. Bitter, bitter was the pain, and wilder and wilder grew her song, for she sang of the Love that is perfected by Death, of the Love that dies not in the tomb.

And the marvellous rose became crimson, like the rose of the eastern sky. Crimson was the girdle of petals, and crimson as a ruby was the heart.

— OSCAR WILDE, "THE NIGHTINGALE AND THE ROSE," ***THE HAPPY PRINCE AND OTHER TALES*** (OR ***STORIES***), 1888.

The language is some of the most lyrical I've ever read. It's gorgeous and it's horrible.

Tumblr regularly throws up the revelation that Hans Christian Andersen wrote The Little Mermaid (original tragedy edition, feet stabbed with glass, outsiders aren't allowed to be happy) as a metaphor for his own queer longing and unrequited love. Oscar Wilde's fairy tale feels like it has the same energy — a beautiful creature so desperate to *give* that it dies for the happiness of others, written by a man whose entire public life was a performance.

I started out to write a story in response to The Nightingale and the Rose — and what I ended up with was a story of longing and pining that argues *against* queer tragedy.

I have to admit, there isn't much of the original fairy tale left in my story beyond the title.

Colours are such an important detail of fairy tales — they help the stories to live in people's heads so vividly. From Red's Riding Hood to Snow White's skin (and hair, and lips), colour often becomes one of those elements of a story that are set in stone even as other elements shift about.

Disney have used this to great effect, to the point that you can tell from the colour of a frock on a non-Disney fairy tale retelling exactly who that character is supposed to be.*

Names are also important, even though many of our fairy tale protagonists don't have them — and when they do, those names often serve as descriptions, changing with every translation. From Cendrillon to Cinderella to Cenerentola to Aschenbrödel to Aschenputtel... modern retellings lean into "her real name is Ella, Cinderella is a cruel nickname" even though the modern name Ashley is *right there*.†

---

* Cinderella in blue, Sleeping Beauty in pink-blue-pink-blue... Belle will be dressed in yellow forever, while Merida and Tiana have distinctly different signature greens.

† See: Season 1 of Once Upon a Time which uses both Ella and Ashley for the double identity of Cinderella. Season 7, featuring a different Cinderella from another dimension, gives her Jacinda as a modern name, (emphasis on *Cinda*/Cinder when her stepmother addresses her). I could write a whole essay on the naming choices in Once Upon a Time, my favourites being Regina Mills & Emma Swan and my LEAST favourite being how the dramatic Rumplestiltskin becomes the cutesy "Rumple" when Belle French is talking to him.

The flexibility around names for fairy tale heroines allows for splendid variety in retellings — though in many cases the Disney version becomes locked into people's minds as the default.

One of my favourite naming choices comes from Robin McKinley's *Beauty* (1978) in which she has all three sisters named after virtues to make 'Beauty' seem less silly,* and goes one step further: the sisters were actually named Grace, Hope and Honour, but as soon as little Honour was old enough to realise her family's naming conventions, she protested that she would "rather be Beauty." Thus, with the ruthlessness of all families, she became Beauty forever.

When I wrote my own Beauty & the Beast (by way of cursebreakers and gargoyles) in the novella *Curse of Bronze*, my heroine was called Bella and her sisters Faith and Charity, in a nod to McKinley and the book that won my heart as a teenager.

Where was I? Colours for names. I've always loved Snow White and Rose Red (see: Rosebuds) for the title of the story as much the idea that any mother might name her kids so prettily. As with Prince Charming, I get a kick out of stories that repeat fairy tale names because then you can pretend they are all the same person... something that my brain literally does with everyone who shares the same first name anyway.

This story began with the idea of retelling Oscar Wilde's The Nightingale and the Rose, and then the new idea about writing a whole new story based on a single quote from that

---

* In the original story by Gabrielle-Suzanne Barbot de Villeneuve, she was of course "La Belle," not merely Belle, but virtues become names in fairy tales so easily...

fairy tale (stories about birds, *boring*) but ultimately turned into 'if you meet someone whose name is the same as yours, translated a different way, you have to be friends, right?'

(And then they kissed.)

SALON FAERIE

Calamine Blue

Ellory awoke. For a moment, a few precious seconds before she opened her eyes, she was able to believe she was lying in her own bed. Home and safe.

The scent of flowers and sugar in the air told her otherwise.

Sun was already streaming in through the huge bay window as she slid out of the silken sheets and went to the wardrobe. Too much to hope that the invisible hands who laid out her clothes each day had gone for practical and comfortable, just this once.

No, it was another gown that looked like it belonged on the cover of Royal Ballroom Couture Monthly.

She washed quickly at the basin, dousing herself with water that smelled of mountains and lemongrass, then shimmied out of the voluminous nightgown to face her fate. Petticoats and shift, hooped skirt, rustling layers of embroidered silk over the top of that.

(Calamine blue, her painter's training brought to mind.

Somewhere between robin's egg and turquoise. A light and airy colour, perfect for sun rooms and porcelain cups.)

The nightgown was gone before she was fully dressed; snatched away by invisible hands. It would be back tonight, all starchy and scented as if it were a new garment all over again. (Perhaps it was new each time, a fresh but identical nightgown woven by, oh pixies or something. The owner of the castle did not seem to care about conserving his resources.)

Ellory glanced in the mirror at the dressing table to note that, as usual, those same invisible hands had worked miracles on her hair, teasing and tangling it up into some wild confection of an up-do.

Poor dears. They probably didn't get out much. This might be the highlight of their day.

Ellory had once attempted to spend the entire day in bed, but the gown and hair and petticoats had all made their presence known rather forcibly. It was not worth it, those small moments of rebellion. She was always the one who suffered for them.

And so, as she did every morning, she complied with their wordless insistence.

This does not touch me. This will not kill me.

She heard them before she saw them: a cluster of chattering, screeching voices, reflected in a cacophony of wild echoes, filling the polished stairwell all the way up. At least she could be certain they would never take her by surprise.

Except by existing at all, but that particular surprise was months behind her. Weeks. Months. Years?

No, not years yet. It could not be.

Mazarine, Pomona

On the ground floor, Ellory hesitated for a moment by the large arched doorway that led into the atrium. This was where the urge to run was always at its strongest; every day, she must master it. Control it. Defeat it.

Running was no solution. There was no solution. She was a prisoner. Acceptance meant survival for a little longer.

One more deep breath, and *through*.

"There she is!"

"It's her!"

"Our little storyteller."

"The entertainment."

"Our queeeeeeen." This last was said at the highest pitch, and followed with gales of laughter because, of course, it was a joke.

Ellory's Pa always said the best jokes had an element of truth to them; if so, this one was a doozy. Ellory herself would never see the funny side.

Humour is subjective, Pa. Case in point.

They lunged and snatched at her, the ladies of the house. Long thin fingers in green and blue (Mazarine, Prussian, Celestial, Pomona, Parrot, Corbeau, Bottle, a line of paint colours frozen in her memory, left over from the days where she was free and had a purpose in life) grabbed at her sleeves and skirts and even the fashionable lock of hair that trailed from the mighty pastry twist on top of her head.

"Here she is!"

"Get her."

"Ladies, please," said Ellory, employing the voice she had used for years when dealing with her Pa's more demanding clients. Soothing but firm. She smacked at the grabbing hands, shoved her way through the press of twisted, leering creatures. Their wings buzzed against each other as they shuffled around reluctantly, making room for her. "I can't tell you the story if you don't let me breathe."

The trick worked; the creatures became docile. "Story!" they exclaimed in their high-pitched voices.

"Such a pretty queen," one of them wheedled.

"Such a good girl."

"Tell us a story."

"Tell us *your* story."

Sycophantic was almost as bad as demanding, but she got less scratches this way.

Head held high, skirts swishing, Ellory walked to the best chair and took her seat. A tray of sweetmeats appeared at her side, and a goblet she usually thought it best to ignore.

The ladies clustered around her, climbing on top of each other, crawling and wriggling and anxious.

"We'll be good."

"Best behaviour."

"Tell us the story!"

"Are you sitting comfortably?" Ellory asked, her story-teller voice taking over. "Ready to pay attention? Then I'll continue."

Carmine, Saffron

"When we left off, Cinderella was... now, where was she?"

"The castle!"

"Shh, no interruptions."

"I was only trying to help!"

"Indeed, we had reached the castle full of red shoes. Only, what do you suppose? All of the shoes were left, and none of them right. There were hundreds, thousands, millions of shoes, but not a pair amongst them. Cinderella sifted and searched and combed and curried her way through the collection, but she could not fulfil the fairy's wish without the matching pair of red shoes. Finally, she came to the very last room in the highest tower, and what do you think she found there?"

"A right red shoe!"

"More left shoes!"

"A cake!"

"An *axe*."

"Shut your noise, you lot, I want to hear what really happened."

"Well, Cinderella climbed over another pile of red shoes
— of carmine shoes, a very particular shade of red — to find
a golden bed. Gold as primroses, gold as the dye of the
saffron crocus. On the golden bed, a sleeping princess. And
on the sleeping princess' foot... a single right red shoe."

"I *knew* it."

"*I* knew it."

"Nobody guessed sleeping princess!"

"Will you all pipe down."

"If I may continue. Cinderella reached out and laid a
hand on the shoe on the foot of the sleeping princess, and
as she did so, another hand lay over hers. It was the
princess! 'What are you doing?' she asked. Cinderella
confessed that she had been trying to take the shoe, as it
was the only way she could save her father's life. 'That is
quite a tale,' said the princess. 'My name is Sleeping Beauty,
and if you take that shoe from me, I will die.' 'How can that
possibly be?' asked Cinderella. And so, Sleeping Beauty
began to tell Cinderella the tale of how she ended up in that
tower..."

Pompadour

It had been a gruelling day. They were all gruelling days.

Ellory was expected to begin her tale immediately after the ladies breakfasted, and to keep talking until they were ready to sup. For a while there, she had hoped they might take on the concept of luncheon, allowing her a break in the middle of the day, but so far they had done little more than mutter about the various mentions of delicious luncheons shared by Cinderella and the princesses she met along her circuitous route through half-remembered versions of every story Ellory had ever heard.

Someday, she would run out of story stuff. She knew this. Even now, she often awoke with empty thoughts, racking her brain for fragments and characters of old tales she had not yet woven into this particular concoction.

She could not think about that. She could only keep her story winding forward, one hour, one minute at a time.

As the bell rang for supper, she wanted to sag exhausted into her chair. Instead, she forced herself to sound light. "Ah, and we are out of time for today, how sad. I suppose

you will have to wait until tomorrow to find out how
Sleeping Beauty escaped the shoe full of children to win the
pumpkin…"

The ladies groaned and muttered, but their thoughts
were already sliding towards their supper: what they would
eat, and what they would drink.

"Tomorrow then," they whined.

"Can we still not kill her?"

"Not until we know how it ends."

"It's no matter. We always get to kill them, sooner or
later."

They rolled and racketed, grizzled and whined their way
out of the parlour, leaving Ellory alone.

She breathed in silence for a moment, glad to ease her
throat. And then she rose to return to her room.

Tomorrow it would start all over again. Tonight, for a
few hours until she slept, she was free.

Today, however, as she set foot on the stair, she saw a
rare glimpse out of the corner of her eye: a flash of pink and
gold.

Him.

She had not seen hide nor hair of him for weeks;
presumed herself abandoned to his creatures.

Her captor.

Ellory abandoned the staircase. She picked up her skirts
and hurried around through the long maze of corridors and
drawing rooms and parlours that formed the West Wing of
this ridiculous house. Was he really there, or had she imagined it?

Finally, she found herself in the last of the libraries.
There was an open decanter of port, a recently-emptied
glass. But no lord of the manor.

Half-relieved, half-infuriated, she turned back... and there he was.

Pink and gold, indeed. He wore clashing velvet and silks, in no recognisable mortal fashion. *Pompadour, Blossom, Nankeen, Apollo.*

His garments were oddly draped and tailored, and yet exquisite, of course. In London, he would turn heads, and not only for his sartorial choices.

His hair was a tumble of gold, falling half to his waist, like a pirate. No man in London would appear so, not even a magician on the stage. But this was no performer. This was a lord of the manor. A king, quite likely, of his own domain.

He was so beautiful, it made her heart catch all over again. But of course, he was her jailer, her monster. Not her lover.

"Wife," he said courteously, moving past her to the decanter. He poured, and waited, then poured again. A glass for each of them.

Ellory knew better than to resist; she had eaten more than seven pomegranate seeds during her time here, even if his servants took a very long time to figure out how often a human needed to eat, to stay alive.

She had considered starving herself, as one form of escape, but the invisible hands were rough when insisting otherwise; she had not tried that again.

"Husband," she said now, in the same even tone.

"They haven't killed you, yet."

"Aren't I the lucky one?"

"You must be exceedingly entertaining."

"So I've been told."

He smiled — a killer smile, and handed her a glass of the

jewel-like liquid. "Here we are. So civilised. I hope you have been enjoying the hospitality of my house."

Ellory sipped. "As your wife, am I not chatelaine of your home? Surely you presume on *my* hospitality."

His face darkened a little, but did not quite tilt into the rage she had seen from him before when she dared to question his behaviour. "There are many duties a wife should perform for her husband," he said. "Where would you like to start?"

"The kitchen, of course," she replied with some confidence. "Introduce me to your cook, and your housekeeper. Show me the accounts books, and the cellar. Give me the keys to hang on my belt."

He gave her an odd, searching look. "Ladies do not need to know of such things."

She scoffed. "You don't know much about ladies."

Her husband moved, quick as a wish, pressed her back across the room with his own body until she was quivering against a book case and he — he continued to push indecently forwards, the buttons of his velvet suit pressed hard against the line of her gown. "I expected them to eat you," he growled. "Or scratch you to pieces. You should not be here still, gnawing at me."

Ellory gathered her bravery; lifted her chin. "So let me go."

He loomed over her, close enough to lick her face. Then he shoved himself away, storming out of the room. "You were meant to be a weapon," he declared. "Not my punishment. Not a chore."

She had messed it up. Her first chance in weeks, and she could not keep her mouth shut. She had meant to be so polite and deferential. That had been her plan. She had meant to *beg*.

"Wait," she called now, running out after him. "Please, husband. A moment of your time!"

But the corridor was empty.

You were meant to be a weapon.

What did that mean?

Gold like Jonquils

"And then what?" demanded the harpies.

Ellory took a careful sip of her water. "Sleeping Beauty was quite lost, in that moment. Alone, wandering in the woods, all scratched with thorns, and fleeing her presumptuous prince. It all could have ended for her. But, as luck would have it, she came across something she had never expected to find."

"An axe."

"A crying baby."

"A ten-foot dragon!"

"A loaf of bread."

"A tower," said Ellory. "A strange, golden tower, with no castle beneath. Alone in the forest, surrounded by almost as many thorns and brambles as her own castle. And in that tower... well. I would tell you what she found inside. But the hour has grown long."

"Nooooo," whined the ladies.

"Just a few minutes more."

"But there is so much more of the story," said Ellory. "It could not possibly all fit into a few minutes. I am very much afraid we shall have to reconvene tomorrow."

Nine weeks now. Four, since she shared a glass of port with her husband and he stormed away from her.

Still a prisoner.

Still the faerie ladies had not eaten her, or torn her to shreds.

Still she told her story.

You were meant to be a weapon.

"And just as Sleeping Beauty was about to pull Rapunzel free of the giant thorn-billed monster that bit and tore at them both... ah, I see the hour has grown long."

"No!"

"Just a few minutes more."

"I couldn't possibly fit it all into a few minutes," said Ellory. "The bell has rung, and your supper is ready. Let us return refreshed tomorrow so I can give you all the juicy details."

"And oh, their dance went on for hours, there in the land of silver branches and gold trees."

"How gold?"

"Gold like jonquils."

"And as the final hour chimed... oh, look at how the sky darkens. I am afraid I cannot complete it tonight. Let us return tomorrow."

"Oh, is that the bell for supper?"

"Ah, the hour has grown long."

"Why, none of us can stop yawning! Let us return refreshed tomorrow."

"Tomorrow."

"Tomorrow."

Saxon

Ellory woke up. Breathed in the scent of flowers and sugar. Wept a little, before rising to wash her face.

She was so sick of stories. Exhausted by the tangled journeys of her fairy tale heroines, merged and borrowed from the tales her own nurse had told her.

Just this once, she wanted a day in which she could walk in the garden and say nothing, think nothing.

"You are lucky to be alive," she told herself sternly as she submitted to the preparations for the day.

Invisible hands in her hair.

Hooped petticoats.

Perfect, as always.

Today, when she walked into the salon, braced for the grabbing hands and darting eyes of the ladies of the house, the room was empty.

For a brief, wild moment, she allowed herself to hope.

"Wife," said a voice.

Not empty after all.

There was her husband, sitting some distance away at a polished oak desk. Every inch the cultured gentleman, though there were thistles in his long golden hair, and what looked like a cobweb smeared on his cravat.

He was a wild thing. She must never forget that.

"What did you mean that day?" she asked immediately. The thought of it had been in her head so long, she must constantly wrestle it out of the way of her story, lest the words themselves become woven into the tale of Cinderella and Sleeping Beauty and the rest of them: those kissing girls, the brave princesses.

You were meant to be a weapon. Not my punishment. Not a chore.

The faerie king (lord, husband, whatever title he wore) sighed and laid down his quill as if merely acknowledging her existence was the dullest of duties.

"Why am I a weapon?" Ellory demanded. He so rarely appeared: it might be weeks or months or years before she got another chance. "What do you want of me? Why even take a wife if you were going to turn me into this — storytelling drudge?"

He turned to her, eyes glowing green. Green of the grasslands. Emerald. Olive. Corbeau and Parrot. Pomona, the colour of apples. And then, finally, a brilliant Saxon green that she ached to daub on a brush.

If she had a paintbrush, she could *stab* him with it.

"I took you," he said. "Because another man wanted you."

Never mind the paintbrush. She wanted to scratch his

eyes out. She could, if only the invisible servants did not trim her nails so neatly every dawn.

"What man?" she demanded, exasperated.

"I hardly recall his name or his face."

"You delivered me to your hungry salon of claws and teeth to spite a man you don't even remember?"

"You were supposed to let them eat you," he said petulantly. "And then I was to deliver you back to his doorstep, all drained and bitten in pieces. Too bad, so sad. The girl he loved, eaten alive. What plays he would have written, what poetry, for grief of you. The pretty painter's apprentice, muse of his heart, all that promise wasted. His never wife."

Ellory began to shake all over. Was this fury, or exhaustion? "But I thwarted you," she said, finally. "I told those stories to your court. Kept the claws from my throat."

"Every day," the king of the faerie sulked.

"And the man you wanted so badly to inspire with my suffering?"

"Oh," said the king, tilting his head. "He died of old age."

No. It could not be. "*When?*"

Ellory had been here months, she knew. Days, weeks, months. She had been keeping track. Surely it could not be years? Surely it could not be decades?

"How long have I been here?" she whispered in horror.

"Counting is for mortals," yawned her husband. "Isn't it a joke? I wanted to make his words better by destroying his muse, but he barely noticed you were gone. Some other man's daughter caught his eye and he was off, writing his plays and verse about her instead. Meanwhile, you've become quite the storyteller. You might be even better than he was in his prime. My court almost tore themselves to pieces when I told them there would be no story today."

"And what," said Ellory, swallowing hard. "What do you intend to do with me now?"

The faerie king scoffed a little; turned back to his desk and his quill. "Perhaps *I'll* write a poem about you. It can't be that hard."

She flung herself at him, ready to squeeze his throat until it snapped with her own bare hands... but there was nothing but air and dust in the room.

Coquelicot

The salon gathered as usual: all the ladies with their thin
fingers (Prussian Blue, Pomona Green) and blood-stained
teeth (Carmine, Claret, Coquelicot).

"What happened next?" they demanded, tearing at her.

"What did the princess do?"

"How did she survive?"

Ellory had a plan, now. A hope. She did not know if she
could ever escape this house. She did not known if she
could survive her story.

But she would not be that man's weapon.

She had a fine gown, and perfect hair. She had a willing
audience, who hung upon her every word. She had a direction for her story. It had always been heading this way.

She would be her own fucking muse.

"Why," she said, in a warm voice of jewels and promise.
"The princess was saved by a court of clever ladies, strong
and beautiful. Let me tell you of their names, and their
strengths."

"I like this story!"

"Are we in the story now?"

"You are, indeed," said Ellory, settling into her story-teller chair. "Today's tale is all about how the princess and the ladies all won their freedom."

Tomorrow's tale would be the same, and tomorrow and tomorrow, until it was enough. Until the job was done.

"How did that happen?"

"What did they do?"

"Why," said Ellory. "They worked together. As a team, they became strong and powerful. They made each other into weapons. They became the best of friends. And do you know what happened next?"

"Tell us, tell us!" chorused the ladies in the salon. Their eyes were bright. Hungry. Inspired.

Ellory smiled a sharp smile. "Together," she said. "They killed the king and took the kingdom for their own. Are you sitting comfortably? Ready to pay attention? Then I'll continue."

Author's Note: your magical gown never needs laundering

This story was inspired by a blog post about the names given to paint colours in Georgian and Regency England.[*]

I've always been fond of a fairy tale frock. There's a certain magic to a ballgown — especially in any fantasy story — that I find captivating. The Fairy Godmother transforming Cinderella, shoes and all...

Once you get past the awful premise that sets the story in motion, Donkeyskin is a story of impossibly beautiful dresses. A princess, threatened by her predatory father who has decided she should take her dead mother's place as his queen and wife, holds him off by requesting what she believes are impossible challenges.

---

[*] http://sarahs-history-place.blogspot.com/2011/09/colours-used-in-regency-and-georgian.html

(Having asked for and received a gown all the colours of sky, it seems rather optimistic for her to believe he would then fail to produce a gown the colour of the moon and then, finally, a gown as bright and brilliant as the sun. And yet, she keeps asking.)

The princess pivots late in the game, demanding that her father slay his beloved donkey (which shits gold) and make its pelt into a cloak. Only then, when the cloak is produced, does the princess realise how much danger she is in.[*]

Amazingly, the princess is able to flee the castle disguised in the donkey skin, even though the king would presumably have been able to very clearly describe four options of what she might be wearing.

Later, working as a skivvy in a different kingdom, the princess secretly wears her gowns at night to remember her luxurious past, and is spied upon a prince who falls to sick with love for her (or for her pretty frocks) that he can only be cured by a cake baked from her hands.

Looking at it here, no one in this fairy tale is remotely sympathetic. Perhaps that's why I focused so much on the frocks.

---

[*]   Robin McKinley's beautiful, terrible Deerskin (1993) steps up and emphasises the sexual violence implied in the king's intention. (Spoilers for the whole book follow) This is brutal to read on the page and yet also feels far more honest than the softened, almost romanticised threat in the fairy tale — which, after the princess is safely married to her prince, resolves harmonious relations between their kingdoms because the king has in the interim found himself a beautiful widow. There is no vengeance, no consequence for his unnatural desires in the fairy tale. Not so in Deerskin, which pays off a horrific depiction of rape and the resulting psychological trauma by making sure that the king meets proper retribution — Lissar is able to expose her father, prevent him from hurting next chosen bride and punish him for his crimes, after which she proceeds to heal and live her best life.

Fairy tales are never only words on a page, or the words of the storyteller. They are vintage illustrations and theatre costumes and hand-drawn animation cells. They are cosplay and anime and Book Week.

So many of the visuals we associate with fairy tales come down to the costume. Whether it's a cloak that conceals or a ballgown that shines, clothes maketh the fairy tale.

Over the decades, countless illustrators have brought the gorgeous costumes of fairy tale characters to life. From Arthur Rackham to Kay Nielsen... Edmund Dulac... Emma Florence Harrison... Ida Rentoul Outhwaite... Aubrey Beardsley...

Those who paint fairy tales often become known as fairy tale artists, regardless of what else they might paint in their lifetime.

One of my favourite modern fairy tale artists is Sally Gardner, whose work is captivating because of the all the minute wordbuilding details she hides in her complex illustrations. I bought her books by the stack when my kids were little, but once they grew up and started paring out all the childhood favourites, I snatched the Gardner books back to *my shelves*. *Fairy Shopping* and *The Fairy Catalogue* are the ones that I return to again and again, but I am also especially fond of her take on *The Princess and the Pea* featuring elegant 1920s slip dresses (yes, it's always the dresses I remember).

Another favourite is Brisbane artist Kathleen Jennings, who cuts ruthless silhouettes out of black card with tiny knives, and whose sketches somehow always look like fairy tale characters even when they are wearing contemporary clothes.

Frocks are a frothy fantasy in many fairy tales, but they can be as much of a trap as the castle, the tower or the forest. They're pretty to wear, but can transform a heroine into an object to be captured or rescued.

Putting the damsel in a fluffy white dress before you sacrifice her is a common trend in 1980s cinema, from Marion in *Raiders of the Lost Ark* (1981) to Vicki Vale in *Batman* (1989). In *Labyrinth* (1986) — truly one of the most iconic and influential fairy tales of the 20th century, Sarah's first white lace dress is of her own choosing; we can read her craving for fairy tales in the way she wears it over her blue jeans and peasant top. Later, a far more brilliant and phantasmagoric white ballgown (object of thousands of fan art and cosplay desires) represents Sarah's captivity and loss of self after she is tricked into biting the forbidden peach.

The actual *Labyrinth* gown is practically a Brian Froud puppet in its own right… six layers plus panniers, those layers including lace, muslin, organza and *literal cellophane*.* Not to mention gold mesh, glass stones, beads, silk flowers and feathers.

Then there's that other 80's fairy tale film classic, *The Princess Bride* (1987), in which Buttercup the farm girl is taken by a prince, largely against her consent (certainly against any form of enthusiastic consent), and transformed into a "princess" by way of gowns and wealth. Once again, this is a trap — the prince does not even want her, but

---

* http://ariacouture.com/sarahs-labyrinth-ball-gown-a-costume-study - and yes, Brian Froud is the gown's co-creator along with Ellis Flyte.

wishes to use Buttercup's false kidnap and murder to start a war. Nevertheless, he is desperately possessive of her, or at least of the version of her he has created by means of pretty clothes and a strong PR campaign.

Even Cinderella's gown, the most famous of magical dresses, is a trap; or at least, a highly conditional contract pretty much designed to get Cinderella caught and/or punished for her effrontery to attend the ball against her guardian's wishes.

A common warning of fairy tales is that that pretty things are never to be entirely trusted.

FROM THE VAULTS: ROSEBUDS, FRUIT & MIRRORS, THE BLUEBELL VENGEANCE

Publishing older work always comes with questions about ethics and authenticity. How much do you edit/change? Do you touch it at all?

One of the benefits of publishing yourself is that it's entirely on you. If you want to touch anything up, you can. It's unlikely anyone will even notice.

(I haven't changed content for these stories, but I have changed punctuation and a few other stylistic touches that would bug me otherwise.)

I also had to remove double spacing THAT'S HOW OLD THESE STORIES ARE.

Reading them for the first time in more than 15 years was quite eye-opening! Stand by for more author's notes.

Content warning

"Rosebuds" includes a non-consensual sexual encounter (due to magic) and some victim-blaming.

Rosebuds

FIRST PUBLISHED IN AGOG!
RIPPING READS (2006)

It began with a bear and a dwarf, as all the best stories do.

I was running after the dwarf. My skirt was mud-smeared and torn. My hair was a mad tangle streaming behind me. I was flushed in the face, huffing and puffing like some farmer's wife in the fields.

Silvy ran a few steps behind me. I knew without looking that her hair was still tidy, her skirt pristine, her pale complexion unchanged, though she was running almost as fast as I was.

That tells you all you need to know about either of us.

At least the dwarf was in worse shape than me. Already today he had been half-drowned, scratched and pelted by an army of forest creatures. And who had saved him from those violent animals? Me, every time.

I wasn't convinced that he needed saving, but Silvia begged me to help the poor little man. My sister's moral compass has always been sharper than mine, so I tend to follow her direction in such matters.

Poor little man, my elbow. After I had rescued him from

the homicidal fish, the manic squirrels and the psychotic eagle (without a word of thanks, I might add), the dwarf's precious sack fell to the ground, spilling its contents into the dirt and revealing its secrets.

I'm not surprised the forest creatures were so vengeful — the sack contained stolen nests and eggs, precious moss from the river, handfuls of the last winter nut hoard. In amongst that lot were several mean, pathetic little treasures from our village — a ribbon locket here, a fountain pen there. I recognised half the items — they had all gone missing over the winter, sparking suspicion between neighbours and friends.

So, the dwarf snatched up his sack and ran for it, and I ran after him. My mother's wedding pin was one of the first baubles stolen, and I was determined to find out if the little crook had it somewhere in his sack.

The dwarf was wheezing now, his sack of stolen things bouncing up and down between his shoulder blades. He threw a panicked look over his shoulder at me, then dove through a clump of bushes, branches snagging at his trousers as he scrambled into the clearing beyond. I threw myself after him. My dress was ruined, after all. What were a few more rips and stains?

I did not reach the dwarf in time. Someone else got there first. A huge, broad-shouldered, magnificent bear thundered across the clearing, towering over the little sneakthief.

I stopped, mesmerised by the sight. Silvy came up beside me, not even breathing hard from her exertions. "Oh," she said in a loving voice. "It's our bear."

To understand about the bear, you have to know that Silvy and I have the most wonderful mother in the world. She is kind and good and everything that I am not. Best of all, she never makes her difficult red-haired daughter feel like she is any less special than the pale and perfect fair-haired one.

My sister was named after the fine white Silvia rose that cost my mother a fortune at the market. I was named for the wild Rosamund rose that snarled in uninvited from the forest, entwining itself through my mother's garden until she was forced to love it. I learned from an early age that most people prefer white roses to red.

It was our mother who invited the bear into our lives, when a thick layer of winter snow covered the rosebushes in the garden. He came to our kitchen door with a mournful look in his big brown eyes, and she let him in to sit by the fire. He stayed with us all winter, lapping soup from a bowl on the floor and gazing at the three of us as if we were his saviours.

If he gazed at Silvy a little more than he gazed at me, I tried not to mind. That has always been the way of things.

It *was* our bear in the clearing now, and there was a terrible look in his eyes. As he advanced on the quivering dwarf, he roared — such a deep and threatening roar that I found it hard to stay on my feet. Oh, he was magnificent.

The dwarf shuddered, and toppled. He fell back on the

grass, his sack falling limply from his shoulders and an awful, frozen grimace plastered over his face. I knew without getting any closer that he was dead.

This was the bear who sighed as I recited Shakespeare to him, the bear who watched my sister as if she was a rare and precious flower, the bear who politely moved his paws this way and that to be out of the way of my mother's broom.

He had just frightened someone to death.

"Rosy," gasped my sister, her fingers tightening on my torn sleeve.

The bear screamed, throwing back his head as if some terrible pain had overtaken him. The fur peeled from his skin like a suit of clothes. His whole enormous frame convulsed and shrank. He threw himself to the ground, crying and sobbing, and it was not the voice of a bear any longer.

He was a man. A huddled, naked man. As he unfolded and came to his feet, I saw that he was familiar in every way except his form. There were the broad shoulders, the deep brown eyes, the strong paws (now hands). There was that humble, almost shy expression. He was devastatingly hand-some. My wicked, night-time thoughts about our friend the bear no longer seemed quite so perverse.

A light shone from my sister's eyes as she stared upon this marvellous, naked man. A similar light shone from his eyes as he looked upon her.

I watched it happen. By the time she had crossed the clearing towards him, and taken the shawl from her shoul-ders to shield his nakedness, they were in love. Sometimes it happens that way. My sister adores romantic novels, and I had always known that the first kind-faced stranger who came her way (boys from the village simply don't count) was doomed to a life of endless, happy matrimony with her.

I just hadn't expected him to be the kind of man who could frighten a dwarf to death with a single roar.

They were speaking to each other now, and I forced myself to listen. Between the usual cooing endearments that are compulsory upon such occasions, we learned that his name was Bran, and he was an actual prince.

Let's be honest, now. Who didn't see that coming?

I checked on the dwarf. "He's dead."

Prince Bran tore his eyes briefly away from my sister to see for himself. "His death broke the spell," he said. "At the beginning of winter, I came looking for the thief who had robbed our castle on the far side of the forest. He used his wicked magic to transform me into a bear."

"That was poor planning on his part," I said. "He should have turned you into a bunny rabbit. I've never seen a bunny rabbit scare anyone to death."

Prince Bran was no longer listening to me. He was too busy holding Silvy's hand, and asking her to marry him.

She bit her lip, just a little. "Rosy. What should I do?"

"Don't look at me," I said. "This is something you decide for yourself."

Silvy's romantic novel-reading came to the fore. She knew what a poor girl does when a rich man asks her to marry him.

Within a minute she had agreed, the prince had kissed her and they were walking arm and arm through the forest. I stayed to pile stones over the body of the dwarf, so that his body would not be eaten by the forest creatures. It seemed the thing to do.

"What about Rosy?" I heard my precious sister ask her betrothed. "She doesn't have anyone to marry."

"She can have my brother," he said. "It's about time he settled down, and Rosy will be good for him. Your mother can come and live with us."

"It's all so wonderful," Silvia cooed.

My sister expected happily ever after, but I had no such illusions. I finished my makeshift cairn, and went after them. Silvy might not realise it, but she was going to need me.

For a start, it wasn't what I'd call a castle. I know, I know. Girls who live in cottages shouldn't throw stones. It *was* a rambling manor house, far larger and more impressive than we were used to. The turrets and battlements were fake, though, added on later than the rest of the stonework, and there was a tower in the centre that didn't match at all. It looked a bit lopsided.

The garden was made up of neat squares of grass and rows of prim, starchy flowers. I couldn't for the life of me see where my mother could put her marvellous rambly roses, even supposing the poor things would survive being uprooted. But there was no time to think of that. My sister and I were about to meet the Queen.

A loud squawk was the first thing we heard as Prince Bran pushed the front door open. He was wearing Silvia's shawl as a kilt, so as not to shock his dear old mother. He certainly shocked the maid. A tray of silverware came tumbling down the wide staircase, and a brassy brunette lass in an apron skirt came scrambling after it. She threw herself straight into the Prince's arms, if you can believe it, wrapping her legs around his waist like a trollop — more so since he was wearing nothing but the woollen shawl around his nether regions.

"Oh sir," she gasped, bouncing up and down. "We have missed you. They said you were taken by bears!"

"Not exactly," laughed Prince Bran, settling her back on the floor. "It's good to see you, Mary. Where is my mother?"

There was a step on the stairs. Silvia looked up and went paler than I had ever seen her before. I followed her gaze.

The woman resembled an alabaster statue. She must have been fifty, but her skin was still tight around her face. Her eyes were like blue glass, hard and cold. She wore the most exquisite dress I had ever seen — all corsetry and narrow skirts, with a boned hem that had gone out of fashion twenty years ago. As she descended the stairs, she carried herself like a queen, and it took me several minutes to pull myself together and remember that she actually was one.

"Bran," she said, presenting her cheek so he could pretend to kiss it. "Where have you been?"

"You're not going to believe this, but I was turned into a bear," he told her.

"Nonsense. You've been off at those gambling halls all winter, just like your father used to." The Queen granted Silvia and me a cursory glance. "I don't know what you've brought home with you, but I advise you to send the miserable creatures away."

Silvy swayed. I moved in quickly and gripped her arm. "If you dare faint on me I will leave you alone with these people." The threat was enough to make her stand upright.

The Prince took hold of his mother's elbow and steered her to one side. "Mother, while you listen to me, try to remember that you will cease to rule this country in less than a year when I come of age. I was transformed into a bear by one of those evil dwarves that have been robbing this kingdom blind. I might not have survived the winter without the assistance of these girls and their good mother. What's more, the fair-haired girl is the one I intend to marry."

The Queen sniffed, looking past his shoulder to reassess Silvy. "I suppose she's pretty enough. Who is the other, her maid?"

"Rosamund is Silvia's sister," said Prince Bran. "I thought perhaps she might marry Kell."

The Queen laughed sarcastically. "Two dowerless marriages? Marvellous. I'm sure we all look forward to you taking the throne, you've such a head for business." She tossed her head. "Honestly darling, I refuse to talk about it. Don't expect me to dine with you and your guests. I'm really very cross with you."

She swept away. Even her backside looked haughty.

"How long were you away?" I asked Bran in a quiet voice.

"Four months," he said, trying not to laugh.

I smirked at him. "Good thing you didn't leave it any longer. That could have been a *really* unpleasant scene."

Silvia burst into tears. Instantly I had my arms around her, the laughter forgotten.

Bran reached out and brushed Silvy's chin, the only part of her face that was not dripping wet. "Don't weep, dearest. Let me find you some rooms and pretty dresses and a nice lunch. You can even have the princess suite in the tower if you like."

"No thanks," I said for us both, remembering the unnatural lean of the tower. "Just some plain old rooms as far from your mother as possible, and we'll be fine."

I had already decided that I was getting Silvy out of there, as soon as possible.

Bran must have had some idea of what I was planning, because after lunch (a quiet affair in our rooms without the presence of his mother, thankfully) he took us straight to the library. As soon as I saw it, I knew I could not leave the castle. Not for a year or two, at any rate. I had never seen so many books in my life, never even imagined that so many books existed.

What a cheap trick.

"Let me show you the poetry nook," said Bran, hooking his arm in Silvy's and guiding her away. I let them go, guessing this would be one of the few chances they had to be alone. I had some exploring to do.

The shelves were all made of polished wood and the books were proper leather-bound tomes with gilt edging and thick paper, no cheap knock-offs. I found myself in the history section, reading titles like *Social Study of Transylvania*, and *The War of the Begonias: an illustrated guide*. Then I found the adventure section and filled my arms with novels by authors with dashing, heroic names.

I found a window seat and curled up with my hoard, drawing the curtain behind me to give Bran and Silvy the illusion of privacy, and losing myself in a sea of crisp white pages.

An hour or two later, my curtain was ripped aside. "What are you doing here?" a young man demanded in a very unfriendly voice.

I hesitated. "My name is..."

"Oh, I know who you are," he spat. "Mother told me all about the drabs my brother brought home with him. Where is your gold-digging sister?"

So this was Kell, the one Bran had confidently declared would be my bridegroom. I was almost relieved to discover that he was brattish and arrogant — if he had been anything like his brother, I might have ended up agreeing to the double wedding scenario. As it was, I owed him a favour for reminding me why this was all such a terrible idea.

I tried to leave with dignity, but his arm was slung across the width of the alcove. "Please let me past," I said.

"You won't get away with it," said Kell. "You and that blonde hussy will be packed off home by morning if my mother has anything to say about it."

I glared at him. "Can you guarantee that? I'd be so grateful if you would."

He dropped his arm, and I shoved past him in a very unladylike fashion to go in search of my sister.

The rooms Bran had chosen for us were pretty enough, but fancier than we were accustomed to. Silvy and I had a bedroom each and a connecting sitting room with a blazing fire that made the room far too hot during the day. Personally, I didn't see the point of a fire without a stovetop slung across it for cooking, but I suppose the ways of a castle aren't designed to make sense to a girl from a cottage.

Silvia was curled up in a white velvet chair, sighing over a small book of poetry. She wore a pink gown I had never seen before, with a full skirt embroidered all over with tiny roses, and the most fashionable sleeves I hade ever seen in my life.

I stared at her. "Where did you get that?"

"Bran sent a maid to take my measurements. She found this and a few other dresses that will do for now, but she's going to make me all new ones. My trousseau, Bran says." She blushed faintly.

I couldn't stop staring. Was this my sister? Was she really this naive? "Silvy, you do *know* no one wants us here, don't you?"

She shifted her shoulders a little. "Bran wants us."

"His mother doesn't. Nor his brother."

"Oh, Rosy, don't you like Kell?"

"I didn't get a chance to like him, since he so obviously loathes the air that you and I breathe."

Silvia sighed. "Bran said he might be difficult. I'm sorry, Rosy, are you dreadfully disappointed?"

I took a few deep breaths, forcing myself not to start screaming. "Silvia, I'm not the one angling to marry a prince here. Tell me the truth. Do you really love Bran?"

Silvia looked shocked. "How can you doubt me?"

"Because you've only been in love for about four hours. How can you be sure it's the real thing?"

Silvia laughed. "Oh, Rosy, it must be longer than that. It feels like forever."

I looked at her carefully. "Did you love him when he was

a bear?" It wasn't completely unlikely. I myself had been half
in love with him as a bear, although the man-version was
distinctly more annoying.

She hesitated, then fluttered her eyelashes a little. "I
think, perhaps I might have been," she said modestly.

Great. I flopped in the second velvet armchair, a deep
pink one. "His mother's going to be mean to you. His
brother, too. You hate it when people are mean to you."

"I don't care," she said. "I won't give him up, Rosy. I'm
going to marry him."

I sank my head into the deep plush of the armchair. "So
what are we going to do?"

Silvia smiled, an unexpected gleam sparkling in her eyes.
"We could take a look at those other dresses. Find something pretty for you to wear?"

I looked down at my grubby day dress and sighed. "I
suppose it couldn't make things worse."

The dwarves did not assault the castle until the following
morning.

The Queen had declined to join us for breakfast, prefer-
ring to take tea and toast in her room where she could sulk
properly. Kell had entered the breakfast parlour long
enough to load up a plate with curried fish, eggy rice and
several beef steaks (rich people have a very strange concept
of breakfast), then made a rude noise in our general direction and took his repast elsewhere to eat it.

This left me and my bacon and eggs sitting at a table

with the cooing lovebirds, who fed each other strawberries and other dainty morsels in between endearments.

Not awkward at all.

"Oh," Bran said, while Silvy was reaching for another strawberry. "I sent for your mother this morning."

"I'm so glad," said Silvy. "I long to see her. Can you believe it's only been a day?"

I looked hard at Bran, willing myself to believe that 'sent for your mother' meant he had actually sent a carriage for her, and a long letter explaining the current situation.

I had a horrible feeling that it actually meant a messenger carrying a curt imperative that my mother drop her daily chores and hasten across the forest (on foot, alone, with her bad back) if she ever wished to see her daughters again.

Why had I agreed to come to this dratted castle? Why hadn't I insisted that Silvy and I go home, and that Bran come courting her like a proper suitor? It didn't matter how well we were dressed, we would never be anything more than the two peasant girls the prince had found in the forest.

The door to the breakfast parlour burst open.

Kell stood there, tense with rage. "You mentioned something about killing a dwarf in the forest yesterday, brother?" he said, the sarcasm fairly dripping off him. "I think you'll find he had a few pals who have something to say about that."

Upstairs, somewhere near the lopsided tower, we heard an explosion that made the castle shake.

Dwarves are known for their mining abilities, for their skill in digging gold and silver and jewels out of seemingly barren earth. In our part of the world, though, there are other treasures lurking beneath the surface, waiting to be mined. Strange, sorcerous materials that just cry out to used.

The dwarves are known for crafting those strange materials into canny and clever devices. This is why you never want to get on the bad side of a dwarf.

By the time Bran, Silvy and I made it to the roof, the castle was under attack. The Queen, clad in perfectly-corseted armour, directed a platoon of sentries, footmen and kitchen maids in defence of the less-than-sturdy walls. Many of the defenders threw pots of hot custard or warm oil (somehow it was never boiling by the time they brought it up from the kitchens) over the parapet, while others brandished garden implements and other improvised weapons.

A glass ball sailed over our heads, and shattered on the tiles beyond. A hissing, spitting pink spell emerged from the broken glass, but a quick-thinking maid extinguished it with a bucket of soapy water.

"If you're going to stay, make yourselves useful," the Queen shouted at us, just as another glass ball sailed straight at her. She smashed it away from her with a swing of an elderly cricket bat, and sprayed the released spell with an industrial-sized perfume bottle. It coughed, and fell dead to the ground.

"You two should go below," said Bran, buckling on the breastplate he had grabbed from the umbrella stand on the way up. "I can't guarantee your safety."

Silvia gave him a look of steel. "If the chamber maids can defend the castle, I'm sure I can."

I have never been so proud of her. Worried, but proud. I picked up a croquet mallet from the pile of spare weapons at the base of the spiral tower. "Let's do this."

There was no diplomacy. The Queen sent several heralds down to parley with the enraged dwarves, but she put a stop to that after the third one was transformed into a butternut pumpkin.

Silvy and I spent hours on the battlements, smacking glass balls out of the sky. If you did it hard enough, the spell would fall down on to the dwarves below. Between the two of us, we were responsible for six dwarves being transformed into small furry creatures, seven falling into an enchanted sleep, nine turning on their comrades in fits of uncontrollable fury, and one being so overcome by a magic-induced lust that he attempted to rape several other dwarves, and was finally left humping the tree that they had tied him to.

Near midday, I swung too hard at a missile of the non-magical variety and lost my croquet mallet over the side. I was so tired and aching that I could hardly stand, but I staggered back to the weapons pile to find something else. Kell was there. He was exhausted too, a long scratch bleeding down the side of his face. He was staring at my sister.

She was worth staring at. Silvia stood on the battlements, her fair hair flying in the breeze, a tennis racquet brandished in one hand. Her pale, perfect cheeks were sunburned.

"She's magnificent, isn't she?" said Kell in a slightly strangled voice.

I tried not to take offence, though I had been defending the castle with every bit the enthusiasm and stamina that Silvy had. People always expect me to cope with difficult situations and hard work, while they expect Silvy to faint, act distressed, and need to be looked after. I was guilty of that expectation myself, at times.

I gave Kell a hard look. "So you're admitting that your brother's chosen bride isn't as useless as you thought she was? How gracious of you." I snatched up a rolling pin, and headed back into the action.

I was distracted, and didn't see the glass ball in time to stop it smashing against the stiff daffodil-coloured skirts of my princess dress. I flailed at the sizzling green spell with my rolling pin, but it latched on to my ankle with a squeal of triumph.

Breathing hard, I waited. After half a minute, I was fairly sure that I wasn't a pumpkin, or an ostrich, or a puppy. Something worse, then. My skin was hot all over, and I could feel my veins twitching.

Some of the spells made you crazy — turned you into a berserker who tore violently at your own friends and allies. I had to get away from everyone until I knew what horror had been visited upon me.

I turned back to the weapons pile, but Kell was gone. My eyes were watering madly, but I still saw the door to the crooked, lopsided spiral tower. I stumbled forward, and wrenched at the door handle.

Inside, the tower was cool and dark. I was shivering, but my skin still felt scratchy and hot. I collapsed on to the steps. I was dying, obviously. I would never see my mother again. I thought of her struggling through the forest in her second best boots, a sensible lunch packed in her basket, hope in her eyes.

Boiling tears dribbled down my face. I was so selfish.

The castle was under siege, Silvy was in danger, and all I cared about was that I missed my mother.

I scrabbled at the bodice of the princess dress, desperate to be free of it. I half unlaced the bodice, but could do no more. It wasn't helping, anyway. My breathing was wild and uncontrolled, and sweat rolled off my skin. What difference did a layer of brocade make? I was going to die of the heat anyway.

Somewhere, a door opened and closed. A voice spoke. "Rosy?"

Bran. I forced myself to open my eyes and look at him. I wanted to warn him to stay away from me, but the words dried in my throat.

He had seen the glass slivers clinging to my skirt. "What kind of spell was it?"

I shook my head. "Don't know."

I did know. How could I not? The very sight of him had quickened my pulse, set my feverish skin singing. Damn it all to hell and back. It was the tree-humping spell. And I was alone with my sister's betrothed.

My hands, almost of their own volition, caught him by the breastplate and pulled him towards me. His eyes were bright and strange. Would I find glass shards clinging to his clothes too? I didn't care one way or the other. My fingers found the lacings of his breastplate, even as my mouth found his and dragged him down to my level.

He was kissing me now, his body responding to mine, and I knew that he had been caught by a lust spell too. What were the odds?

There was room for guilt in this scenario, but I pushed it into a tiny corner of myself, somewhere near my elbow. Part of me knew that spell or no spell, I had wanted this. I had wanted him as a bear, wanted him as a man — wanted, more than anything, for one single person to notice me more than they noticed my sister.

The spell sang along my skin as I freed him of his breastplate, and scrabbled at his trews. He was lifting my skirts and ripping at my underthings, grinding himself against me as he sought his way within.

The steps grated hard against my back, and it hurt in other ways too; ways I didn't want to think about. But the heat was driving me wild, and I bucked and groaned against him as if it was anything but my first time.

At one point, there was a moment of stillness as if something wonderful had been achieved, and then we were mad creatures again, tearing at each other in our desperation to be rid of the spell.

If you've read enough cheap melodramas, you know how this ends. At the height of my madness, as I clawed his back to drive him deeper inside me, I looked over his shoulder and saw my sister Silvia standing in the doorway to the tower, colour flaming in both her cheeks.

I pounded on Bran's shoulders with my fists, and he turned to see her too. But by then, she was gone.

"Silvia!" I shouted, even as I scrambled out from under the hot, wet body of her betrothed and flung myself out through the tower door.

For a moment I couldn't see her. I could see Kell and the servants still fighting the dwarf spells, and the Queen shouting at the troops.

The air was thick with glass shards and spells. Two of the footmen were fighting as if they wanted to kill each other, and two more were kissing against the chimneys like the world depended on it.

I saw her then, a pale figure in a pink dress, teetering on the edge of the parapet. For one awful moment I wasn't sure if she was defending the castle or preparing to jump. As I opened my mouth to scream that I was sorry, that I loved her, that it hadn't been my fault, I saw a glass sphere shatter hard against her golden hair.

The spell inside was silver and sharp edged — I had not seen one like that before. It engulfed her, trapping her inside a glittering mesh and yanking her back over the edge.

"Silvy!" I screamed in a voice that felt like it came from outside my skin. I ran to the parapet, reaching it just as Kell did. A moment later, still breathing hard and rearranging his breastplate, Bran joined us both.

Silvia was still falling. The silvery mesh lowered her slowly to the grass below, and the dwarves snatched her body out of the air. Many of them did an ugly little war dance, and shrieked expletive-riddled taunts up at us.

One of them cast a glass sphere at the grass, opening up a huge wound of fresh-turned earth, and every single dwarf leaped into the hole and was gone. They took Silvy with them, still struggling in her magical net.

Bran and I stood there for one long moment, staring in mutual horror at the hole in the earth that had swallowed our beloved girl. It was Kell who broke the silence. "Well? Are we going to rescue her, or not?"

Of course we were. Of course, of course. I wasn't going to leave something this important to the men. I would rescue my sister and see her safely home to our mother.

(Rescue or no rescue, I didn't see how I could ever possibly look her in the eye again.)

I need not go into detail about how angry the Queen was that both her sons were abandoning the castle to rescue my sister from the dwarves. We could still hear her shrieking from the battlements as the three of us leaped into the gaping hole that had torn up a large portion of the front lawn.

The tunnel was deep and wide, arching down into the soft earth in a slow spiral. Our feet sank into the dirt as we hurried down and along in the wake of a hundred tiny footprints.

I don't know what I was expecting at the bottom of that tunnel, but the lake took me by surprise. We came out into an enormous cavern, at the shore of a lake so huge and dark that we could not see the end of it.

"I'll go around this way to see if there's a route through," said Bran, having reclaimed his customary note of leadership. "Kell, go around to the left. Meet back here in ten minutes."

As easily as that, I was alone. I took a step or two towards the glistening, black waters of the lake. I slipped my shoes off — ridiculous, impractical slips of yellow satin-thin leather — and let the water curl around my toes.

Glancing around to be sure that neither of the princes were within sight, I leaned down into the water and cupped it in my hands, rinsing hastily between my legs.

There was blood and other stickiness on my fingers as I washed myself clean. A sudden urge to cry, or to vomit, rose up in my throat, and I scrubbed my hands so hard I almost lost the skin from my palms.

The water of the underground lake was cool and tempting. For a moment, I wondered if it might be possible to lose myself in its depths before Bran or Kell returned. Then I shook those thoughts clear of my head, angry at myself. I had to save Silvia first. The lake could wait.

"I know what you did," said a voice, cutting through the splash and the silence.

I whirled around, my skirts soaking, to see Kell sneering at me.

"Do you think we don't all know what kind of slut you are?" he said.

"I was under a spell," I said angrily, stepping out of the water. "Feel the glass shards in my hem if you don't believe me."

"Can you tell me that you didn't want to steal your sister's man?"

I opened my mouth to deny it, but my tongue choked on the words. It was true. I was the worst sister in the world. Part of me had not only enjoyed possessing Bran for those stolen moments, but had relished the fact that I got there first — for once, I had snatched something before it was given to my sister.

"Up here!" Bran called to us. "There's a passage through, and a hundred dwarvish footprints leading the way."

Kell turned without a word and headed around the lake towards his brother.

I followed, my wet skirts swishing at my ankles.

The tunnel went on a long way, and was so low in most places that we had to crouch and crawl. A steady whirring sound of machinery surrounded us, but it was only once we emerged from the end of the tunnel that we realised what it was.

This cavern was just as enormous as the first one, only instead of lake it was full of... well, you always think that dwarvish devices are going to be small and canny, like the glass missiles they besieged the castle with. This particular dwarvish device was the size of a city. Every part of it whirred and clanked and hummed and rattled. A steady stream of junk and treasures — gold, jewellery, weapons, cutlery, broken glass and china, torn books, grass clippings - poured from the ceiling into a large vat that munched it into unrecognisable slag.

The slag oozed down metal pipes and along clockwork conveyor belts before being channelled into other machines: one spat out glass spell balls, another produced small and gleaming wands, and a third produced bowls of a grey, strange-smelling substance that might in some universe be considered porridge.

"Gods and demons," breathed Bran. "What is this place?"

I sympathised with Kell's withering look. I was beginning to suspect that my sister's betrothed was an idiot.

"Where is everyone?" I asked, hoping it sounded like less of a nitwit question than Bran's. "Surely there should be dwarves... I don't know, tending this lot."

"Not a lot of point to automation if they have to be here," said Kell, reaching out and lifting a glass ball from a packing case it had just landed in. "But I take your point."

Somewhere in the distance, a scream rang out.

"Silvia!" said Bran, darting towards the sound.

I helped myself to three glass balls and a dwarvish wand before following him. The glass was still warm to the touch.

When I caught up to them, the brothers Prince were arguing at the mouths of two tunnels. "The scream came from this one," Bran said angrily.

"All the more reason to approach from the other," growled Kell. "They'll be expecting us, you fool."

"You'll have to get used to obeying me one day," said Bran in a dark voice, and threw himself into the tunnel he had chosen.

Kell hesitated, then took the other.

Neither of them had looked at me for an instant. I considered my options, and followed Kell.

"Tired of my brother's bravery already?" he said when he heard me coming after him.

"Let's just say I'm losing faith in his tactical decisions," I replied.

We emerged from our tunnel on to a shaky layer of scaffolding. The roar of voices was at first overwhelming. When I recovered my senses, I realised we were in a cavern many times huger than either of the previous ones, and that this one was full of dwarves.

They hung from the walls on scaffolding and slings; they filled platform after platform, many of them chattering or shouting angrily amongst themselves. It was like a council meeting at the village hall, only a hundred times busier.

In the midst of it all, my sister Silvia hung miserably from the ceiling, wrapped in that same silvery metal net. She was wide-eyed and startled, as if she had recently awoken from a dead faint to find herself in this bizarre place, surrounded by angry dwarves.

No one had spotted Kell and I yet, as we were lower than most of them. Literally beneath their notice. "What do we do?" I asked him.

"Wait for my brother to do something stupid, and then clean up the mess he leaves behind," he muttered.

A roar broke into the chatter and chaos of the dwarves — a male, human roar with more than a hint of bear in it. Prince Bran exploded out of a tunnel higher up in the chamber, appearing on a balcony in full view of everyone. He saw Silvy's predicament, and his face went bright red. "Let her go, you mutant devils!" he screamed, brandishing his sword in the air.

Beside me, I heard the quiet slap of Kell hitting his own face with his palm.

A dwarf who might have been some kind of leader — or possibly just the one with the best decision-making abilities — gestured with one hand. A second silvery net fell from the cavern ceiling to entangle Bran's limbs. It fought him as if it were alive, pinning his limbs together.

"Foolish man thing," snarled another dwarf, possibly a woman. "Do you really think all this was about capturing *her*?"

"Oh, Bran!" wailed Silvia, but everyone pretty much ignored her.

"Her only use to us is as a witness to your crimes," said the first dwarf, with some satisfaction. "You shall be tried for the murder of Viggi Sigurd Friggland III, and she will give us the evidence we need to prove your guilt."

"No!" I yelled up to them. "That's not right!"

I thought I heard Kell mutter something along the lines of, "Oh, cobnuts, she's as bad as he is," but I ignored him.

The dwarves peered down at me with some interest.

"And what do you have to say in this matter?" asked the one who was probably a woman.

"Silvia wasn't there when Vig... Sig... when your brother dwarf died!" I yelled. "Or, at least, she wasn't as close as I was. If you let her go, I'll be your witness."

"Interesting," muttered many of the dwarves.

"Don't trust her," muttered some more.

The 'head' dwarf looked from me to Silvy and back again. Silvy looked cowed and fearful, more than a little confused. "Fair enough," the dwarf said, finally. "Let down the blonde one, and bring up the redhead!"

Several dwarves pulled levers and winches, and Silvia was slowly lowered in her silvery net all the way down to where Kell and I were standing. "What exactly are you planning?" he asked me under his breath as we waited for her to reach us.

"I don't know," I said desperately. "What do you think I should do?"

Kell looked up at his imprisoned brother, then at Silvia, and finally at me. "Tell the truth," he said grimly. "At this point, I don't think it can actually make things worse."

Silvy gasped as her feet touched the platform, and the silvery net fell away from her. She hugged me hard, and then fell back as she remembered that she hated me right now. The look on her face was somewhere between awful and hilarious.

"Get her out of here," I told Kell. "Take her home, please. And - when I say home, I mean our mother's cottage. Not that castle of yours."

"I understand," he said.

"I don't," Silvy flared. "What's going on, Rosy? What

about Bran?" She hesitated, and her cheeks flamed red. "I mean... I don't want anything horrible to happen to him."

"And what about me?" I said. "Do you want anything horrible to happen to me?"

She looked stricken. "I — I don't know. I just want to go home. Can't we all go home?"

"Not yet," I said, looking up at the dwarves. "But you can. Go with Kell, show him the way. I'll be along in a little while."

Kell took Silvia's arm, and she allowed him to guide her back through the tunnel that had brought us here. I turned back to the enormous council chamber to see a thousand dwarves staring down at me. "So what do we do now?"

I had expected them to imprison me in another of those metallic nets. Instead, a small platform was painstakingly lowered for me. Once I stepped on to it, I was raised to the level of the higher-status dwarves — the one who sounded like a leader, the one who was probably a woman, and an engineer who held a basket of glass balls. He held it out to me, and I reluctantly placed the balls and wand I had stolen into it.

If I was getting out of here alive, it wouldn't be by fighting. I had figured out that much.

Bran was dragged to another platform near the three dwarves who seemed to be in charge. He snarled at his captors like some kind of wild animal.

"Will you submit to truth spells?" asked the engineer dwarf.

"I don't care what hexes you put on me," growled the Crown Prince. "I have nothing to hide."

"Why do you need a witness if you have truth spells?" I asked.

The three dwarves looked at me as if I was crazy. "For the paperwork," said one of them. Sure enough, many of the dwarves around us were taking detailed notes, tapping sentences into complex devices.

"Cross referencing," said another.

"Legal ramifications," said a third.

"All right," I agreed, in the hopes that they would stop explaining. A glass ball promptly smashed against my chest. A green flicker of a spell emerged, spitting and giggling, and latched itself on to my larynx.

A second spell was likewise released over Bran.

"State your names," said a dwarf.

"Rosamund of Rose Cottage," I said.

"Prince Branweather Floribund," said Bran from within his net.

Several dwarves snickered at this. I couldn't blame them, really.

"Miss Rosamund," said the dwarf who was probably a woman. "Did you see the death of Viggi Sigurd Friggland III?"

"I saw the death of a dwarf," I said. "But if you mean the one who stole the trinkets from our village, and who was left buried under a cairn of stones in the forest, then yes, we're probably talking about the same one."

"How did Viggi Sigurd Friggland III come to die?"

"Prince Bran scared him to death." Part of me wanted to stop talking right there, but the truth spell got hold of my throat and threw out a few more details. "That is, well, it was all Viggi Whatsit's fault, though, wasn't it? If he hadn't turned Bran into a bear then Bran wouldn't have been able to scare him to death. So he brought it on himself, really." I wanted to explain my joke about how it would have been better to turn Bran into a bunny rabbit, but the truth spell mercifully allowed me to repress it.

The possibly female dwarf turned to Bran. "How did Viggi Sigurd Friggland III come to transform you into a bear?"

"I found him in a cave," Bran said in a sulky voice. Like me, the truth spell was drawing more out of him than he obviously intended to say — it had stripped away the veneer of charm that he usually layered over every conversation. "Stupid little mutant. He'd been stealing from our castle, and I caught him red handed. I yelled at him and made him give me his sack, and he was so goddamn useless that he dropped it. One of those glass balls rolled out and broke on my foot. Next thing I know, I was a bear."

I was staring at him. "What? Is that really what happened?"

"Amazing what comes out under truth spell," said the dwarf engineer cheerfully. "Prince Bran, did you intend to do harm to Viggi Sigurd Friggland III?"

"I didn't intend to kill him," said Bran reasonably. "I just wanted to put the wind up him, give him a good fright. Serve him right for turning me into a bear. Though, I'm not weeping any tears over the shortarsed freak, let me tell you."

"Thank you for being so honest," said the possibly female dwarf, smirking a little. "I think that wraps things up nicely. One more question, Prince Bran. Are you the one who made a gesture towards honourable behaviour by placing a cairn of stones over our brother dwarf?"

"Um, no," I spoke up. "I did that."

Bran looked at me in surprise. "Did you? What on earth for?"

"I would like to propose that Prince Bran be considered guilty of 'Causing Death by Inappropriate Action and/or Carelessness," with a secondary charge of 'Unprincely Behaviour,' my fellow dwarves," said the possibly female dwarf.

"Seconded," said the engineer.

I half raised my hand. "Um, while he's under the truth spell, can I ask him a few questions?"

The dwarves looked at each other, and mostly shrugged. "If you like."

"Rosy, what are you doing?" Bran asked in a strangled voice.

"Judging from what I've heard today, this is the only way I can get a straight answer without you honeying it up with that charm you do so well. So try this one: were you affected by a dwarf spell when you found me in the tower?"

He clamped his lips shut, but they flew open of their own accord. "Of course not. I never said I was."

"And you knew what kind of spell I was under."

He couldn't help it — he actually smirked. "That was pretty obvious."

"You took advantage of your betrothed's sister while I was in the throes of a lust spell?" My voice had risen into something of a shriek, but that didn't prevent me from hearing the collective indrawn breath of a thousand dwarves.

Bran smiled that gorgeous smile of his. "I didn't know Silvia was going to find out about it..."

The possibly female dwarf raised her hand. "I would like to propose that the charges against Prince Bran be promoted to 'Very Unprincely Behaviour' as well as 'Causing Death by Inappropriate Action and/or Carelessness," she said in a very firm voice. Oh, yes. Definitely a woman.

"What's that supposed to mean?" Bran demanded. "Who the hell are you little runts to decide what constitutes 'Unprincely Behaviour'? I'm the fucking prince around here."

"Can we consider a tertiary charge of 'Ungentlemanly Language in a Public Arena?" suggested the dwarf engineer.

Many of the dwarves near him agreed that, yes, they probably could.

Bran turned his anger on me. "What the hell have you done to me, you stupid bitch?"

"Let's pause for a minute and think about what exactly was done to whom," I shot back.

There was much muttering and discussion amongst the dwarves — not only those near us, but every dwarf in the chamber. They went back and forth for ages, arguing and shaking their heads, getting into minor riots, and passing little notes up to the paperwork dwarves.

Finally, the dwarf who was probably in charge took a deep breath. "Miss Rosamund, given the circumstances, we have decided to let you be in charge of sentencing Prince Bran. We are prepared to enforce any punishment or... transformation that you decide upon."

Bran sounded almost cheerful. "But she can decide to forgive me and set me completely free, right?"

"If that is what she wishes," said the probably in charge dwarf.

I thought about it. I really did. I thought about letting him go. I thought about him bursting through the cottage door, and explaining the whole thing to Silvy in such a way that he ended up as the hero. I thought about her married to him, unable to escape, and only then learning what kind of person he was. I thought about her making excuses for him for the rest of her life.

I thought about how much nicer he seemed to be when he was a bear. I thought about him showing no remorse at having caused the death of a fellow person. I thought about the very real possibility that I might be pregnant.

If Bran didn't learn a harsh lesson about how to treat people very soon, in less than a year he would be in charge of our entire kingdom, and then we really would be in trouble.

"Let him be a rose," I said, in a clear speaking voice.

"What?" Bran howled.

"Let him be a rose in my mother's garden," I said. "Let him watch and listen. And... once my sister Silvia is so deeply in love with someone else that she could never be convinced to go back to Bran, let him be a man again and make what he can of the rest of his life."

The dwarves nodded and smiled to themselves. "Good," said the female one. "With a mind as devious as that, you should have been a dwarf."

Bran was staring at me, his jaw dropped so wide open that he could have fitted a whole roast chicken inside it. He mouthed words at me, and they weren't pretty. But he was already changing form, his limbs twisting in on themselves to form green, spiky branches.

When the dwarves were finished with him, he was quite beautiful. His flowers were a dark purplish colour. He would look well among the white Silvia and red Rosamund of my mother's garden, for a while at least. The engineer dwarf passed a wand over the rosebush, and it vanished.

The female dwarf took my hand, and led me along a

winding rack of scaffolding to a series of freshly-ground tunnels in the wall of the cavern. "The one on the left will take you straight to your mother's garden," she said. "It's a short cut. You'll probably be home before your sister."

I thought of burying my face in my mother's apron and confessing all to her, before Silvy reached the cottage to tell her how wicked I was.

"Where do the other tunnels lead?" I asked the dwarf.

She shrugged. "Other places. Other kingdoms, I suppose."

My hand brushed the left hand tunnel, and a wave of longing overcame me. But, after a moment, I pointed at the tunnel furthest from the one that would take me home. "I think I'll try that one."

There was nothing but kindness in the dwarf's face. "What are you looking for?" she asked me. A better question, I suppose, than "what are you running away from?"

"I don't know," I told her. "Perhaps I'll find out when I get there." Me, and anyone else I might happen to have brought with me.

I crawled into the tunnel mouth and started to climb up towards the daylight, thinking about a kingdom of limitless possibilities. A kingdom without mothers or sisters or bears or castles or princes.

A kingdom where no roses grow.

Author's Note: On Rosebuds

Wow, this story is peak Tansy in many ways. I see so many elements that still appear in my stories — of course the castle has a library, of course the royals eat kedgeree or something like it, of course the frocks are lovingly described.

It's not a story I would write now — I certainly don't think I'd write the original dwarf as I did (even if he got justice in the end) and I'd probably be less scathing about the silly 'good' sister and so on. I wouldn't toss rape spells around with quite such a lack of awareness.

I like to think I'd let Rosy be less hard on herself, too. But oh, you can see my dislike of the Prince Charming concept baked into the bones of this one, can't you?

I thought this story was terribly smart and grown up and even a little gritty when I wrote it, but then Margo Lanagan wrote *Tender Morsels* which absolutely eviscerates this particular fairy tale and only goes to show that my talents are better served writing cozy than grit.

Fruit and Mirrors

FIRST PUBLISHED IN AUREALIS 2006

Tiffany Grey-and-White followed the scent of ripe mangoes from one end of the Bazaar to the other, searching for the Tropicana fruit bar. Galloway was there, his long body slouched drunkenly on a bar stool as he sucked at the gobs of flesh that still clung to a half-chewed melon rind.

"The Queen's little lapdog," he slurred. "Where's my letter?"

Tiffany eyed the pile of fruit skins that littered the ground around him. "Back on the hard stuff, Galloway? I thought you'd given up."

"Given up everything," he chortled, waving madly at the bartender. "Hey! More cantaloupe over here. Slice me a double."

The bartender rolled his eyes. "I think you've had enough, mate."

Tiffany agreed, taking Galloway's arm. "Let's sober you up, shall we?"

He shook her off angrily. "Where's my letter? I sent a very stern letter to the Queen and I should get a reply.

That's how these things work! Letters are sacred things and deserve a proper response."

"I'm the response, pear-head," she hissed furiously in his ear. "Come on. We're taking a trip, you and me."

He brightened slightly. "She wants to see me?"

"Not exactly." Tiffany managed a smile in the direction of the bartender. "Sorry about this."

"As long as one of you pays his bill, love."

Tiffany looked hard at Galloway, who giggled. "My pockets are empty."

"You have to be kidding."

"My brain's empty too," he said earnestly. "Not a whiff of inspiration. Not even a couplet."

Growling, Tiffany dug a crumpled sonnet out of her back pocket and put it on the bar. At the bartender's sceptical expression, she added another to it. "Fine bloody day when I have to pay a poet's bar bill," she grumbled. "Come on, Galloway. Let's walk."

She was strong enough to help him walk as the two of them made their unsteady way out of the Bazaar, but his height meant that he was practically draped over her small frame. "What did she say?" he demanded, his breath smelling of stale fruit as he turned his face against hers.

"You gave a Queen an ultimatum," Tiffany reminded him. "You can hardly expect her to be pleased about it."

"She has to choose," he insisted. "She has to make up her mind which one of us she wants."

Tiffany hauled him along efficiently. "She has chosen, you useless pip. She chose weeks ago, or hadn't you noticed?"

Galloway reeled away from her, his face shockingly pale like an unripe apricot. "What do you mean?"

"What do I mean? She's married to the greatest poet in the land. Did you honestly think she would risk her position as the King Laureate's consort for the sake of a few loving lyric verses and a roll in the hay?"

"I'm a great poet," Galloway said stubbornly. "I could be the Laureate."

Tiffany glared at him. "And even if you knocked our King off his laurels, she would still be his wife. Don't you get it? You can't win. You've already lost."

"So where are you taking me?" he mumbled, looking a little broken around the edges.

She grabbed his collar, securing it with her steely grip. "Where you can't do any more harm."

"Exile." He was sobering rapidly, remembering who she was. Everyone said that Tiffany Grey-and-White was the hardest, coldest, toughest damn soldier in Illusion. Finally, as his brain began to shake off the effects of his overindulgence at the fruit bar, Galloway began to be afraid of her.

"Exile," she agreed. Time enough later for him to find out about the long glass knives that hung beneath her cobweb-coloured uniform.

The water that lapped around the hull of the boat was the colour of lime skin. The boat was also green, but paler, like shelled peas. The shore was a distant line on the horizon. Galloway huddled at one end of the boat, sulking. Tiffany fingered the glass knives through the soft fabric of her clothing. "It's for the best, Galloway."

"Is it?" He still stank of fruit fumes, but his eyes were clear and accusing. "We used to be friends."

"You used me to get close to the Queen. That's not a friend."

"You're so quick to follow her orders, Tiffany Grey-and-White. If she ordered you to kill me would you do that too?"

Tiffany slid a glass blade from the small of her back, slid a second from her wrist. The knives were cold in her hands. "She did order me to kill you."

He hardly believed it at first, stunned by the glint of pale sunlight on the sharp glass edges. "You can't do that!"

"The Champion is not just a lapdog who carries messages to and from the Queen's lovers," she said in a voice as cold as her knives. "The Champion is her body-guard, footsoldier, assassin."

"You've done this before," he accused.

Tiffany's smile did not reach her eyes. "She's had many lovers, Galloway. The only difference this time is that she blames me personally for introducing you to her circle."

He flung himself backwards, but there was nowhere to go but the lime-coloured ocean. His hand brushed the side of the boat, and came away green. He stared at it, then laughed hysterically. "She *does* blame you!"

Still gripping the hilts of her knives, Tiffany stared around in horror. The pea-green boat was melting from under them, dissolving into the darker green water.

"We've both been exiled," Galloway shrieked as the last planks gave way, and they were both submerged into the icy green ocean of Illusion. "See you in the next worlds, Queen's Champion!"

Emma woke up, shivering. The water had seemed so real, and so very green. She rolled out from under her warm doona and slid her feet into battered ugg boots, wrapped her body in a voluminous towelling robe and went out to make herself a cup of tea.

"Eleven thirty," called Stevo from the living room as she switched the kettle on. "New record for the dedicated post-grad student on a Wednesday morning."

"Sleep-ins stimulate creativity," she yelled back to him.

"Yah, keep telling yourself that."

She made him a cup as well and took it into him. He was sitting on the floor in front of the Playstation wearing pyjama bottoms and a t-shirt so old that the lettering had faded into a series of cobwebby holes. Emma put his cup of tea beside him and then curled up on the couch with her own. "How's the new novel coming?"

"How's the thesis?" he shot back, not taking his eyes off Lara Croft.

"I'm allowing my ideas to percolate."

"That's what I thought." He plunged Lara Croft underwater and sent her lithe figure swimming down to pull a lever at the bottom of the artificial lake. Bodies of dead crocodiles floated on the top of the surface, pixellated splashes of red blood leaking from their shotgun wounds. "I'm researching underwater action scenes for chapter five."

"So, we're both working very hard."

"You said it."

She drank some tea, warming her hands on the cup. "I had the strangest dream just before I woke up."

"Was that after the third alarm went off, or the fourth?"

"Um, the fifth. It was like I was dreaming a whole story."

"That's brilliant," he said, suddenly interested. "I did that with the end of my first book. I didn't know how to end it and then wham! I had this amazing dream and I just typed for eight hours straight and there was my big climactic scene."

"Wasn't that the scene that the agent wanted you to remove?"

"I didn't say it was a great scene. I said it was a great dream."

"Mine was really detailed. It was this strange world where fruit was something you could get drunk on, and they used poetry for currency."

"That's stupid," he complained, bringing Lara Croft up out of the water fast enough to draw her magnums and blow away an inoffensive panther. "Now, short stories I could understand..."

"Do you think I should write it down?"

"Sure. It's not like I can use it. Sounds like fantasy." Stevo wrote science fiction action thrillers, and had been on the verge of having his first book published for the last three years. "Fantasy's very popular right now, if you can write a novel that's two hundred thousand words long and then write two more to make it a trilogy."

"I'm having enough trouble with a sixty thousand word thesis," she sighed.

"Well, that's your subject matter, babe. I did an English degree too, and I know that no one seriously thinks Galsworthy is worthy of critical attention."

"People are doing PhDs on *Star Trek* and *Neighbours*

these days," she said firmly. "I think I can justify *The Forsyte Saga*."

"I saw that crap on TV last year, Emma. No one can justify *The Forsyte Saga*."

Tiffany's cobweb-coloured uniform had vanished. She was wearing a long, swinging coat made from processed animal skins. It smelled pungent and disturbing, and clung to her body in ways she didn't like. She fingered her glass-hilted knives, and found they had transformed into black metallic cylinders, holstered to her belt.

"The new bounty hunter," sneered a massive man with metal rings hooked into his nose and lips. "Creed will see you now."

Tiffany stared at his mutilated face in fascination. There was something she was forgetting. "How long have I been here? Wasn't I just... somewhere else?" *I am a warrior. I know that much. And this is a place for warriors.*

"You've been standing in this damn line for hours," he grunted. "Creed likes to keep his new workers waiting. Do you want this job or not?"

To her sensitive nose, the metal cylinders at her belt smelled worse than the animal skins she wore as a coat. It all seemed far too easy. "No," she said aloud, and backed away from him, running out on to the street.

This world was a hard place, full of metal and mirrors and hissing electricity. Bright pink and orange signs leered at her out of the blackness of the street. Screeching vehicles tore past, blinding her with white light and thumping music.

She gripped the hilts of her metal cylinders, wishing for the familiarity of long, glass knives. *You're a soldier, damn well act like it.*

Somewhere inside, her bravado was a plaintive wail. *This isn't my world!*

If only she could remember what her world was. Somewhere, she could smell apples. It was a scent that reminded her of home. She followed it, stumbling into a dark cave of a bar, just in time to see a tall, gangly stranger accepting a mug that smelled of spoiled fruit.

He wasn't a stranger. He was Galloway. The sight of him brought it all back. Illusion, and exile. It was all his fault. She strode forward and slapped her gloved hand on his shoulder, making him sputter and spill his drink.

He groaned as he recognised her. "Tiffany Grey-and-White. Why did you have to find me? I was quite happy not remembering who I was."

"They want us to forget," she snapped. "This world is trying to fit us in, find a place for us. We are supposed to lose ourselves in new lives, new personalities."

Slowly, he lowered the glass to the bar. "Is that such a bad thing?"

Rolling her eyes, she grabbed his arm and hauled him off the stool. "I'm not ready to give up on me yet. Unfortunately, that means I need to hang on to you. Together, we can fight this."

He rolled his eyes. "So you don't want me for my winning personality?"

"Run," she urged, grabbing his hand and pulling him off

his bar stool. Dragging him after her, she ran across the bar and leaped headfirst into the nearest wall of mirrors.

"Sounds like cyberpunk-lite this time," grunted Stevo when Emma told him of the latest instalment of her dream. "Some kind of soft, girly version of Blade Runner. You're mixing your genres."

"I'm not the one doing it," she protested.

"Your subconscious, then. I wouldn't worry about it. Probably just anxiety about your thesis."

"I wrote two hundred words this week."

"How many did you delete?"

"Oh, about twice that."

"You should get out a bit, see a movie. Go to the library. You hardly ever leave the house these days."

"You're one to talk! The only time you turn off the Playstation is when there's something good on TV."

"True enough. Beer?"

"Okay."

The sun was hot on the back of Tiffany's neck, a slow and sleepy kind of heat. She relaxed into the sand, allowing the blissful lethargy to overcome her. *Finally, I can rest. I can be happy here.*

"No." Galloway stood over her, digging ruts into the

sand with his suntanned foot. "I won't let you do this. It's not fair."

She stared up at him, all pale and earnest with sunburn already pinking his ears and nose. His tall, lanky shadow engulfed her. The sight of him brought it all back, not only Illusion and exile and the world of darkness and lights, but the world of desert armies and the world of alien conquest and the underwater world of mermaids and tridents. She had been a guard, a mercenary, a freedom fighter, an assassin.

This is the first world where they didn't make me a warrior. They finally found something to tempt me with. It was so delicious to be weaponless: simply a girl on a beach with no sharp edges, no responsibilities. "You're standing in my sun," she said calmly. *I will not go back.*

"How many worlds has it been now?" Galloway demanded.

She rolled a little to one side, so that her body was once more engulfed in a halo of sunshine. "I don't care."

"Twelve, Tiffany. And every time, you pulled me away. I could have been happy in nearly all of those places. I had things that I wanted — love, comfort, pineapple slices — and you ripped me away, time after time in your stupid quest to get us home."

"You were right," she said drowsily. "Stupid home. Like it here."

He leaned over, grabbed her by the shoulders and forced her to stare at the twelve ruts he had dug into the sand. "All those worlds, Tiffany. We've survived every temptation the universe has to offer. Home might be just around the corner."

She sagged against him, her bare skin radiating heat

against the soft, cool clothes that he wore. "I don't want to fight anymore. I don't want to run. There's nothing for us there, nothing but glass knives and sonnets. Go on without me." *Let me forget again. Let me have oblivion instead of being reminded of my true self every time I gaze into those bright green eyes of yours.*

He stared at her, not answering.

"What's wrong, poet?" she challenged him. "Can't find the words?"

"You've been strong for me. Kept me from losing myself. If I leave you now, there will be nothing left of Tiffany Grey-and-White."

"So what?" she flung back. "What's worth saving? A hired assassin — a failed, hired assassin, no less. There's nothing to lose here, Galloway." She arched her neck up to the glorious, blazing sun and giggled. "Besides, we can't leave. No mirrors. No way out, no way home. You'll just have to take off that stiff shirt of yours and get a tan."

"You're right," he said, surprisingly.

She peered at him. "Huh?"

He was peeling off his dark shirt, letting it fall to the sand. "Let's swim."

She flung her arms around his neck. "We can stay?"

"We can stay."

She relieved him of the rest of his clothes in a rush, and let him pull her towards the sea. *If we stay here long enough, I can forget again.* Too late, she saw her own reflection bouncing back at her from the uneven surface of the rolling waves. "No!" she screamed, but Galloway's hands were tight on her thrashing waist. "That's not fair!"

"That's what I said when you tore me away from the paradise of flowers and the Great Library and the land of grape juice and elegiac verse," he growled as they struggled. "Remember Marina, who loved me? You made me give up everything to go home, Tiffany. I won't give up on you now, and I won't let you forget who you are." His voice was cruel, but there was a softness there too.

"Let me stay!" she bellowed, twisting in his grasp. She wasn't a warrior in this reality, so she couldn't fight him properly. Her traitorous body had to resort to wriggling and writhing and scratching and kicking, all of little effect as he hauled her resisting body further and further into the water. "Let me go, you don't need me! I don't want to be me any more..."

"I can't do this without you," he yelled back. "You're my strength and my willpower and my protector all rolled into one. I need you to remind me of home."

"I'm not anything," she wept.

"You're everything," he insisted, and kissed her as they fell back into the salty surf.

Emma blinked and stared at the ceiling. The couch was uncomfortable beneath her, an awkward shape for her long and curvy body. She pulled her towelling robe around her for comfort, and continued to stare at the ceiling for some time. When she looked around, she saw the frozen image of Lara Croft paused on the television screen.

"Another instalment in the adventures of your exiled elves?" asked Stevo as he emerged from the kitchen with two plates piled high with toasted cheese sandwiches.

"They're not elves," she said. "I don't know what they

are. I just wish they'd find their way home and get on with it. I want my sleep patterns back."

"Maybe getting home isn't the happy ending for them," he suggested, handing her one of the plates and then sitting on the floor in front of the couch, setting Lara Croft in motion once more. "Or maybe the story shouldn't end with a happy ending. Readers like dark twists, you know."

"Hmm." She bit into a sandwich, relishing the hot cheesy toastiness of it. "There's some kind of romance creeping in, which makes not no sense at all. Are they friends or enemies or lovers? I just don't get it. I don't think it's a good story."

"That's what editing's for, babe. Write it down, worry about fixing it later."

"Huh," she grunted. "I think I'll stick to the thesis. Seems to be a thankless task, being a short story writer."

"Could be worse. You could be a poet."

"Very funny."

"Hey, it's not all bad. The paradise of flowers and ice crystals that they were in a couple of worlds ago, the one with all the court politics and poisonous plants. I reckon you could get a five book epic out of that one alone."

"I don't want to write a fantasy epic!" she complained. "The sexual significance of women's clothes in *The Forsyte Saga* is quite enough to be getting on with."

"Weren't you supposed to be meeting your supervisor today?"

"Tomorrow," she said, taking another bite of melted cheese and crumbs.

"Yeah, but weren't you supposed to meet him tomorrow *yesterday?*"

Emma frowned. "That can't be right, can it?"

"Suppose not." Stevo effortlessly manoeuvred Lara Croft up a cliff face, to fetch a piece of a golden idol that was hidden in a pixellated seam between two rocks. "I'll give you a lift into uni tomorrow if you like. We need to do a shop as well. We're almost out of bacon and teabags."

"Can't have that."

"Nope."

Emma watched the screen as Lara Croft did an elegant backflip into a deep pool of water. "Stevo?"

"Hmm? Don't talk, this is a tricky bit."

"Haven't we been almost out of bacon and teabags for a really long time?"

"Don't know what you mean."

"It's like we've been on the verge of running out of groceries forever, and I can't remember the last time we did a shop."

"We do a shop every two weeks."

"I know we do, I just don't remember it." She sighed. "Maybe I'm overworked."

"Maybe you should write some thesis so you can justify calling yourself overworked?"

"Cheeky."

"Hey, I wrote four pages of my new novel this morning. I can be officially smug for another eight hours."

Emma had a horrible thought. Having had that thought, she found it incredibly hard to shake it loose. "Let's go for a walk. We never go for a walk."

Stevo gave her a funny look over his shoulder. "There's a good reason for that. What happened to the girl who said 'people who exercise should be put down at birth,' huh?"

"If we walk really slowly it would hardly count as exercise. Come on, just for ten minutes. A stroll around the block, to get some fresh air. We hardly ever go outside any more."

Stevo grunted. "Maybe when I get to the end of this level."

"In fact," Emma said in a slow and painful voice. "I'm not entirely sure that we've ever been outside."

"What are you talking about?"

"Think about it. Do we visit anyone? Does anyone ever visit us?"

"So, we have no social life..."

"It's more than that. I don't know if my thesis supervisor is a man or a woman. I don't have any childhood memories. I don't know what colour our front door is!"

Stevo turned around very slowly and stared at her in the way she had most feared — as if she was crazy. "These dreams are making you nuts, Emma. Forget them."

"I can't," she protested. "I really can't. Not now I think I've guessed the truth. Emma doesn't exist." She ran out of the room, with Stevo lunging after her. He didn't catch up until they reached the front door.

It was brown and elderly, with bubbled glass framed in the top. Like their living room, there was no clear view of the outside world. What colour was it on the other side? She really couldn't imagine it, even as she leaned over to unhook the security chain.

"Don't spoil this," Stevo panted, standing between her and the doorknob. "We're happy here, Emma. We're together and we're happy. What more could you ask for?"

"Galloway," she said in a steady voice.

He flinched as if she had stabbed him with her glass-hilted knife. "No. There's no pain here, no glamour. Just you and me and cups of tea and toasted cheese sandwiches and Lara Croft. We don't have to know what else is out there."

"We already know," said Tiffany Grey-and-White, in a chilly voice. "Otherwise we wouldn't be having this conversation." She reached past his unprotesting body and turned the knob. The door opened inwards.

On the outside, the door was green. Beyond it, a lime green ocean filled all available space, bright and tempting. "The is the way home," she said with a numb kind of triumph. "We can go back to it all. The Queen will forgive us, I know she will. We can return to our life."

"What life?" he said sullenly. "We're not those people any more."

"We could be."

"*Why*? You couldn't be happy in the worlds that I loved, and I couldn't be happy on your damned everlasting beach, but we're both happy here, aren't we?"

Tiffany gazed into the rolling lime green ocean. "Just one step, Galloway. That's all it would take. This is the last world."

He hesitated, still fluctuating between Galloway and Stevo, not quite one or the other. "I have a novel to finish."

"You're supposed to be writing poetry," she said in frustration.

He glared at her. "That's a horrible thing to say to anyone."

"Our world is waiting for us."

He placed his hand on her arm. "So let it wait a little longer."

"What?"

"It's not going anywhere, is it? Don't you want to find out how your thesis turns out?"

She hesitated, almost tempted. "We can't, Stevo. What if we forget who we are again?" *Galloway, his name is Galloway.*

"We won't forget. We know who we are, don't we?"

She looked at him, and he gently leaned forward to close the door. "Let's have a cup of tea and think about it, huh? There's no rush."

"I suppose not." She allowed him to lock the security chain again. It couldn't hurt to be Emma for another day or two before it was time to return to duty and honour and long glass knives. "Do we have any biscuits?"

"Possibly one or two. Nearly out of teabags, though."

"We can get some tomorrow. Will you let me have a go at Lara Croft?"

"Maybe if you write another four pages of thesis."

"Bully."

"That's me."

"If there aren't enough biscuits, we could have Froot Loops."

"I've gone off fruit. All those vitamins can't be good for you."

"I'm pretty sure there's no fruit in Froot Loops. Or vitamins, for that matter."

"Better to be safe than sorry."

"Shortbread creams?"

"Now you're talking my language."

Author's Note: Fruit and Mirrors

I started noodling on a short story draft last year, built around the concept of poetry as currency, thinking it was an idea I'd always wanted to use. Look, I used it seventeen years ago! (Here, fruit is also booze which is kind of hilarious.)

This one's not so much a fairy tale as a Tale of Faerie, and you can spot much of my cultural stash about faerie folk here, just as in the more recent "Salon Faerie."

"Fruit and Mirrors" is a cobbled together mish-mash of *A Midsummer Night's Dream*, Christina Rossetti's *Goblin Fruit*, and Pamela Dean's gorgeous *Tam Lin* novel.

I enjoyed re-reading this one, so dreamy and strange but also packed with little details that are very 2006 me (or perhaps a nearly-forgotten 2004 me that was already beginning to drift away).

2006 was, incidentally, the year that I finished my doctoral thesis, which was not on *The Forsyte Saga*.

The Bluebell Vengeance

FIRST PUBLISHED IN ASIM #28 (2007)

There was something irresistible about humans. Mendra
Melody loved them. They were irresistibly round and pink
and luscious, like ripe Christmas strawberries.

Take the specimen she had just woken up next to. He
wasn't classically perfect (she didn't like them too pretty)
but he had an interesting face and wild, curly hair. You
could tell just by looking at him that he was an artist, or a
writer – anyway, that he didn't work for a living.

Mendra examined his long, tapered fingers. She could
still feel the imprint of them inside of her thighs. His nails
were speckled with blue paint, here and there along the
cuticle. Definitely an artist.

While he continued to sleep, Mendra slid out from
under his doona and headed for the bathroom. This would
be where she would find evidence of a girlfriend, if one
existed. She did hope so. It was hardly worth giving him a
second tumble if there wasn't some sweet, naïve little
chickadee to drive crazy about it.

Oh, yes. There was a girlfriend. She obviously stayed

over on a regular basis – the bathroom cabinet was too tidy to suggest otherwise. There were the rose soaps and bubble bath pellets crowded next to the razors and general man-things. There were the freshly laundered towels, lined up on the rail. A house-proud girlfriend. This was going to be fun.

Mendra glanced in the mirror. The goth makeup from the night before was a nightmare scrawl across her face. Her Blood Mandarin lipstick had been kissed off her mouth and deposited somewhere near her ear. Her long black hair needed not only a brush, but was greasy from the frantic dancing and the sweaty, Olympic-standard sex.

She flicked her fingers at the scary reflection, and it shimmered into something far more respectable: Day Goth chic, her lipstick and mascara a little less intimidating than the night before, and her hair braided back.

Much better. She yawned and smiled at herself, then turned back towards the bedroom. She had a human to play with, and a girlfriend to plot against.

Who said romance was dead?

After the human in question woke up, and they located almost all of their discarded items of clothing, the two of them walked the short distance to the nearest cappuccino bar for breakfast (note to self: he lived in a very trendy area, convenient for vintage clothes shopping, art cafes and gay novel-writing waiters). By the time the coffees and crois-sants arrived, Mendra had discovered:

a) Her new lover's name was Glen

b) He was indeed an artist, though his cagey use of the

word 'painter' made her suspect that houses got painted rather more often than, say, masterpieces

c) He was a very good liar. He said he didn't have a girl-friend with such sincerity and conviction that any woman who hadn't looked into his bathroom cupboard would believe him in a heartbeat.

Mendra found this very intriguing. Every pore of Glen's body suggested 'good guy' and yet he could present a major lie without a single guilty tell – not a blink or a twitch or a smile. She did like a mystery.

"So, Mendra," said Glen once his credentials were established. "What do you do?"

She sipped her cappuccino to disguise her panic. She couldn't think of any of her usual stories. What was wrong with her? Was he such an accomplished liar that he had put her off her game? "I work for a family business," she said. Godsdamnit, that was the truth! Bad enough that she had given him her real name.

"What kind of business?" he asked, a perfectly reasonable question.

And now she had to lie, though something inside her was screaming for honesty. She smiled into his brown eyes, wondering how he would react if she told him the whole, unvarnished truth. "Mail order stuff." *Curse frocks, poisoned cloaks, trick wands, bondage gear made from frogskin leather and unicorn bristles...* "Fashion."

"Oh, interesting." He popped a bit of croissant into his mouth (he ate them like she did – dissecting the crunchy bits away until the buttery white flesh was all that remained). "When can I see you again?"

Mendra opened her mouth, debating between 'never' and 'when your girlfriend says it's okay for a threesome.'

Her mobile sang out with the theme tune of The Addams Family (da-da-da-dum click-click) and relief washed over her as she reached for it. *No. You can't see him again. He brings out the worst instincts in you. You practically held his hand on the way here! You think he's cute. You never think people are cute. You hate cute! Could you stab a bunny rabbit in front of this man? I think not.*

The voice of reason in her head was so loud and demanding that it took a little while to recognise the voice on the phone as that of her cousin Chat.

"What's up?" she asked, breaking into his flow of panicky description.

"Weren't you listening?"

"Not really."

"Get over here now, Menge. It's an emergency!"

She snapped the phone shut. "Sorry, Glen. Emergency."

"Family or fashion emergency?" Glen asked, and his smile crinkled the sides of his eyes.

"Um, both."

"Can I have your number?" he asked.

"Sure." She scribbled a mobile number on a napkin and only after she had walked away did she realise she had given him the right one by accident.

"This had better be important, Chat," Mendra said as she entered the kitchen of the Big House on Hemlock Street.

Her cousin was waiting for her, wide eyed and wired. "It's Granpap. You know that big curse he'd been working on for the VIP client? It hit a shield spell. A good one."

"No one's good enough to block a Granpap special," Mendra scoffed.

"Someone is," said Chat. "Really, Menge. You've got to do something. He's a mess. And if we don't fix it before Granmam and the pares come home from Europe…"

Mendra shuddered at the thought of Granmam in a rage. Not to mention her parents and Chat's, almost as bad as each other. "Okay, how bad is it?"

Chat led her through the house. "It's bad."

"Not those eBay wizards again? The anti-curses they've been selling are a joke."

"I don't think it's wizard work at all."

"One of the other Dark Families, looking for revenge?"

"Worse," said Chat. They rounded the corner together, into the Library.

"Oh, my —" said Mendra at the first sight of her Granpap. This was a man who had been cursing kittens, princesses and Hollywood starlets since the Roman Empire was new. He was the most feared of all the Dark Lords who had survived the Great Transylvanian Massacre. A man so very, very evil that even the Sex Pistols used to watch their language around him.

He sat in the middle of the floor, surrounded by bluebells. Bluebells. They grew up out of the carpet, twiddled between his bare toes, and lay in scattered handfuls across his lap. A braided wreath of them lay upon his silver hair, and more jutted out from his long beard. He was smiling as if he was genuinely happy.

"Crap," said Mendra. "It's the fucking fairies."

"Don't be like that, my sweet," said Granpap, his eyes briefly meeting hers with a warm glow. "Why can't you just relax and enjoy the scenery? It's so peaceful."

"Hippie fucking fairies," agreed Chat with a nod. "That's what I thought."

Mendra sniffed the air. Along with the bluebells, which just barely masked the normal everyday smell of Granpap, there was something sweet in the room. Aniseed, and lemon drops. "Mum's regular supplies aren't going to cut it," she said heavily. "For this, we need the garden centre."

"Zebedee's Plants and Garden Supplies" wasn't not your everyday garden centre. Due to the owner's herbalist sensibilities, and his wife's deep commitment to medieval botany research, you could get just about any strange or unusual plant that you needed.

Mendra was carrying a box of wild widow-wart, African hearth grass and poisonous daisyblades to her car when she noticed the smell of bluebells. The heady, sickly scent of the fairy flowers hovered over her Renault like a soggy cloud. Small tendrils of leaf and stalk were twisted around one of her back tyres, and there was a pattern of tiny blue petals pattered against her windscreen.

"Bugger!" The spell had followed her. She put her box of plants on the ground and opened the driver's side door. A clump of bluebells sprung out of the cigarette lighter. She turned her key with little hope, and was utterly unsurprised when the engine failed to turn over. Fairy magic was notorious for fucking with all forms of modern technology.

"Gah." Mendra leaned her forehead on the steering wheel. She could call Chat to come and pick her up in the family bus, but he was already panicky since Mendra's and his parents were coming home tomorrow. For a twenty-four year old, Chat was still deadly afraid of his mum and dad.

She hoped this thing with Granpap would be relegated to an amusing dinnertime story about how Mendra and Chat saved the day, rather than further evidence to support the general family theory that the younger generation was so not cut out for the stickier side of the family business.

But bluebells were the worst. If they didn't peel this spell off Granpap soon, there wouldn't be a Big House left to greet the pares on their return, just uber-meadow from one end of Hemlock Street to the other.

"Mendra?"

She jumped at the sound of the friendly voice. "Gah! Glen?"

Her one-night-stand leaned over the door of her car. His smile was so warm she could feel it heating up her stomach from the inside out. "I didn't expect to see you so soon."

"Um, me neither. What are you doing here?"

"I just finished a job – painting. You know. I paint. Walls, mostly." He revved up that smile again, though it faltered a little when he spotted the state of her dashboard. "Are those bluebells?"

Mendra pushed herself out of the driver's seat so fast she practically ended up in his arms. Not intentional, that move, oh no. "Car. You have a car here?"

"Well, a truck."

"Brilliant. I need a lift. If I don't get these plants to my Granpap straight away, he'll..." *be stuck with the personality of a giant flower-sucking garden gnome for all eternity,* "...be really grumpy."

Glen laughed. "Heaven preserve us from grumpy grandpas."

Mendra managed to stop flirting for thirty seconds, just long enough to give him a long-suffering stare. "You have no idea."

"What did you bring him for?" Chat demanded as Glen carried Mendra's box of sinister plant life into the Big House on Hemlock Street.

Glen smiled in a friendly, non-confrontational way. "You must be the brother."

"Cousin," said Mendra, thanking all the blood-sucking saints that Glen wasn't likely to meet any of her brothers any time soon. "Don't mind him. Can you pop the plants in the family room?"

"Righty ho," said Glen.

"What are you doing with a man who says 'righty ho'?" Chat demanded, as soon as Glen was out of earshot. "Our Granpap is turning into a frigging flowerpot hugger, and you're taking time out to get laid?"

"I didn't take time out." Mendra wondered if making out at the traffic lights counted as a delay. "Maybe I multi-tasked..."

"Mendra!" said Glen, from the family room. "Do you know this old fellow?"

"Granpap!" Mendra gasped, heading down the corridor.

"He must have escaped the bathroom!" said Chat, following her. "*None* of this is my fault!"

The family room was normally an oasis of simplicity, compared to the high Gothic grandeur of the rest of the house. The furniture was red velvet and black leather, and the walls were decorated with family portraits rather than the usual collection of Dark Lords and Evil Queens that Granpap emulated.

Today, bluebells hung from every surface and corner like a riot of springtime. Plagues of baby's breath and violets joined them. Granpap dangled upside down from the spiked light fittings, his long white beard dripping with petals and posies. He was singing a song about sweet little squirrels. It had the word nonny in it.

Glen held the box of plants in a death grip. His eyes roamed the walls anxiously. He didn't seem overly comforted by the watchful presence of Auntie Batwing and Great-Great Uncle Spyderwart. Did mortals never pose for portraits with their favourite horned blood-parasites proudly displayed on their laps?

Granpap hiccupped, and tiny pink bubbles escaped from his nose and mouth.

"It's reached the third stage!" Chat yelled. He grabbed a pot of daisyblades.

Mendra snatched at the hearth grass and widow-wart. "Close the door," she snapped at Glen. "We can't risk the fumes escaping." She began the chant, and Chat joined in on the chorus.

"Dark Lord, resist this fairy spell. Blight their power, give them hell." It was a simple charm, one that they had learned in their cradles. Far more useful than Hey Diddle Diddle, which wasn't much use once you had reclaimed all the runaway crockery.

Glen staggered, still only halfway to the door. "I have to get out of here."

"No one's stopping you!" Mendra said as she shredded the hearth grass, tearing out her cuticles in the process.

"Close the door on the way out. Dark Lord, resist this fairy spell. Blight their power, give them hell."

Glen hit the carpet, holding his head in his hands.

Chat threw the daisyblades at their Granpap's torso, one after the other. They pierced his flesh even through the thick layers of beard and bluebells. Tiny droplets of blood ran down Granpap's body, turning the bluebells black.

"Dark Lord, resist this fairy spell. Blight their power, give them hell."

Granpap screamed, a long horror movie of a scream. His body twitched with convulsions. Mendra and Chat hit the floor on either side of Glen, covering their noses and mouths. There was an explosion of bluebells.

Mendra kept her eyes tightly shut even after the noise of the explosion had faded. She wasn't sure she wanted to see the results of their little botany experiment.

"Isamendra," said a deadly voice. "Chatsworth. What exactly are you two playing at?"

It sounded like Granpap – the real Granpap. Mendra peeped through her fingers.

He stood in mid-air, hovering several inches off the carpet, his usual black cape and opera suit billowing around him. His white hair and beard had been restored to their usual well-groomed state. His eyes flashed red. "You do know that I will kill you for this?"

Mendra pushed herself to her feet. "Well, that's hardly fair. I can't think how you could possibly blame either of us for this whole bluebell disaster."

Granpap quirked an elegant eyebrow in her general direction. "I don't blame you, child, or the idiot boy. I blame him." He raised his arm, pointing an unreasonably long and pointed index finger straight at Glen.

Mendra took a deep breath. "Granpap, I think you're a little confused."

"Confused?" said the Dark Lord, his voice dripping with charm. "I do not think I am the one who is confused, you incompetent excuse for a witch. I am not the one who brought a filthy *fairy* into the private sanctum of your family."

Mendra turned, slowly. Glen was lifting his face from the floor. He looked wary and uncertain, but he didn't look anything other than mortal. "You're kidding, right?"

Granpap's voice rose into a debonair roar. "You think this is a joke? Not only do you bring a fairy into this house, but you choose the very one that wrought this evil spell upon me. Look! His fingernails are still stained with vile bluebell juice."

"That's paint," said Mendra desperately. "He paints. Mostly houses."

"Actually," said Glen, standing up. "Mostly flowers. My name is Bluebell of the Clan Glen. That spell you just took off your grandfather was definitely my handiwork. I was hired last week to pop up a shield at the Bank of Greenelves to protect them from warlocks, witches, goblins and terrorists. Um. I am a fairy. Sorry?"

A guttural roar burst out of Granpap. He whirled toward the lanky fairy in a tornado of rage and curse magic. Without even thinking, Mendra summoned up her own power as a shield and pushed herself between Granpap and Glen.

Granpap reared back as if he had been physically struck. "Traitress," he hissed. "Oathbreaker!"

"What oath?" Mendra yelled. "Thou shalt not protect thy boyfriends from thy *nutso* grandfather?"

A strange look came over Granpap's face. "Family is everything," he said. "Family comes first, Isamendra. You broke one of the Inviolate Rules to protect a clover-sniffing, dirt-humping, tinsel-snorting *fairy*. You are no longer my granddaughter."

Mendra blinked, and she was standing outside the Big House. A moment later, Glen crashed into the gutter, his arms and legs flailing. She stepped towards the house, but an invisible barrier held her back. "No!"

"What's wrong?" Glen asked from the gutter.

"He's revoked my family status," she said. "He's shut me out." It was too big to contemplate.

There were only two Inviolate Rules in the magical world — *family comes first*, and *promises can't be broken*. Mendra was sure she hadn't broken any oaths, not technically. But as head of the family, Granpap could interpret *family comes first* any way he liked.

"Um." Glen stood up awkwardly. "Can I give you a lift somewhere? To your place?"

Mendra felt numb. "My flat is family property too. I won't be able to get in."

This had happened to her third cousin Serenilla, after she was caught in bed with a leprechaun. Serenilla's entire apartment block had been surrounded by a hedge of thorns ever since. She took up pole dancing and librarianship to make a living outside the family businesses. Mendra didn't even know what a Dewey Decimal *was*.

"My place then."

"You're a fairy," she said accusingly.

"I'm a fairy with a truck."

"Fair point."

Granpap's word was law. That ran through Mendra's mind as the truck growled away from Hemlock Street. Mendra's pares had never once stood up to him about anything that mattered. Chat's pares were almost as bad. And as for Granmam... well, she would stand up to Granpap in a heartbeat if she ever disagreed with him. In seven hundred years, she never had.

So that was it. She was no longer a curse witch. No longer a Melody. Just... Mendra.

She was so busy with her own thoughts that she was out of the truck and halfway up a disturbingly floral garden path before she realised that Glen had not brought her to his flat. "Where the hell are we?"

"I said I was taking you to my place. Home."

She stared at him. For a non-human, there was something awfully mortal about that stray lock of hair that kept flopping in his face. "Your place is a flat. The neat freak place with the scented bathroom."

"This is my home too. I just have to stop in for a few minutes. I didn't think you'd want to stay in the truck..."

She stared at the house in a panic. What was this, Goldilocks Avenue? Primroses grew around the windows, and there were hollyhocks everywhere. The letterbox was pink. "Oh, no. This is your *family home*." Talk about rubbing it in. "Glen, I can't cope with fairies right now."

"My parents are away," he said in a soothing voice. "I said I'd feed the pets, that's all. We'll can be out of here in fifteen minutes."

Relieved of the horror of meeting glitter-farting parents,

Mendra allowed him to steer her inside. "Don't you have a girlfriend to get home to?"

"I don't have a girlfriend," he said. "I told you that."

"You were obviously lying. Why else would your bathroom smell of... flowers. Oh shit," she said miserably. "You are a fairy."

After that, there was nothing for it but to have a cup of tea. Glen made it while Mendra sat at the country pine kitchen table, debating whether or not she should beat her head against it.

Glen put the steaming cup in front of her, followed by a packet of Arnotts Cream Favourites. "Sorry, we're out of fairy bread."

She knocked back the tea. It barely touched the sides. "How can you joke about this? Did you know who I am – what I am – when we got together?"

"Of course not." He sounded shocked. Fair enough, really. Her Granpap's reaction had been bad, but Mendra couldn't imagine how fairy parents would cope with their son fraternising with the enemy. "I didn't suspect until the garden centre."

"So, it's a coincidence that Granpap ran up against *your* curse shield?"

"Not entirely. I'm only one making major-league curse shields in Hobar apart from the eBay wizards. And no one buys from them if they can avoid it. But you and me? A horrible coincidence."

Mendra tried to recall the night before. Why had she

picked Glen out of the crowd? Why would her subconscious hook her up with a card-carrying member of the Bright Families? "Just the other day, I complained that the Universe kept sending me blokes who were wrong for me," she muttered. "Ever notice that the Universe has an evil sense of humour?"

Glen reached out, and touched her hair. "Right now, I'm not complaining."

The Universe paused for a moment or two, to laugh at them. Mendra wasn't listening.

The front door crashed open. "Bluebell, is that your mouldy old truck outside?" screeched a female voice. "Put the kettle on, will you?"

Mendra jerked away from Glen in a panic. "Fairies!" she said urgently. "Mustn't see me here. Bad. Fairies bad."

"It's worse than you think," said Glen. "That's one of my sisters."

Luciana of the House Glen was a fairy. There was no denying it. Her brother Bluebell (Mendra was still firmly calling him 'Glen' inside her head) may get away with looking vaguely artistic but his sister had been doused with the glitter gene.

She was blonde and thin, with tapering fingernails and a giggle that could shatter frozen vodka. When she sat at the table, Mendra could hear the burr of invisible wings vibrating against her chair back.

She wasn't fooled in the least when Glen introduced Mendra as 'my friend.'

"Does she know?" she shrilled.

Mendra rolled her eyes at the lack of tact. "That he's a fairy?" she said sweetly. "Oh, yes. He told me on our second date." *If you count getting a girl evicted from her family home a date.*

"Aren't you sharp for a mortal?" said Letitia with something halfway between a smile and a leer.

Mendra managed to keep her mouth shut at that one. They wanted to think of her as a redblood, fine.

"Have you heard from Mummy and Daddy?" Luciana went on, dismissing Mendra entirely.

"They called my place earlier to say they were finished with their business in Prague and would be home tomorrow," said Glen as he handed around cups of tea to his sisters.

Mendra almost swallowed her own tongue. *Prague.* That was where the pares were, last she heard – supporting the revolutionary magic-workers of the city against the smug Sweetness and Light corporation that had bought out half the country to use as a back lot for filming inspirational movies. There had been open fighting in the streets, last she heard: warlocks, witches, goblins and werewolves vs. fairies, pixies, talking bunny rabbits and the occasional Hollywood vampire.

"Are you all right?" Glen asked her.

Mendra wanted to break something. How dare he be so considerate of her feelings? Didn't he realise they were at war? "I have to go," she said, pushing herself to her feet.

"Don't let us stop you," sneered Luciana. "If I'd known you like them prickly, Bluebs, I would have set you up with a curse hag."

"I'll see you out," said Glen.

"Don't bother," said Mendra, heading for the door.

He followed her out anyway. "Where are you going?"

"Anywhere's better than here," she snapped. "Our parents have probably been trying to kill each other over in Prague."

"Saves us having to wait for them to come home to do it," he joked.

The smell of hollyhocks in the front garden made Mendra's shoulder blades itch. "Funny. It's just hilarious the way you have totally screwed up my life."

"Stick around. Maybe I can help repair some of the damage."

"What's the point? Why are you being so nice to me? It was a fuck, Glen, a lousy one night stand. Don't try to make this more than it is."

He gave her an annoyingly patient look. "If what we have is so meaningless, why have we barely spent an hour apart all day?"

"Because you tried to kill my Granpap!"

"That's not entirely true."

"I can't get my family back until you are out of the picture."

"Are you sure you want them back after the way they treated you?"

Any regrets she had about dumping him instantly grew wings and flew to Cuba. "How would your lovely folks react if they knew I was a witch from a Dark Family? Would you give them up for me?"

"Mendra. I've never felt this way about anyone."

Emergency, emergency... red lights flashing, get out of there! Mendra hesitated on the doorstep, momentarily caught by Glen's deep, sincere brown eyes. In a parallel universe, this was the point where he kissed her and she kissed him back, and somehow it all worked out for the best.

This wasn't that universe. This universe was the one where he leaned in as if to kiss her, and she socked him in the eye before transforming herself into a flock of bats.

Bat travel was the worst. There were the orienteering issues of trying to find your way across a stretch of unfamiliar suburbia when your consciousness was spread over a multitude of small flying rodents. Also, bats, when it came right down to it, weren't at their best in the mid afternoon.

But, hell. It was a great exit.

Somewhere between Fairyville and Mendra's inner city flat, her mobile rang. The vibrations of the Addams Family theme tune threw the last skerricks of bat radar into utter confusion, and she fell in a shower of membranous wings, scratchy claws and long black hair.

Luckily, a cemetery broke her fall.

Mostly reassembled, Mendra answered her phone on the fourth ring. "Yes?"

"Dahhhhling." There was only one woman who could pronounce four 'h's in the word 'darling.'

"Hi, Mum."

"We've heard all about it, sweetness," said Valmai Melody. "Chat sent us a very detailed email. It's obvious that the old man's finahhhhlly lost it. Does he expect us to believe our little girl is stupid enough to get hot and sweaty with a sparklebunny?" She laughed for quite a long time.

Mendra resisted the urge to stab her own veins with her

fingernails. "Will you be home soon?" The thought of the older generation rampaging to the rescue was suddenly a huge relief.

"Of course, dahhhhling. We'll be home any minute. Keep yourself busy for an hour or two – go shopping, buy yourself something nice. Your father and I will handle evehhhhrying, and you'll be back in the bosom of the Family before you know it."

"What... exactly do you mean by handling everything?"

"Oh, honey pie, this shield spell that blew up in the old man's face has clearly knocked something sideways. He needs some good old fashioned hexing to get him back on the straight and nahhhhrrow."

Mendra squeezed her mobile tightly in her fingers. "Who are you all planning to hex?"

Even over the phone she could hear her mother's frosty smile. "Who else, sweetpea? That son-of-a-bunny who set the wretched shield up in the first place. Bluebell of the House Glen."

Mendra flew back to the Big House in Hemlock Street so fast that her bat wings had stretch marks. Chat was waiting for her by the gate. "Did the pares reinstate my family status?" she asked breathlessly even as she reassembled her arms and legs from the last few bats.

"Not exactly," said Chat, sounding fed up. " Granmam used her Senior Crone's pass to create an Exception Door in the barrier Granpap threw up, but he's the only one who can actually reinstate you."

"Fan-frigging-tabulous," said Mendra. She reached forward and felt the air between Chat's left ear and the letterbox. Sure enough, there was a narrow doorway. "Do you know what they have planned for Glen?"

Chat looked embarrassed. "I'm not sure if I should tell you. It's... you know, family. And he's a fairy. Why do you care what happens to some stupid daffodil-shagger?"

Mendra reached out and flicked him Chat in the forehead. "He's a person, you spineless wonder. Can you really stand back and watch our dearly beloveds take him apart?"

"If it's a choice between him and me, damn straight," Chat said, rubbing his forehead. "Rebellion isn't wise in a family where everyone has their own ceremonial axe. They want me to eat this joker's major organs, I'm going to say, 'spoon or chopsticks?' So would you, a couple of days ago."

Mendra hesitated. "Maybe. But not now."

"So what happened? A big cloud of fairy dust and suddenly you're less of a bitch than you were before Tinker Bell showed you a good time? He can't be that well equipped."

"This isn't about sex," she said firmly, heading for the front door.

"So, what? You're in loo-ove?"

Mendra whirled around. "Don't say that word near this house! Don't even think it!"

Chat looked panicked. "Shit, Mendra, I was kidding."

She gave him a shifty look. "So was I."

"Oh, you liar!"

"Just... shut up, can you do that, Chat? For me?"

The kitchen was the largest room in the Big House, and that was saying something for a building that included two Great Halls and three Ballrooms.

Exactly three square metres of the kitchen were dedicated to the preparation of food, most of that was the fridge. The rest was a huge expanse of tiled floor (easier to hose blood off) and one massive granite ceremonial table.

Granpap was tied to the table, gibbering like something out of a 1930's Frankenstein movie. A fresh crop of bluebells sprouted out his ears and nostrils. Mendra's mother, gowned in her best ceremonial Versace, was stirring something evil-smelling in a microwave-safe Tupperware. Her father, as usual, was sitting out of the way, and reading a newspaper. He wiggled his fingers at her. "Hi, honey."

Uncle Chatsworth and Auntie Dimelza drew arcane symbols out on the floor, using two pastry brushes and the blood-coloured contents of another Tupperware.

"So," said Mendra, in what she hoped was a bright and non-threatening voice. "What exactly is the plan here?"

"That should be obvious," said a menacing voice right behind her.

Mendra was proud of the way she glanced casually over her shoulder, as if she was only barely interested in who was standing there.

It was Granmam, in full battledress, ready for action. There was no sight in the universe more terrifying, or ominous.

The fishnet stockings were a particularly intimidating touch.

Granmam had been around since the days of Marie Antoinette. Even in jeans or pyjamas, she carried herself as if a full boned corset and wide metal crinoline were taking the weight. Today, she was in black lace and leather mode: short skirt and long boots. This was the woman who had parachuted into WWII France to steal hippogriffs from the Nazis. Her hair was perfectly set in a bounce that was more Bond girl than nanna.

Actually, she had been a Bond girl. Travelling via film crew was the most convenient way to smuggle enchanted firearms into Europe during the Cold War. These days, she was more into animal cruelty, and to that end had a chain of pet boutiques ranging from one end of the country to the other. Any remotely fashionable witch's familiar who was remotely fashionable had their fur styled and ears pierced at Trim N Catwax.

Granmam's heels clicked against the granite floor of the kitchen. "Don't tell me you've forgotten the basic precepts of vengeance spells," she said with a sneer. "The only way to cure your grandfather permanently is to take the snivelling creature who perpetrated the original spell, cut him open, turn him inside out and hold him upside down until every drop of magic in his body is a congealed puddle on the floor. Then we can build the hex to end all hexes, send his accursed family into oblivion and protect ours from their ridiculous sparkledust antics **FOREVER**."

Mendra noticed a hint of black powder clinging to Granmam's nostrils. She was snorting the mandrake root again. It would be a miracle if anyone got out of this alive. "You're speaking metaphorically about the turning him inside out and upside down?" she suggested.

Granmam smiled, thinly. "Henri, what do we have in the way of meat hooks?"

Mendra's Dad glanced up from his newspaper. "I'm sure we can scrounge something up, Arguerite."

No reason to panic. Mendra needed a brilliant plan in brand spanking time. Maybe she could sidle outside and send Glen a text from her mobile, warning him to leave the country for a decade or two. That could work. If she had his number.

Shit.

"Where's the prisoner?" Grandmam asked.

"I'll get her," said Chat, sounding depressed.

Mendra whirled around. "We have a prisoner?"

"How else to lure our little flower artist into a trap?" said Granmam with a smirk.

The Addams Family theme tune rang out from Mendra's handbag. "I have to get that," she said gratefully, and fled through the French doors to the garden.

Outside, she scrabbled for her phone. It was an unfamiliar caller number, but she had no doubt who it was. She could feel him glaring down the aether at her. "Glen?"

"Mendra, what have you done with my sister?" He sounded angry and forceful, in a Mr Darcy kind of way.

Mendra tried not to swoon. No time for this now, but she was going to have to remember for the future that his 'bossy' voice was sexy as hell. "Sister? What sister?"

"The one who is now missing. Luciana." [if you do delete the earlier sister bit, this would need a bit of tweaking, obviously...]

"Haven't seen her..." Mendra's voice trailed off as she stared through the French doors into the kitchen. A petite, struggling blonde fairy in a pink ballet dress and Prada sandals was being handcuffed to the light fittings. "Oh, crap."

"She's there, isn't she?"

"Glen, stay away. It's a trap, obviously. My family plan to kill you."

"What am I suppose to do, trust you to help her escape?"

"That's optimistic of you. She wasn't very nice to me when we met."

The French doors burst open. Valmai Melody stood there, her designer suit fluttering around her. "Thahht's him, isn't it?" she demanded of her daughter.

Mendra lowered the phone. "It's a phone sex line. I was feeling needy."

Granmam appeared beside Valmai. The two striking figures in black looked like Best Actress nominees at an Oscar's after party. "Be True," Granmam cursed.

Mendra held up the phone. "Glen says hi. Can he have his sister back?"

Granmam threw back her head and howled.

Valmai stepped forward, her slasher movie fingernails outstretched towards the phone. She mimed as if pulling something long, heavy and resistant through the air towards her.

A scream started in Mendra's phone and stretched outward, the painful sound vibrating up her wrist.

The phone bulged, twisted and pulled apart to reveal a hand, and then an arm, and then a Glen.

He collapsed in a pile of yaargh! on the grass at Mendra's feet.

"That was a brand new phone!" Mendra yelled at her mother. "And this is getting way out of hand." She didn't like the looks that her mother and Granmam were giving her. The ruthless looks that women only gave each other when there were no male witnesses.

"So, your Granpap was right," said Granmam in an "Ah, so many Dalmatians, so little time," kind of voice. "You have been fornicating with the fairies, grand-daughter of mine."

Mendra rolled her eyes at the word *fornicating*. Honestly, it wasn't like Granmam didn't watch *The O.C.* She didn't have to speak like a 17th century Puritan play. "I think you broke him." She crouched down beside Glen. If he had any handy escape plans to whisper to her, now was the time.

"They're coming for you," he warned in a hoarse voice.

There was a buzzing sound overhead. Several dozen balls of light smashed against the invisible shield that domed over the Big House. Then several more dozen, all pink and purple and blue. A veritable hailstorm of fluffy balls of light exploded above them.

There was a cracking sound.

"Get — in — side!" cried Valmai, dragging on Mendra's arm. Granmam had Glen slung across her broad shoulders. They crowded into the kitchen together.

"The fairies are besieging us, then," said Mendra's dad, turning another page of his newspaper.

"It took them half an hour to break through the shield last time," noted Uncle Chatsworth. "When was that, 67?"

"1969," said Auntie Dimelza. "We had to set that whole man on the moon thing up to distract the neighbours."

"The shield's a lot stronger than it used to be," said Uncle Chatsworth. "Should take them at least forty five minutes."

There was another cracking sound, louder than the first. "More like fifteen," said Auntie Dimelza "Fairy shield-crackers have improved too. Haven't you been keeping up with the journals?"

Granmam dumped Glen on the floor and marched towards the struggling, bound figure of Luciana. "Now then, Young Chatsworth. How would you like to have a go at your first fairy sacrifice?"

Chat looked horrified. "Um, what an honour. I've never done any Old Style spells at all, you know, just the modern nuts and berries kind of stuff."

"I'll sharpen the knives for you," she said almost kindly.

Mendra edged towards Glen. "I don't know how to stop it," she said in a frantic whisper.

He gave her a dirty look. "Do you expect me to believe that you want to?"

"I don't know what I want!"

"Obviously."

Granpap, whom no one had paid attention to for some time, suddenly hiccupped. His body, still bound to the table, bucked against its bonds.

It started raining bluebells.

"Hurry," said Valmai. "Maman, you must start the hex now. The shield is giving way."

Granmam spat out a mouthful of bluebells, and handed a wicked carving knife to Chat. "We need blood, bone and a gobbet of flesh. Get working."

Chat looked from Granmam to the tied and struggling Luciana. "Okay," he said miserably, his finger trembling on the hilt of the knife.

There was a loud cracking sound as the anti-fairy shield above the Big House broke open. Balls of light skittered everywhere, smashing against the windows and squiggling through the crack under the door.

The air buzzed and hummed like the nagging of a thousand bumblebees.

The Melody family threw defensive hexes, jinxes and curses through the air. Bluebells and sparkle dust showered around them.

Mendra found herself under the table, holding hands with Glen as if her life depended on it.

"We have to do something," he said. "Our families are going to tear themselves apart!"

Mendra swallowed. Hard. "Give me a ring," she said.

"Look how well that turned out last time…"

"Not on the phone, you nong. Give me a *ring*. Of the engagement variety. I like rubies, personally, but I understand you might have to improvise."

Glen's mouth fell open. "Do you know what you're asking?"

"Can you think of anything else that's going to keep this lot from killing each other?"

Glen looked at her. Many emotions crossed his face. Mendra was pleased to see that they didn't include horror and nausea. "Right," he said, and balled his hand into a fist. When he opened it, his hand contained a shiny silver ring with a sapphire the size of a bluebell. "I tried for a ruby," he said apologetically. "Bluebells are kind of my default…"

"I'll take it," she said, sticking out her hand.

"You're really sure about this?"

She looked through the sparkles and madness to where Granmam held Chat by the wrist, miming the actions he should use to cut bits off Luciana. Chat had already thrown up once, but Granmam was never going to take no for an answer. "You're the one who suggested this should be more than a one night stand."

They climbed out from under the table together, and

once they were on their feet, Glen slid the bluebell ring on to her finger. "Mendra Melody, will you marry me?"

"Yes. Glen..."

"Bluebell."

"Shit, sorry. Bluebell of the House Glen, will you marry me?"

"Yes."

"Promise?"

"Promise."

Family comes first. Promises can't be broken.

"No!" shrieked Valmai Melody from the other side of the room.

Everything stopped. The hexes and curses dribbled into the corners of the kitchen. The balls of light solidified into proper-sized, pissed off fairy people. Bluebells kept raining from the ceiling, but everyone was used to that by now.

Every member of the Dark Family Melody and the Fairy Clan Glen stopped what they were doing and stared at Mendra and Bluebell.

"We have an announcement," Glen said with a sickly smile.

"You can't be serious," said Valmai. "You can't do this!"

"Just did," said Mendra. "Welcome to the family, everyone."

Family comes first. Promises can't be broken.

Glen squeezed her hand. It felt kind of nice.

Valmai Melody sank on to the kitchen stool with her head in her hands. "I don't believe this is hahhhpening."

A fluffy fairy woman, whom Mendra guessed was Glen's mother, looked equally unwell. She clung to a wiry, hippie-looking fairy male in a Hawaiian shirt and daisy-studded beard, who might be Glen's father. Or his disreputable older brother who'd had a hard life. "Do you have anything to drink in this place?"

"Young Chatsworth," said Granmam in a lordly voice. "Put the kettle on."

As if in a dream, Chat moved to obey her.

Granmam herself went to untie Luciana's wrists, but. T the blonde fairy dissolved her own bindings. "Don't worry about me, Arguerite. Check the old man's doing okay."

Granpap sat up and spat out a last mouthful of bluebells. "I'm fine, young Lucie. You did very well."

She blushed and giggled. "I always wanted to be an actress, you know."

Mendra looked from one to another. "Now, hang on a minute."

"Are we missing something really important?" Glen demanded.

Valmai stared at Granmam and Granpap, who looked suspiciously pleased with themselves. "I'd like to know that myself."

"Luciana Violet Grimaldia Fiappacina Mabel of the Clan Glen," said the fairy who might be Glen's mother. "What have you done now?"

"You're always complaining about how he's not settling down and giving you grandkids," Luciana said sulkily. "I thought you'd be pleased I got him married off. And then this opportunity came up... a very lucrative business opportunity, you might say."

"Indeed," said Granmam. She pulled a sheaf of documents from her corseted bosom. "Will you sign, my dear?"

"Of course," said Luciana. She signed several of the papers, then handed them back to Granmam, who did likewise.

"There," said Granmam, finishing her last signature with a flourish. "As of Monday, Luciana's patented Lucie Violet range of hand-herbed shampoos, conditioners and curl potions will be available in every Trim N Catwax salon in the country."

Luciana took her copies of the contracts and simpered. "Of course, it's illegal for Dark and Bright Families to do business with each other..."

"Unless they are connected by a tie of marriage," said Glen in a hard voice.

"Betrothal's good enough for a holding period of six months," Granmam said brightly. "It's not like either of you can get out of it now."

Mendra blinked several times. "You set all this up — the bluebells, the hexing, the engagement... for cat shampoo?"

"High class cat shampoo," said Luciana. "I also have a range of herbal polishes for toads and bats."

"We must discuss those," agreed Granmam.

"*Cat shampoo?*" shrieked Mendra.

"Let's take a moment outside," said Glen, steering her out the French doors.

Chat was already out there, sitting on the steps and looking somewhat greenish. "She knew," he said unhappily. "Granmam knew I didn't have it in me to be the Big Bad like the rest of the family. She counted on it."

Mendra cuffed his shoulder as she went past. "I wouldn't be too upset about it. Why would you want to be like anyone in this family?"

"Keep moving," Glen said firmly, dragging Mendra further down the garden and out of Chat's earshot. They settled near the frog pond.

"Were you in on this?" she demanded.

"Don't be ridiculous."

Mendra's stomach swirled. She sat down in a hurry on the mossy rocks and buried her head in her hands. "I don't believe this is happening to me."

He touched her hair. "Is it really so bad?"

"Are you kidding me? I'm legally obliged to marry a man whose sister tricked him into it. It's not only a blatant violation of my Magic Citizenship Rights, it's bloody humiliating."

"Mendra, when I woke up this morning, do you know what I thought?"

"Aargh, I've been taken hostage by an evil goth girl?"

He laughed. "No. I thought, wow. I want to get to know this girl better."

"Oh."

"Do you know what I found out when I did get to know you better?"

"If you keep asking questions, I'm going to keep right on making sarcastic retorts."

Glen rolled his eyes. "If you'd shut up for thirty seconds, I could tell you that I think you're funny and strange and somewhat twisted. And I'm crazy about you. Hadn't you noticed?"

Mendra stared at him. "I think I need to lie down." He hugged her close, and she let him. She buried her face in his neck, and breathed in the scent of man and bluebells. "Our families," she moaned.

"They kind of deserve each other, don't you think?"

"Can we kill them all?"

"After the wedding."

"After the wedding," she agreed.

It seemed appropriate to kiss for a while, so they did that.

"Just so's you know," she said some time later. "I'm not wearing a tutu and wings to the wedding."

"I'm not wearing a pointy hat."

"I hate hollyhocks."

"Doesn't everyone?"

"If you think I'm going to read our children those stupid fairytales with witches being pushed into oven and fairy godmothers being all 'la di dah, here's a dress that is entirely impractical because you can only wear it once' and what's wrong with giving her a pair of jeans or a coupon or whatever so she can buy her own clothes..."

"Mendra, do you ever stop talking?"

"Hah, you said you'd marry me, too late to back out now..."

He kissed her again, which was fine with Mendra. As long as he was kissing her, she could forget that she had a wedding to plan, two incompatible families (cat shampoo transactions aside) to unite, and a host of fairy in-laws who were going to hate her until the day she died.

Kissing was better than thinking. If she squeezed her eyes shut tight enough, and pressed hard enough against Glen's warm, inviting body, she might be able to fool herself into believing in Happily Ever After.

For at least thirty seconds.

Author's Note: The Bluebell Vengeance

This story was a turning point for me about the kind of stories I wanted to write. I intended for it to be a series of fun rom-com witch meets fairy suburban fantasy stories set in Hobart — and the fact that it was set in Hobart was a big deal for me, I'd always shied away from that with my SFF.

I didn't end up developing Mendra and Glen's world as a series for one reason or another — I've always had more stories to write than I have time to write, and eventually the moment passed.

Re-reading it now, I can see how some of the vibes and ideas carried over to the Belladonna U series (ironically not set in Hobart, but also about messy families and suburban magic, exploring how magic might react to modern technology).

I can also see a shape here of the Blights, a dysfunctional magical family I wrote into "12 Days of Witchmas" in 2023 without thinking once about "The Bluebell Vengeance" from 15 years earlier.

What goes around comes around.

CROWN TOURNEY, OR: HOW TO WIN A CROWN, A KINGDOM AND A WICKED FAIRY IN TEN "EASY" TOURNAMENTS

Tournament of Flowers

SITE: THE POPPY MARSHES, UPPER BELGROR

PRIZE: A GOLD TULIP, 24 CARAT, THIRTEEN INCHES BY FOUR INCHES

"Nameless knight, wife of the fairy Carabosse!" cried the herald. "No great tournaments fought before, no wins to her name."

I never expected to find myself here, a decade after I cursed the princess, shivering on the stands with the tourney wives. Waiting for my champion to beat her opponents bloody.

When I first agreed to this foolhardy plan, I did not imagine she would stick it out. No one had ever heard of a princess — or any woman — making it through more than a few preliminary bouts of the tourney season.

She would be bruised, I thought, and battered — either in her ego or in her curvaceous behind. Either way, it was no skin off my nose.

And yet. This was the boon she asked of me, in return for destroying her life. I owed her one.

(I owed her ten.)

When the princess Aura of Argentia was fifteen years old, the wicked fairy Carabosse transformed her into a silver swan.

There are three kinds of tourney wives:

1) the Camp Hags, who join the caravan of champions from day one, hanging in there through the rain and mud and mealy campfire potatoes and entire lack of glory attached to the pre-season. While their champions prove their mettle by sword and lance and staff and bow, the Camp Hags prove *their* mettle by putting up with grunge, gunge and altogether grim living conditions. They adore every damp-socked minute of it. Every Camp Hag I've met so far is all too eager to share horrifying anecdotes about

how to survive the season, including top tips for ridding yourself of lice, and where to bargain for the best porridge oats.[*]

2) the Banner Queens, who don't join the fun until the prelims are done and the final lists have been decided for the Ten Great Tournaments of the season. They're a little more hoity-toity, expecting a better class of catering and waterproof canvas, but the Banner Queens will muck in with the rest of us when all's said and done. They over-compensate for the lack of mud on their hems by going all out with the pageantry — every hand-sewn banner is bright, every chant is word-perfect. The Camp Hags roll their eyes and smirk at how earnest the Banner Queens are about the whole business. After all, most knights are happy with a hot cuppa and a snog at the end of the day. They might have their differences, but both groups of tourney wives have little time for:

3) the White Nightingales, who never get their boots dirty. These glamorous goddesses fly in/fly out for each of the Ten Tourneys, modelling pristine gowns and tailor-made banners at every occasion. (No Nightingale would ever stoop to DIY). Their appearances are brief — they prome-nade during the lists, tie favours around the biceps of their champions, and rarely stay longer than the first remove of the celebration feast. Their winged carriages flap away long before the party warms up, and you won't see them again until ten minutes before the next show.

---

[*] I did not name the Camp Hags. They named themselves, claiming 'hag' as a badge of honour. They have their own merch.

I knew all this already. I might never have been a tourney wife before my princess claimed her boon, but my path has crossed many an active champion over the years. It's amazing how much work there is in the world of tournaments for a wicked fairy who specialises in curses. Not all knights are bastions of morality... (and besides, it's mostly the wives who hire the help).

I don't recall if any of this generation of tourney wives ever hired me to nobble the competition (once you pass three hundred years of age, it's tricky to keep track of current events) but I erred on the side of caution this season, reverting to an old disguise.

If the body I chose to wear for my new life as a tourney wife was one of my prettiest, from the days when I was young and wild with spiky black hair and a rack to die for, well... sometimes, wicked is allowed to mean 'selfish.'

The Tournament of Flowers was the first Great Tourney of the season. I'd earned a little respect from the Camp Hags by mucking in through the early bouts, though they wouldn't consider me one of them until I'd lasted a few years on the circuit.*

This was the big leagues. A proper jousting field, paved instead of a rough square of grass cut to size. Stands for the ladies and the local crowd, built in creaking wood but undoubtedly solid. Cushions, even. Beer and nuts for the hoi polloi. A raised dais for the royals — several in attendance this year, not unexpected, considering the stakes.

---

* Hopefully *that* wouldn't be necessary!

Belgror liked their flowers, and so the jousting field was decorated with poppies and roses, tulips and blowsy camellias, enchanted by several local fairies to keep them from wilting.

Every wife was given a wreath of pansies with which to honour her champion.

"Which one is yours?" asked a cheerful redhead who skidded in late with two children at her skirt, and a banner that spoke of many hours of hardcore embroidery.

I nodded towards where the knights were levering themselves into dented armour, covering up the dings with hand-sewn tabards. Most of them were cheerful with each other, bumping elbows amiably and chirping about who would happily knock whose heads off.

Princess Aura, her chin set in determination, stood to one side in her fiercely polished breastplate, practicing her hilt grip like her life depended on it. (It did, obviously.)

"Mine's the blonde in the corner that everyone's pretending isn't there," I said, cheerfully enough.

The redhead's mouth formed a perfect 'o.' "That's nice," she said quickly. "How long have you been married?"

"Six weeks."

"Lovely."

The knights trooped past the wives, each stopping before their lady to bow the head and receive a crown of pansies. When Aura knelt before me, her fair hair already tucked deep inside her silver helm, my hands shook only a little as I laid the garland upon her.

She glanced up for a moment, that familiar look in her eye when she saw me — somewhere between hatred and gratitude, yet not quite either of those things.

"Stay safe," I murmured, and her lips curved up in the slightest of smiles.

I should have known better. *Safe* was not what we were aiming for.

When the dust cleared, and the air stopped ringing with the shouts of the crowd, my lady was still on her feet. She came fourth in a field of sixteen at the lance, and sixth at the sword, not bad at all.

We didn't win the gold tulip, but that was not the prize we were after.

Tournament of Steel and Stag

SITE: MAILLY-ON-THE-MIST

PRIZE: A SILVER STAG

The Tournament of Steel was held in a series of boggy paddocks in the outer borderlands of the kingdom of Mailly-on-the-mist, far from civilisation and hot pease bars.

Aura and I shared a battered tent — it had lived a long life before we got our hands on it, and Mailly's peat-stinking grounds and ever-drizzling rain did it no favours.

I offered to dry the canvas off on the inside, repair the worst of the cracks. I still had my magic, if little else.

Aura gave me a dirty look, reminding me that she had spent years of her life *marinated* in my magic, and it was the last thing she wanted to think about before she went to sleep each night.

She did not have to speak the rebuke aloud; I had heard it before. The slog through the preliminary circuit had been long and arduous and gave us plenty of time to air our grievances.

Her grievances, mostly. All deserved. I understood then as I did now that this quest was not only for Aura to recapture her kingdom.

It was my apology tour.

It was my punishment.

The princess was hunted across the shining lake for three years by three princes from other lands. They had each been promised marriage to a princess and the crown of the kingdom of Argentia if they killed the silver swan.

Against all the odds, the sun was shining over the boggy paddocks of Mailly-on-the-mist when the knights took to the jousting field. There was still plenty of mud under hoof, churned up by the horses.

Aura held up well at the lance, unseating two opponents and holding fast against a third who stubbornly refused to go down. She placed second, awarded a bottle of mead as she stood a rung below today's champion: a beefy knight with a tooth missing.

Only those who placed in the top three of each event were allowed to join the final sword melée: the ring of steel. Twelve contenders stepped inside a circle formed of steel antlers. They fought, blood and blade, sweat in their hair, armour grinding into the dirt. Once you fell, you were dragged back over the antlers to safety, and your wife.

Aura stayed on her feet until cornered by that same beefy knight; he grinned at her as if he knew he could beat her again.

And there I stood, with a banner covered in ivy leaves and feathers, powerless to help her.*

The two of them swung, passed, swung, passed, always circling. I wanted to close my eyes, but if she could do this then I could be brave.

"Why is this kingdom so obsessed with deer?" I asked in frustration, with the antler fence burning its way into my retinas. "There isn't a tree for miles around?"

"They chopped down all the trees years ago," said Lorna, the red-haired Banner Queen. "The last king offended a witch, and she sent a blight to wither all the forests. There have been no deer in these parts since before their last king came to the throne."

Aura lost the final bout; the beefy knight accepted the silver stag in triumph and handed it to his wife, a sylph-like White Nightingale adorned with silk flowers. Somehow, she

---

* I had used my magic to sew most of the details in place; Aura could hate my abilities all she likes, but she would look quite the fool if I gave my natural embroidery skills free rein. I would never be a Banner Queen, but I was quite proud of the results.

had got through the afternoon without a speck of mud on her pale floral gown.

My Aura stood at the prize-giving, exhausted and bloody, covered in mud. She was awarded six gildyrs for the trouble; her final placing was third.

The feast included haunches of venison, served with turnip and cress. It had the distinct odour of food that has been created, not harvested from reality. No one else seemed to mind.

Tournament of Dragons

SITE: THE WHIRLING MOUNTAINS, IGRIZEL

PRIZE: AN ENCHANTED SADDLE

Normally they do not bring dragons into play this early in the season. I'm not saying that the schedule was changed specifically to scare my princess away, but I'd seen the looks, heard the mutters.

No one understood how she was still here. Clearly they only saw what they wanted to see: a cursed princess not smart enough to stay down. They were not paying attention.

They didn't see the muscle beneath her armour, the tilt of determination in her jaw. The tattoo on her left ankle that she got after her third year of training under one of the greatest tourney champions our kingdoms have ever seen.

She was a princess, therefore: she must be in need of rescue.

Princess Aura broke her own swan curse and returned to her kingdom as a human, only to find she had been replaced as the heir of Argentia by her cousin Odile.

Many of the jousting knights, especially those representing the highest families of the richer kingdoms, were able to provide their own dragon, resting their usual hardworking horse in favour of a more pampered beast.

All equipment including steeds were supposed to be provided by the champion and their patrons, but dragons were rare enough that an exception was made for any who didn't happen to have one at home.

This was Igrizel, after all: a kingdom rich in nothing but dragons. For an extra list fee of twelve gold floryns, one could hire a dragon for the day. The one they brought to Aura was an amber creature with fire in its eyes as well as its belly, and wings spanning three carriages wide.

Other first-year champions had been offered tamer beasts; everyone was sniggering behind sleeves.

"You don't have to," I murmured to her. "I could —" But what could I do? My magic had its limits. Short of transforming myself into a dragon, I had little to offer her; and should I do that, she would be disqualified for having no wife in the stands.

"I'm not afraid of flying," Aura said scornfully. "I'm not afraid of anything."

How could she be? She had already lost everything that ever made her feel safe in the world.

Aura strode up to the amber dragon, staring it directly in the face. Without her helm, her blonde hair whipped around her, enwildened by the mountain breezes. Her stride was as confident, her back as broad, her gaze as steady as any man in this tournament; stronger than many.

"I can see we're going to be good friends," she said to the dragon, daring it to contradict her.

Later, as Aura jousted in mid-air, unseating four knights and keeping her saddle in the midst of the flame and the smoke and the screaming, I found myself unexpectedly short of breath.

"Impressive," noted Margie, one of the Camp Hags, chewing on a piece of homemade venison jerky. "If your princess knocks my Bran into the ditch," she added. "I'll pull her hair out."

Beneath the arena, several dozen servants in silly hats ran around with nets outstretched, to catch fallen champions and, where possible, douse any flames that came with them.

I liked Margie. She was probably my best friend at the camp. "If you touch a hair of my princess's head," I said, ever so slightly feral. "I'll turn your Bran into a newt."

Tournament of Cobwebs

SITE: CASTLE BLACK, THE DREAD REACHES

PRIZE: AN ENCHANTED CAT

Of course, the first tournament she actually won was the one with a live animal as a prize. Just my luck.

No one recognised Princess Aura's face, or her voice, or her words. Not the nurse who had raised her as a baby. Not her own parents. In final desperation, she threw herself off the highest tower in the kingdom, transforming back into the *silver swan... and then they knew exactly who she was.*

I don't want to talk about the cat.

(I have to talk about the cat).

I knew the cat was going to be trouble when I overheard it talking to some mice.

And that was before I caught it trying on my best boots.

Then, just as I opened my mouth to tell Aura of my concerns...

The cat opened its mouth, and pearls spilled out on to the floor.

Oh, I thought. *We'll never be rid of it now.*

But at least there would be buns for tea.

Tournament of the Lady of the Lake

SITE: THE LANGUID LAKE, BILLEMAUDH

PRIZE: A KISS, OR A WISH.

"Nameless knight, wife of the fairy Carabosse! Winner of this season's Tournament of Cobwebs in the Dread Reaches."

"We had become a trio, by the time the Languid Lake loomed on our horizons. The cat was Aura's new best friend, curled up in her lap while I trudged ahead, leading the mule-drawn cart (with Mallowart, the jousting stallion, roped alongside) to our next destination.*

Billemaudh, the legendary kingdom of the mists.

A sad king ruled here, surrounded by sisters and nephews. He had never married, his bride-to-be having been seduced away by his favourite knight.

There she was, I noted as we set up camp: Lady Gwynit of the grey kirtle. A Banner Queen, rather than a Camp Hag or Nightingale, though I had not seen her nor her dashing knight at any of the other tourneys in the circuit; they never travelled far from home.

Lady Gwynit was middle-aged now, her fair hair turned ash-blonde in the sunlight. She still looked like the heroine of a ballad, however soft around the edges. All the wives hushed and whispered together when Sir Lancel rode up to kiss her hand and claim her favour.

And the sad king looked sad.

"He won this tourney twenty years ago," Hilda told me — another of the Camp Hags who had warmed towards me after the twelfth or fourteenth time she saw me emptying night soil in the correct manner, or scrubbing my wife's armour until my knuckles bled. Oh yes, I had quite a few allies now, among the old lags of the circuit.

"I heard he refused to kiss the Lady of the Lake as his prize," added Margie. "And he wouldn't say his greatest wish

---

* The cat barely tolerated me, but I had learned to appreciate its presence; a steady source of pearls had helped with our travel budget no end.

out loud, so as not to betray his king, *but she granted it anyway.*"

"I can see the whole situation resolved itself beautifully," I snarked, noting the miserable glances exchanged between the king, his knight, his knight's wife, all bundled up in two decades of awkwardness.

"My Bran won this one three years ago," said Margie. "Kissed the Lady of the Lake for a full minute."

"This one punched him afterwards," snickered Hilda. "Right in the face."

"And I'd do it again," said Margie with a nod, wiping the nose of one of her children. "He'd better take the wish next time. We need a new mule."

The princes shot at the swan, still wishing to win their prize, but the wicked fairy Carabosse appeared, refusing to allow further harm to come to the cursed princess.

Later, as I handed Aura into her saddle, I suggested lightly that if she won this tourney, she might be better off taking the kiss than making a wish.

"Yes," said Aura, looking amused. "That's what Puss thought you would say."

My wife won at sword, but only came third in the joust; Sir Lancel unseated her so roughly I thought she might need to grow wings again to survive it; she walked off the field in the end, but limping bravely.

Margie's Bran won at the bow, and Hilda's Erik crushed all comers at the staff. In the final melee, Sir Lancel was victorious over all.

The waters of the Languid Lake parted, and the Lady Underneath emerged, greenish and heavy with silt. She greeted Sir Lancel as an old friend, and he bowed his head to kiss her without hesitation.

No wishes would be made today.

"And now," said the sad king. "A feast!"

Tournament of the Golden Vine

SITE: THE VINEYARDS OF MYLDOVIA

PRIZE: A GOLD CORNUCOPIA

This one was a rough day.

Our mule cast a shoe on the way to the tourney grounds.

The cat stopped talking to us, and stopped dripping pearls; the only thing he spat up was the ruined remains of a field mouse, right on the corner of my new-sewn banner.

One of our tent poles shattered. I spent an hour hunting for a useful branch that could be transformed into a replacement.

I had a headache that lasted five hours.

Aura did not place in any of her bouts.

The wicked fairy Carabosse cast back the arrows to protect the silver swan, and all three princes fell dead at her feet. In the chaos, the replacement princess Odile also fell from the tower and none were able to save her...

Late into the night, as we lay side by side in our sagging tent, Aura sighed the sigh of a woman who has lost faith.

"I'm not good enough," she whispered to the canvas. "I'll never be good enough. I'm such a fool."

And I whispered back: "Don't talk about my wife that way."

The Bluebird Tournament

SITE: THE EYRIE OF FLORINE

PRIZE: A SAPPHIRE-STUDDED CORONET

The prince of Florine was a bird. No one ever talked about it. No one seemed to find this strange. During the early bouts, I saw my princess falter as she realised the glorious blue-plumed bird sitting on a cushion on the Royal Terrace was not a pet, but a prince.

Still, she recovered well enough to take second place at the sword, though the local knights closed in hard around her; it was a while since she had faced opponents who were shocked to see a woman on the field.

As I readjusted Aura's armour before the joust, tying my ribbon more securely to her arm in preparation for her first bout, I saw her glance once more at the bluebird prince, and shudder.

"You never asked why I cursed you," I murmured into the back of her neck.

"No," she whispered back. "I never wished to know."

With Odile's body barely cool on the ground, Princess Aura and the wicked fairy Carabosse fled the kingdom in opposite directions. The heartsick king and queen announced to their people that their heir, the princess Odile, was dead.

It was her cousin, of course. It is a hard thing, to be a motherless cousin to a princess who has everything. Odile brought me silver and desperation, begging for me to rid the kingdom of Princess Aura so she might take her place.

I had never met Aura. Had never set foot in the kingdom of Argentia before, in all my centuries. But I owed Odile's dead mother a favour.

And I have always thought that swans are beautiful.

After the final joust was over, my Aura stood up to receive the winner's coronet from the bluebird prince. It was his wife, Princess Doromel, who placed the gleaming circle on Aura's golden hair.

Other wives might have come forward, to share their knight's glory; I hung back by the wagon, watching from afar. I deserved no share of her success. My only job was to repair what I had broken.

"This isn't going to end well," remarked the cat, from where he was curled up upon my folded cloak. Genteelly, he spat up three pearls which rolled away along a crack in the planking.

"Haven't you ever heard of happy endings?" I replied, my eyes still on Aura — bruised, battered, glowing with pride.

"For her, perhaps," remarked the cat. "Not for you, I'll wager."

Tournament of the Silver Pear

SITE: THE VERDARY PLAINS

PRIZE: THREE GOLD PLUMS, ONE SILVER PEAR

"Nameless knight, wife of the fairy Carabosse! Winner of this season's Tournament of Cobwebs in the Dread Reaches and of this season's Bluebird Tournament at the Eyrie of Florine."

They had built a maze, for the Tournament of the Silver Pear. The audience, royals and wives and peasants all together, climbed up towering staircases to high glass terraces overlooking the wide, complex knotwork of the maze.

It was made from trees, not hedges, conjured into rapid growth by a troupe of wizards. Jewelled fruits and flowers hung from every bough, as did all manner of enchanted traps: spider webs that wrapped around arms and would not let go; snakes that darted out to coil tight around ankles.

We clung to each other, watching as our champions collided in an endless melée of sword and staff, aiming to slow each other down while they clawed their way out of the wild green pathways. There was no joust today, and the bowmen were busy trying to prevent the winged monsters from descending in attack.

I had never been afraid of heights before — but last time I stood atop a tower, a princess died.

"She's fierce, your wife," observed the Earl of Verdary, a graceful man with long silver beard and a sharp eye for a good fight.

"I never thought I'd see a woman fight like a man at the sword," agreed his wife, the Countess Shalott.

"That one don't fight like a man," grinned my pal Margie. "She fights like a princess, don't she?"

My head went up in alarm. Margie knew who we were?

Did everyone know our story?

Seven years after the death of Odile, the king and queen of Argentia fell ill. A proclamation was *issued that they would enter the kingdom in the upcoming season of Great Tournaments, with their crown as prize.*

The feast that followed the conquest of the enchanted maze was lavish and long. The prizes were awarded based on whom the Earl and Countess felt had provided the greatest entertainment, though bonus points were awarded for those who got out of the maze early.

Aura squashed against me on a bench, her face rosy and her breath warm with mead. "You'd better keep this for me," she said, pressing a golden plum into the palm of my hand. "We'll need to go to the city before Fleur-of-the-West, get a new horse. Old Mallowart has been steady, but he's not strong enough to take me through the end."

I scratched the gold of the plum, just a little, to be sure of it. "We can replace your armour too, I think, if we're careful on our purchases. Plenty of pearls in the travel purse."

Aura laughed a little, leaning into my neck and tucking her face there as if she belonged. "You're good at this. How are you so good at this if you've never done it before?"

I kissed her hair. "I might ask you the same question, princess."

Tournament of Air and Lilacs

SITE: FLEUR-OF-THE-WEST

PRIZES: THE LILAC GIRDLE, THE SAPPHIRE
SCABBARD, THE SWEET PEA QUIVER, THE
WISTERIA CHAIN, THE CROWN OF AMETHYSTS

The kingdom of Fleur-of-the-West loved tourneys at a level
to which no other kingdom could ever truly aspire. The
Fleur-of-the-West annual Tournament of Air and Lilacs
lasted nine days. The first day was devoted to the examining
of the weapons, as well as three separate parades.

The tourney field was an enchanted meadow floating
three feet off the ground. Somehow, the horses did not
object.

Enormous, otherworldly flowers bloomed everywhere you looked. Colour, scent, joy. But mostly, purple. I stitched an extra row of harebells on to our banner on the second and third day, while waiting for Aura's sword bouts to begin.

Aura won at the joust. She won, she won, she won.

Her points at the sword were high enough that she won the Tourney Crown as well.

We drank deep at the feast. The tables were decorated with cloth of purple, every table carried trays of roast purple carrots in honey, even the mulled wine was dark violet. And as for the cakes? Sugared lavender crystals stuck to *everything*.

When we returned to our tent she draped me in her prizes, clearly designed to be gifted to a knight's wife. Still warm from the feasting fires, I wore a light shift as Aura wrapped me in the Lilac Girdle, bright with purple beading, her fingers warm against the thin fabric.

With ceremony, she placed the Crown of Amethysts upon the dark curls of my hair.

"You were right to buy a new horse," I told her, grinning. "You need to look grand when you conquer Argentia."

"I always look grand." Aura's fingers tangled in the girdle and she drew me to her, hip first, her mouth finding mine.

Victory tasted sweet. Aura tasted sweeter.

Princess Aura, who had been training in secret at the sword and the lance, climbed seven

magic mountains to find the wicked fairy
Carabosse.

The wicked fairy was intrigued to see the
princess on her feet, so strong and determined to
win back her kingdom, no matter the cost. But only
married champions could enter the Great Tourney
circuit.

And so the fairy
The fairy
(She said yes)

"Why did you do it?" she gasped against me as we came
together, naked and wanting in a tent I had wrapped in
every silencing charm I could muster. "Why did you agree
to help me?"

Why, why, why?

She had never asked me why I cursed her, but this... the
answer was worse. More self-serving, harder to explain.

"You were beautiful," I moaned as my wife kissed her
way down my neck and breasts. "You were sad. You were
asking. And I --"

(I, I, I, a moment lost to a scream and a shudder.)

"I wanted," I managed finally, when I had my breath
back.

Aura looked up at me, smug in the results of her endeav-
ours. "You wanted?"

*I wanted to do one thing in all my centuries that was not
wicked.*

"I wanted you," I confessed.

I wanted you to have everything you deserve. Everything I took from you in a careless moment. I wanted to be good.

Aura's hands, stronger than they had been a few months ago, parted my thighs. "I wanted you too," she said, and descended on me like a swan upon pondweed.

Tournament of Crown and Thorns

SITE: ARGENTIA

PRIZE: THE CROWN & KINGDOM OF ARGENTIA

It took nine days for us to travel from Fleur-of-the-West to the borders of Argentia, and another three days to travel across the kingdom to the castle grounds, where the tournament was to be held — the first tournament to be hosted by Argentia in nearly a century, and the first time in twenty years that a kingdom was on offer as a prize in any of the great tournaments.

We made love on the road, every night, wild and passionate behind the walls of our tent. Frantic, frenzied, desperate for each other.

(The cat found somewhere else to sleep.)

Once we crossed the border into Argentia, my wife would not touch me.

Knights poured in from all around; unless you were a local, it was generally not the done thing to enter a Great Tourney (especially a final tourney) if one had not properly entered all ten that season.

But a crown and a kingdom were on offer; the usual etiquette did not apply.

Knights poured into the kingdom, and with them their wives. Even the Nightingales joined us early, risking the hems of their pale, pretty gowns as they hovered on the periphery of the action.

Aura was not scheduled to fight until the third day. She spent most of her time polishing her armour and avoiding the tourney field. Specifically, avoiding any chance of seeing who sat in the royal box.

I was less circumspect; after all, my wife was ignoring me. Why not assuage my curiosity? I joined Margie and Hilda in the stands with the other tourney wives, to observe the early bouts of bow and staff.

If I looked closely, I could see what remained of Argentia's royal family: the king and queen, dressed in careful perfection, both pale and sunken-cheeked. The scent of high-end medical magic rolled off them so thickly I could smell it across the field. Someone was spending a lot of gold in keeping those two upright until the kingdom could be passed on in the only traditional way that did not include blood descent, or adoption.

The stands were old, but rugged: made from wood older than I am, and kept in prime condition over the centuries thanks to a series of magical protections. Thorns and roses were carved into every piece of polished oak: a symbol of the kingdom's history, I understood. Roses and thorns, thorns and roses. Classic fairy tale stuff.

Twelve generations ago, a princess of this family had been cursed to sleep a hundred years, and awoke to find her home wreathed in thorny hedges that only a prince could cut his way through. Anyone who survived an event like that was bound to ensure that their descendants remembered it through symbol and story, passing it down until it sounded entirely untrue.

Perhaps, if (when) my princess won her tournament, her descendants would decorate their castles in silver swan wings, along with crossed swords and lances.

What would I be in their stories? A wicked fairy is rarely remembered as anything other than a monster.

I watched Hilda's Erik take on six different challengers at the staff, all of them large and sweaty men who grunted as they hit each other with sticks. Any one of them might win the day, depending on his second weapon and how many points he amassed.

What a foolish way to choose a king or queen.

"You must be tempted," Margie murmured. "With all that magic at your fingertips. To help her on her way. It's her kingdom, after all. Her birthright."

I looked at her, narrow-eyed and suspicious; I had never told her who I was. Somehow the tale had got around, I knew, that Aura was a princess in disguise, but me?

They should not be wondering about me, at all.

Margie shrugged, and her eyes briefly shifted from hazel

to bright green and back again. "You're not the only one with a touch of magic in your blood, love. If wives were allowed to join combat, imagine what a mess we could make. My magic, your magic, Hilda's fingernails..."

"I'd dip them in poison," Hilda said calmly, without taking her eyes from her husband's bout. "For maximum damage."

"But we must let them do it on their own," Margie went on, as if she had not blown my mind. "It's the only way. They'd never forgive us, otherwise."

I was already beyond forgiveness; how could one further crime make a difference?

"I've seen a lot of shit over the years," Margie went on. "So many tourneys. The story doesn't always turn out the way it should. Best to keep any secret weapons you have as the back up plan."

The princess married the wicked fairy under a blossom bower. Princess Aura entered nine tournaments, one after the other, winning several prizes and astounding those who thought a woman should not be able to lift a sword...

At her side, always: the wicked fairy Carabosse.

That's it. You're up to date.

Back up plan. What was mine?

Walk away, I supposed, as the dust settled from the final joust. I had no skin in this game. Aura could win or lose and either way, we owed each other nothing once the season was over.

If she lost, she had lost everything all over again. No wicked fairy wife could change that for her.

If she won... well, what was I but an embarrassment? A complication. A bad memory.

On the third day, Aura was already awake and dressed by the time my eyes cracked open. Usually I had to shove her off the bedroll so she'd have time to break her fast before strapping on the armour.

"Are you ready?" I asked, knowing what a loaded question this was.

She looked at me, head high as if she was already queen of this kingdom. "I can't lose," she said calmly.

"Of course you can," I replied, and watched her face fall. "Losing is easy. All it takes is one mis-timed jab of the lance, and Margie's Bran will be marching into your palace, wiping his boots on your mother's rugs, and quaffing his ale from your father's favourite tankard."

Aura stared at me, silently outraged.

"You *won't* lose," I added, in a kinder voice. "Not today. You won't let yourself. I know that, if I know anything about you."

She took a step towards me and gave me a quick,

bruising kiss. "When I win," she said. "You'll still be here when it's over, won't you? You'll stay?"

I had lived for centuries. I had fought warlords and dragons and my own conscience. I had killed armies, flattened mountains. I had cursed *babies*. Not to mention one rather resilient teenager.

She was not a teenager any more. She was a warrior woman. A knight in shining armour. And here I was, helpless against her.

"I married you, didn't I?" I muttered.

Aura gave me a smile I can only describe as a little bit wicked. "Oh," she said. "Was that you?"

Part of me wanted to whisk her away, so that she never had a chance to lose.

One way or another, this tournament was going to break her heart.

The third day was for the sword bouts. The ring, formed from enormous dried thorny boughs, had been set up in full view of the stands, and the royal box.

Aura stood with the other knights, sword gleaming, ready for a fight that never came. She did not look up at the King and Queen, who had erased their daughter from the family history as soon as she was turned into a swan.

(Who had sent princes to hunt her down as an animal,

ensuring she never returned to embarrass their family or claim her birthright.)

As always, the herald announced my wife, along with her more recent honours: "Nameless knight, wife of the fairy Carabosse. This season's winner of the Tournament of Cobwebs in the Dread Reaches, of the Bluebird Tournament at the Eyrie of Florine, and of the Tournament of Air and Lilacs in Fleur-of-the-West."

The king and queen of Argentia looked startled at the mention of my name. I was paying attention, and saw the moment that they recognised their daughter.

Aura stepped into the ring of thorns. Her opponent, Sir Melchin of Verdary, stopped short of it and bowed to her. He spoke quietly, and walked away. Aura looked stunned.

This had not happened before; there had been mutterings early in the season about fighting a woman, but none of the champions had actually *refused*.

After some shuffling among the heralds, the next opponent came forward, Sir Bastien of Delmaa. He, too, bowed to Aura and left the field without fighting her.

There was a-murmur, among the wives and the greater audience. No unkind looks, no cruel stares. Several of the ladies looked quite emotional. "What is happening?" I hissed under my breath at Margie, who was unconcerned.

"I don't know why you're surprised," she shrugged. "Everyone knows who she is."

"And only now do they decide they're too good to fight her?"

Margie looked pityingly at me. "Oh, my dear. You *have* got the wrong end of the stick."

Aura was shaking with humiliation when she left the sword ring with eight wins to her name (all from withdrawals) and headed straight for our tent. A little while later, with no other volunteers forthcoming, I was sent by the heralds to convince her to return and accept her prize.

"They're ruining this," she said, pacing the tiny space from tent wall to tent wall, wringing her hands. "Why do this to me now?"

"Margie explained it to me," I said, staying calm enough for both of us. "They all know you're the lost heir. They know that this is your kingdom. It's not that they don't want to fight you. They *want you to win*."

Aura turned on me, wild-eyed. "So, what? The whole season was for nothing?"

I scoffed as if I had not needed the matter carefully laid out for me by a Camp Hag several centuries younger than myself. "You think the men would have stood aside for you if you strolled in with clean armour on the third day of the tenth tournament? You've proved yourself to all of them over these last few months. You got knocked down, you picked yourself up. You spat *teeth* on one very notable afternoon which personally I have never recovered from. They respect you because you put in the work. You earned this."

Aura blinked rapidly, staving off tears. "You can't really believe that, Carabosse."

"I'm a fairy," I replied. "All the stories I know are about hard work rewarded by magic."

The King and Queen of Argentia had already withdrawn to their sickbeds for the day, when Aura emerged to receive her prize — a silk ribbon — for winning at the sword. It was an elderly prime minister who handed over the trinket, while staring at her like she was a miracle.

"Will you joust tomorrow, lady?" he asked in a quavering voice.

Aura stood up, straight-backed. "That depends on my opponents," she said, glaring around the field.

By the last day, the heralds knew what to expect; no sooner had one knight bowed to Aura and dropped his lance to demonstrate that he would not fight her, a new shield was whipped into place.

At the dinner hour, she returned to our tent to scream silently while everyone else was chewing mutton bones and quaffing ale. "I understand they mean well," she sighed finally, letting me tidy her hair back under her helm. "But I wanted to fight for my kingdom. I wanted to prove myself."

"You kept your head up today, before the people who ordered your death because you were the victim of a spell," I told her, pressing my cool hand to her cheek. "If that's not fighting, I don't know what is."

The crowd might be as much on Team Aura as every knight in the land, but they were still growing restless without much of a show. Other knights could ride against each other, of course, but no one wanted to see that, either.

Finally, as the afternoon light began to dim, one knight rode forth on a gleaming white horse. His armour was golden, his banner perfectly sewn.

(The crowd hissed in response, recognising his banner.)

"That's Sir Lancel," I gasped. "He never leaves Billemaudh. Why is he here?"

"*She's* here in the stands," Margie said in my ear. "Look!"

At first, I only saw the hood of a pristine white cloak more suited to a Nightingale than a Banner Queen; she turned her head and I recognised her, the ash-blonde Lady Gwynit, a satisfied look upon her face.

"They choose now to finally leave that sad king in peace?" I grumbled.

On the field, Aura bowed her head. "You will joust, sir knight?"

"My lady wishes to live in a new kingdom," said Sir Lancel, his voice frosty. "This one will do as well as any other."

They came together, gold knight against silver, three passes at the joust. The first was a double knock. The second, inconclusive. And the third...

I doubt there has ever been a more satisfying sound in the world as that of the people of Argentia catching their breath as a gold-armoured knight sailed out of his saddle and landed hard on the dirt field.

Nor of the cheers that followed.

The King and Queen sat as still as statues as their rumpled, victorious champion knelt at their feet. I was with her, my arms tangled with those of my lady. I did not even remember running across the ground to hurl myself into her arms, but apparently everyone else did.[*]

"Will you give us your name now, champion of Argentia?" asked the Queen in a soft and quivering voice.

The winner of the Tournament of Crown and Thorns met the Queen's gaze without flinching. "You know my name," she said, then raised her voice louder. "You all know my name."

Thus, the last sound that echoed around the tourney field that day was the crowd chanting the name of Queen Aura, their new ruler, over and over again.

In all the chaos, I slipped away. That is what a wicked fairy does, when the tale is over.

---

[*]   Reader, they wrote ballads.

Aura found me in our tent, hours later, arguing with the cat.

"What would you even do with a tent?" I snapped at it.

"What would you do with it?" it purred back. "You are no longer a tourney wife. Go back to your magic cave, witch."

"Fairies do not live in caves!"

An amused cough interrupted as both. "Packing?"

I straightened up, caught with an armful of hand-made banner, hugged to my chest. "Moving on," I said crisply. "It's time, don't you think?"

The cat rolled his eyes at us both and strode out of the tent, but not before licking it to prove ownership.

Aura had eyes only for me. "I think," she said in a dangerous voice. "You have forgotten that you married me."

"You're a queen now."

"I am, indeed. The former monarchs of this land have relinquished the castle to end their days in a comfortable hospice." She pointed with one arm, still armoured. "The castle is ours."

"The castle is *yours*," I corrected. "This was your quest, Aura. This is your new life, won by right of combat."

"All true," she said, removing her helm and the cap beneath. Her hair emerged, golden and sweaty. She would need it brushed for her, so that it didn't matt into clumps.

That, of course, was what maids were for.

"And so our deal is ended," I pronounced. "My apology tour is over."

"Then why can you not forgive yourself?"

"Why should I? What does it matter?"

She raised one eyebrow. "Because the wife of a queen is also a queen."

My breath dried in my throat. "You can't be serious."

Aura spread her arms wide, dramatic as always. "In all of this — in the mud and muck and gruel and blood and bruises have you *ever* known me to be unserious?"

It was true, my wife had little sense of humour.

My wife.

"You can't mean to install me in a solar as your consort," I scoffed. "I'm the wicked fairy who turned you into a swan!"

Aura's face softened. She took a step and brushed her fingers gently along the side of my face, tucking a stray curl behind my ear. "Yes, you did. And then you worked hard, to make up for it. And now, you are to be rewarded. That is how stories work."

"Not for me! At the end of the tale the wicked fairy *disappears*."

Aura's eyes flashed. She took another step, her armour pressing against my chest. "Have I not done enough to earn your devotion? Do I need to take up another quest? *Do I need to fight ten more tournaments?*"

I laughed then, and I was lost. "No," I said, when I could breathe. "No, you have fought enough tournaments. Exactly the right number."

"And will you leave me alone, weeping on my throne like the sad king of Billemaudh?"

"A fate worse than death," I admitted.

"So, will you let castle servants tidy this tent away from us, so you may come and view your new kingdom?"

That, at least, I could refuse. "A good knight takes care of her own equipment," I teased. "What would your trainers say if they knew you left this work to servants?"

Aura's eyes narrowed and her voice grew thick. "I

imagine they would say: *I see Sir Aura bedded her wife with a roof over their heads, and about time too.*"

Unable to help myself, I reached out and began to unstrap her breastplate. "*But first,*" I teased. "*She reminded her wife how good it had been in a tent.*"

The next hour was lost to us both entirely, but at least we were in good company.

We let the cat take the tent, on condition that it never told us what hustle it intended. Sometimes it is best to remain ignorant of the schemes of others.

Especially if you are a queen.

Later — much later — after we gathered our belongings and moved them into the castle that would be our home, I slipped away to stand at the high window, looking out over the kingdom of Argentia.

My wife came and found me; I have learned that she will always find me, when I grow pensive.

"Queen Carabosse," she said, in that husky voice of hers.

"Queen Aura," I replied. "Do you miss flying?"

Her eyes widened only a little in surprise; she snugged herself behind me, arms loosely grasping my waist. "Do you?" she murmured.

"I'm a fairy," I reminded her. "Flight is always an option."

My wife squeezed me tighter. "I'm a swan, my love," she said in a whisper. "If you fly, I will follow."

After that, there was little to do but live happily ever after.[*]

____

[*] Including, we can only assume, the cat.

Author's Note: On Sports Romance and Wicked Fairies

I always wanted to write a story called "Tourney Wives" which was probably a romance, set in the world of tournaments — specifically the world of tournaments as portrayed in the 2001 classic film *A Knight's Tale*.

I fell in love with this film many years ago, and only later realised how well it fits into one of my all time favourite genres: the sports romance. I didn't even know I loved them until well into my thirties because I was so firmly established in my own head as a Bookish Person With No Interest in Sport.

I have, however, spent my life falling in love with sports movies and sports narratives, from Enid Blyton's lacrosse games to *The Mighty Ducks* through to *Ted Lasso*, with plenty of stops along the way for *Check Please*, *Bend it Like Beckham*, *Yuri on Ice* and every novel ever written by Sarina Bowen.

I even briefly went through a phase of being obsessed with actual sport, but I mostly gave it up after a few years due to the difficulty of time zones vs the English Premier League.

There's something about the tensions and contained worlds created by sports movies that I enjoy. I've often found myself delighting in the invention of fictional sports in my SFF books — such as fleur-de-lis/cinquefoil/Zero-G TeamJoust in *Musketeer Space*, or Rookery in *Castle Charming*.

A Knight's Tale was the first time I saw jousting presented as a sport, and it stuck with me. I rewatched it recently and it holds up in ways that most 25 year old films don't — it's still the same film I watched the first time around, only this time I'm anticipating the soundtrack instead of surprised by it.

Oh, the characters! The friendship! The honour. The *world*. No wonder it has occupied space rent-free in my head for so long.

Sports stories, and romances in particular, are full of fairy tale characters: the entitled prince, the queen bee, the underdog, the traitor. They include mentorship and friendship and intense feels put through the wringer.

Beating the champion, though the odds are stacked against you. Winning the prize. Losing it all, but finding something more important.

You don't get more fairy tale than that.

The main difference between this story and all the others in this collection is that I wrote it after I had assembled the rest of the manuscript and written all of the author's notes. I knew the shape of the book, therefore, and needed a story that brought it all together.

NO PRESSURE.

As with most of my fairy tale stories, this one features scraps and snippets snatched from a lifetime of loving fairy tales.

The cat who spits pearls, you may recall from my discussion of *Tuppeny, Feefo & Jinks* — though I haven't re-read the book, so it's from my memory combined with the sass of Puss in Boots, one of my problematic faves. A little Arthuriana (not technically fairy tales... or are they?) snuck in along the way. Flowers and fairies, thorns and towers.

I've never particularly loved *Swan Lake*, as I do not have the ballet-appreciation gene, but I have always loved the name Carabosse, and I can appreciate a wicked fairy.

Many of my thoughts and feelings about princesses are tied up here — I've always preferred stories where they save themselves, and you can see shades of "Waking Flora" and "Daredevil Duchess" overlapping with this particular story.

As with everything I write, I didn't know what the shape of it would be until I wrote it. I wouldn't have it any other way.

Keep reading fairy tales! There's always something new to find, and borrow, and steal.

Tansy's Grand & Majestic
Fairy Tale Book List

Adams, Georgie & Gardner, Sally - *The Real Fairy Storybook: Stories the Fairies Tell Themselves*

Ahlberg, Janet & Alan - *Each Peach Pear Plum*

Atwater, Olivia - *Half a Soul*

Banks, Lynne Reid - *The Fairy Rebel*

Black, Holly - *Tithe*

Blyton, Enid - *Tuppeny, Feefo and Jinks*

Brennan, Sarah Rees - *In Other Lands*

Brewer's Dictionary of Phrase and Fable

Burgis, Stephanie - "The Wrong Foot"

Burgis, Stephanie - *The Dragons with a Chocolate Heart*

Calvino, Italo - *Italian Folk Tales*

Carter, Angela - *The Bloody Chamber and other Stories*

Cushman, Carolyn - *Witch and Wombat*

Dahl, Roald - *Revolting Rhymes*

Datlow, Ellen & Windling, Terri (eds) - *A Wolf at the Door and other Retold Fairy Tales*

Datlow, Ellen & Windling, Terri (eds) - *Snow White, Blood Red*

Datlow, Ellen & Windling, Terri (eds) - *The Faery Reel*

Dean, Pamela - *Tam Lin*

De Lint, Charles - *Seven Wild Sisters*

De Godard, Aliette - *In the Vanisher's Palace*

Eager, Edward - *Seven Day Magic*

Evans, C.S. & Rackham, Arthur - *Cinderella and the Sleeping Beauty*

Forsyth, Kate - *Bitter Greens*

Forsyth, Kate - *The Rebirth of Rapunzel: A Mythic Biography of the Maiden in the Tower*

Frank, Natalie (illustrator) & Zipes, Jack (translator) - *The Island of Happiness: Tales of Madame D'Aulnoy*

Freeman, Pamela - *The Willow Tree's Daughter*

Froud, Brian - *Faeries*

Froud, Brian & Terry Jones - *Lady Cottington's Pressed Fairy Book*

Gardner, Sally - *A Book of Princesses*

Gardner, Sally - *Fairy Shopping*

Gardner, Sally - *The Fairy Catalogue*

George, Jessica Day - *Tuesdays at the Castle*

Goldman, William - *The Princess Bride*

Hale, Shannon - *The Goose Girl*

Hale, Dean & Shannon - *Rapunzel's Revenge*

Healey, Karen - *When We Wake*

Ibbotson, Eva - *Which Witch?*

Jennings, Kathleen - "Some Ways To Retell a Fairy Tale"

Jones, Diana Wynne - *Howl's Moving Castle*

Kelly Link - "The Faery Handbag," *Magic for Beginners*

Kelly Link - "Travels With the Snow Queen," *Stranger Things Happen*

Lanagan, Margo - *Sea Hearts*

Lanagan, Margo - *Tender Morsels*

Lancaster, A.J. - *How To Marry a Winged King*

Levine, Gail Carson - *Ella Enchanted*

Lo, Malinda - *Ash*

Lo, Malinda - *Huntress*

Mantchev, Lisa - *Eyes Like Stars*

Marillier, Juliet - *Daughter of the Forest*

Marillier, Juliet - *Wildwood Dancing*

McAlister, Jodi - *Valentine*

McKillip, Patricia - *The Tower at Stony Wood*

McKillip, Patricia - *Winter Rose*

McKinley, Robin - *Beauty*

McKinley, Robin - *Deerskin*

McKinley, Robin - *Rose Daughter*

McKinley, Robin - *Spindle's End*

McKinley, Robin - *The Door in the Hedge*

Medley, Linda - *Castle Waiting*

Mudge, Faith, Valente, Catherynne M & Jennings, Kathleen (illustrator) - *To Spin a Darker Stair*

Munsch, Robert & Michael Martchenko (illustrator) - *The Paper Bag Princess*

Nesbit, E - "Melisande, or Long & Short Division" in *Nine Unlikely Tales*

Novik, Naomi - *Uprooted*

Pratchett, Terry - *Lords & Ladies*

Pratchett, Terry - *Maurice & His Educated Rodents*

Pratchett, Terry - *Witches Abroad*

Rackham, Arthur (illustrator) - *Fairy Tales From Many Lands*

Rackham, Arthur (illustrator) - *Rackham's Fairy Tale Coloring Book*

Rossetti, Christina - *Goblin Fruit**

---

* There are many gorgeous editions of this poem but may I recommend

Sapkowski, Andrzej - *The Last Wish*
Scarborough, Elizabeth Ann - *Song of Sorcery*
Shelley, Mary - "Roger Dodsworth: The Reanimated Englishman"
Slatter, Angela - *A Feast of Sorrows*
Slatter, Angela & Jennings, Kathleen (illustrator) - *Flight*
Slatter, Angela - *Sourdough and Other Stories*
Slatter, Angela - *The Tallow-Wife and Other Tales*
Tepper, Sheri S - *Beauty*
Valente, Catherynne M - *Deathless*
Valente, Catherynne M - *The Girl Who Circumnavigated Fairyland in a Ship of Her Own Making*
Valentine, Genevieve - *The Girls at The Kingfisher Club*
Vernon, Ursula - *Castle Hangnail*
Warner, Marina - *From the Beast To The Blonde*
Wrede, Patricia C - *Dealing with Dragons*
Wrede, Patricia C - *Snow White and Rose Red*
Wilde, Oscar - *The Happy Prince and Other Tales (or Stories)*
Wodehouse, P.G. - *Summer Lightning* (Blandings Castle)*
Yolen, Jane - *Not One Damsel in Distress: World Folktales for Strong Girls*
Zipes, Jack - *Breaking the Magic Spell: Radical Theories of Folk and Fairy Tales*

---

the audiobook Miriam Margolyes Reads Christina Rossetti

* Not a fairy tale, but I do adore these books so much and if you're going to mention Wodehouse, even in passing, you have to be prepared to back that up with recommendations. By far the best place to start with Blandings Castle is the excellent Stephen Fry audiobook collection P.G. Wodehouse Vol 2 which includes a selection of the best Blandings novels and stories. (You can listen to this before/without Vol. 1 which is a selection of Jeeves & Wooster stories but that one's also excellent)

I have probably forgotten many essential texts which should be on this list, and you will certainly have your own. Please, make your own list and spread it far and wide.

Also if you didn't believe me the first time about watching Rik Mayall perform "Sweet Porridge" in his Grim Tales series, he is still waiting there on YouTube to delight and repel you.

You're welcome.

About the Author

Tansy Rayner Roberts is an award-winning Australian fantasy author. Her favourite fairy tale is the Twelve Dancing Princesses. She lives with her family in Tasmania.

- Listen to Tansy on Sheep Might Fly, a podcast where she reads aloud her stories as audio serials.
- Read Tansy's stories before anyone else when you pledge to her Patreon.
- What tea is Tansy drinking? Find out when you subscribe to her excellent newsletter: tinyurl. com/tansyrr
- Follow Tansy on Bookbub so you never miss a release.

facebook.com/TansyRRoberts

instagram.com/tansyrr

patreon.com/tansyrr

bookbub.com/authors/tansy-rayner-roberts

Curse of Bronze

Who cursed the celebrated cursebreaker Charlotte Hathaway, right in the middle of the Eldritch Library? No one knows, despite the murder happening in a crowd of witnesses.

Charlotte's niece, Bella Hathaway, is on the case after inheriting her aunt's townhouse full of dangerous artefacts and talking teapots. Only problem? She's not a cursebreaker. Bella has always been the quiet member of the daredevil Hathaway family, translating magical languages, wearing sensible skirts and avoiding perilous adventure.

Now, with the help of the beast next door and his sprawling library, it's time for Bella to step up to her family legacy, translate an untranslatable demon language, locate two archaeologists who went missing twenty-five years earlier, and figure out exactly why her aunt was messing around with a gang of gargoyle-stealing werewolves.

Bella Hathaway might be out of her element in this city of paranormal creatures, but she's not going to let that stop her from solving this cold-blooded crime.

Castle Charming

Welcome to Castle Charming, where fairy tales don't care who they hurt.

The scandalous young Royals are self-destructing, messily, as reported in the local newspapers. This would be the worst time for a horde of foreign princesses to roll in, hoping for marriage.

Kai joins the press corps to report on the drama. He's not expecting to find a family, fall in love with a palace guard, or save the kingdom.

In this magical kingdom of cursed spinning wheels, violent beanstalks, deadly queens and disaster princes, the most dangerous thing of all might be a Happily Ever After.

Gorgons Deserve Nice Things

*"We lived in a world that did not allow women to breathe;
how could we be anything but monsters?"*

Tansy Rayner Roberts retells the stories of seven women
from Greek mythology, giving voice to the scorned, the
sidelined, and the monstrous.

A young gorgon finds acceptance at the Medusa Club.
Atalanta spills the truth behind the myth of the Argonauts.
Scylla suffers through a series of terrible college roommates.
Handmaids in Sparta get more than they bargained for
when they interfere in their queen's correspondence with a
Trojan prince. A comparative mythology graduate finds
herself at a speed-dating night packed with dodgy gods.
Behind a velvet rope, a queenly Minotaur presides over a
roller disco. Persephone shares her story via a series of
pomegranate recipes.

"Deliciously mythic and delightfully funny, *Gorgons Deserve Nice Things* (Brain Jar Press) delivers new takes on ancient stories, reinvigorating them with modern perspectives and settings. Showcasing the craft and insight that made her one of Australia's most beloved short fiction writers, this collection sees Roberts at her wry, subversive best."

On Patreon

This book would not exist without the ongoing support of my Patreon members, whose subscriptions, comments and feedback have inspired and encouraged an ongoing flood of bonus stories, strange projects, random manticores and a slightly erratic podcast over more than a decade.

If you want to find out what all the fuss is about, find me at patreon.com/tansyrr.